U0164537

香港華人名人史略

黃慕松題

獻此於吾族兄吳鐵城主席

TO

MR. WU TEH SHING

CHAIRMAN OF THE GOVERNMENT OF KWONGTUNG PROVINCE

FROM WHOM I HAVE RECEIVED KINDNESS.

編者小史

編者小照

吳醒濂·字肇醒·粵中山縣人·現年四十五歲·民國三年·畢業交通部上海工業專門學校（即今交通大學）·旋留學美國·民國九年·在滬創設南洋商科高級中學·歷任該校校長達十五年之久·民國十三年·赴滇出席第九屆全國教育會聯合大會·雲南督軍兼省長唐公繼堯·聘充省長公署顧問·後再度漫遊歐美·民國二十三年·受美國加省士丹佛大學之聘·充任漢文文學教授·曾著『芝加高世界博覽大會之批評』一文·分登美國各報·並著有『美國檀山菲島華僑合誌』一書·其在滬所手創之南洋商科高級中學·因一二八之役·受日軍轟燬·損失甚鉅·難以為繼·現已讓上海市總商會接辦·改稱為上海市總商會商業中學矣·民國二十五年來港·微編是書·

香港華人名人史略（一九三七）

PROF. WOO SING LIM, THE AUTHOR.

Born in Canton, 1893. Graduated from the Government Institute of Technology (now Choa Tung University) Shanghai 1914. Special student of Columbia University N.Y., U.S.A. 1916. Principal of The Nanyang Commercial Academy Shanghai 1920-1935. Adviser of the Governor of Yunnan Province 1924. Professor of Chinese literature of Stanford University California U.S.A. 1934. Author of "Criticisms of the A Century of Progress International Exposition Chicago" 1934. Author of "The Chinese in America, Hawaii, and Philippine Islands" 1936. Author of "the Prominent Chinese in Hongkong" 1937.

序

囊史官世其家，崇其位，厚其祿，史之重可知也。周末，孔子修春秋，正名份，嚴一字之褒貶，使君君臣臣，以喜以懼。史事遂屬學者，喀萊爾（Carlyle）謂世之史，大人先生傳記耳。華夏自司馬作列傳，始易左傳紀一事物，而傳大人先生也。大人先生傳記耳。華夏自司馬作列傳，始易左傳紀一事物，言，功，苟有一可式世者，傳，傳也。其道可稽，昔儒以德，言，功，苟有一可式世者，胥足傳，傳固非易也。史，執正而持中。司馬遷寧逆漢武以獲罪，不易『今上本紀』，持史筆者不畏禍，毋劫於勢，不喜功，毋誘於利。然後其義生，史之信亦難矣哉。宗兄醒濂，幼嘗同學鳳山書院，長嘗共事修來學校，既橐筆海上，曾遍遊歐美各大埠，以稽華人海外掌故。曾成『美國檀山及菲島華僑合誌』諸書，世頗有嘉其勾稽得間。使遠民之德，弗潛於世者，吾兄今復以修『香港華人名人史畧』告，梅鶴曰，史為德音，音出宜響乎其聲，英人哥德斯密（Godsmith）謂『史應孕道德，生產，智力』。德人陸宰（Lotge）張為慎察智力，產業，美術，宗教，政治五者，而史之響，乃應乎其聲。夫聖賢尤以博選為本，以正世為用，人益顯其誠能，其道乃弗可去，兄之述，其有志於斯乎，則豈局於一地一世，直百世之器矣。

民國廿五年十二月中山梅鶴吳曆昌謹叙

自序

曩者考察教育。觀光文化。幾度漫遊歐美。目覩各大都邑紀載名人事績之刊物。至為普遍。即我國出版界。近亦有中華當代名人傳等書面世。其適應潮流。獨標一格。所以滿足後學之楷梯。當為大雅所許。寧以史官自居耶。香港開闢。將達百年。現蔚為遠東第二大商埠。吾華人才蓁萃。名流迭出。其間能造成社會幸福。推進中英邦交者。不鮮其人。況乾嘉近風俗日偷。人心不古。而無專書。分別紀述。久易湮沒。殊為可惜。此是書之所由徵編也。文人無行。昵節趨時。侈談神怪。艷說風流。更有以公妻共產之學說。導近青年於陷阱者。有心志士。恐然以為憂。思矯其弊。遂有少年叢書。小學生文庫之傳記類等籍刊行。其體裁分紀中外聖賢。惠美矣。未盡善也。何則。以古代異方之人物示範。徒供仰止。以近世當地之人物表率。切實親近。易於仿模。如孔子，孟子，諸葛亮，岳飛，文天祥，耶穌，華盛頓，林肯等。於一世之雄。馬稍補耳。抑有進者。(濂)不慚學力淺薄。謬然主撰是書。以貢獻於香江人士之前。亦冀世道人心。於才兼文武之曹操。屏而不錄。尚友錄一書。遠渺艱深。備列其中。殊非人人可得。又其次在立功。(濂)名譽隨之掃地。曹操於此點乎。我國之標準名人錄也。歷朝人物。均應基於道德。否則功業失其價值。(濂)對於中人選。敢不就就於此點乎。若紀其行狀。蓋人之立身建業。太上在立德。其次在立功。其次在立言。今僑居香港之華人。多出於商賈一途。自古真名之所歸。欲建三不朽之業。殊非人人可得。(濂)既以香港華人名特別技能。或自創基業。因機會所限。致力公益者。傳之也。而非全中國或全世界之名人。範圍人史署八字名其書。顧名思義。而能獻身社會。可知其中所載。皆香港之名人。而誰曰不宜。至(濂)既有專門學問。或之大小既清。則詫異與讚嘲之來。可以止矣。然則謂香港華人名人值得錄於是書者。將盡於此區區八十餘人耶。是又不然。此次主撰是編。搜羅資料。窮八月之光陰。工作人員。聘五人為助理。終因困於見聞。不免掛一漏萬。且港中縉紳名流。及商業鉅子。或因公忙。或因謙遜。徵求未必即應。滄海遂多遺珠。事與願違。實深抱歉。而同時對於寄表同情慨然加入者。愈覺感激。其次對於盧伯禎，郭子超，楊應聰三先生。及姚秀容，黃志惠兩女士。或佐編中英文稿。或代訪今古史實。亦應致謝。微諸名流之應徵。此書不能蔵事。微數子之襄助。亦未易成功也。

中華建國二十六年吳醒濂序於香江客次

PREFACE

Included in this book, are the photographs and biographies of about eighty prominent Chinese in Hongkong. Political, commercial, financial, industrial, educational and professional circles are represented herein. As the existence of this book, distributed throughout Hongkong and China, will act as an encouragement, to some one, as well as a deterrent, to many; the author has endeavoured to make careful selections.

The biographies of this book are principally written in Chinese. For the sake of convenience of those who learn English language, an addition of English translation to each biography is necessary. However, as the English translations are only the outlines of the ideas of the Chinese texts, they are not to be translated words by words and sentences by sentences.

It is very difficult to determine in just what order to place the biographies. Certainly I cannot please all in this matter; but I wish to state that the order in which they are placed does not indicate the order of importance in the affairs of Hongkong. It is merely what I believe to be the most satisfactory manner of arranging them, and was done with no intention of being partial to anyone.

I wish to acknowledge the co-operation given to me by every one whose biography included in this book. I also wish to thank Messrs. Chi Chew Kwok, Ying Chung Yang, Park Ching Loo and Misses Yao Shou Yung and Wong Chi Wai, without whose assistance in compiling and collecting the materials, my work would not have been a success.

Hongkong, April, 1937. WOO SING LIM.

名留海宇

孫科題

滄海之廣不息

其源萬蠱之底

不忘其本

于右任

嶺海俊彥

王寵惠題

海外球圖

香港華人名人事略

香港人物

曹善允題

還至名歸

範瑩

編例

（一）此書之編‧中文為主‧西文為輔‧兼以編排關係‧英文祗可撮領提綱‧愧未能全篇對照繙譯也‧

（二）是書紀載之次序‧係以覆函應徵之先後而定‧究與其本人在港中地位無關‧編者對於袞袞諸公‧一致景仰‧更不欲有所軒輊‧稍存成見‧

（三）書中人物‧年齡有老壯之分‧功業有多寡之別‧撰述或簡或繁‧實非輕彼重此‧

（四）此書延攬之今古名流‧必以其人一生事業‧多在香港‧或現居香港者為限‧不敢勉強牽附‧如孫總理中山‧幼讀於皇仁書院‧並曾留港業醫‧如伍博士廷芳‧卒業聖保羅書院‧後曾著九龍巡理府‧又充定例局議員‧為華人代表第一人‧終因其大部份勳績‧屬於全國‧未敢加入‧餘可類推‧

（五）其他名流史畧‧未經調查而脫畧者‧諒尚有其人‧將來擬再努力徵集‧在再版時補充‧以彰賢才‧

何東爵士

SIR ROBERT HO TUNG

何東爵士○字曉生○現年七十六歲○來籍廣海○僑寓香江○父平見背○遺孤七人○母氏殊賢○亦探不精寬假○爵士少喪親○以家清倫○佐

就學私墊○母日與銅錢三○作午餐用○彼報有存積○合數旬將四十餘錢○一日遇過老乞丐○狀甚貧苦○博之○彼以乎數相贈○其尚俠興好義○於幼時已見其端倪矣○迨七齡○其母忍治生計○擬令輟學○政習英文○師定其材○嗣免所費○仍俟留讀於墊中者數載○故爵士於漢學朋具洞源○十二歲將入中央學校○（即今皇仁

書院）六年畢業○博覽西史○洞通群籍○爲謀敎水之數○曾曰枝克助敎○越年○改進粵垣海關○襄理稅務○兩年後○以治事精勤○賢勞攝著○爲上關○襄理稅務○因應友召○告辭近港○延任怡和洋行總司理人風其名○亟謀倚重○延任○爵士固辭不獲○乃就職任事○贊

襄助理○戚慶得人○又越二年○香港火險，廣東水險，兩公司分行○迆以組理要席聘請兼領○而辦理船務糧務○復剛重要○爵士總任數載○規畫精詳○興利剔弊○洞中肯綮○業務蒸蒸○

士益展鴻才○且至公元一九零零年○始以積勞告退○嗣行重遷其悉○勉從所辭○然銘鐫紀功○其盛德之感人○勞苦功高○有如此者○嗣後爵士自營商業○字然奇計○范盡○華人商其中者日多○五方雜處○疾疹時有○

怡和洋行復推之爲正買辦○爵士在新界建築兄童幸福會一所○以乎數身充本港貧女敎育費○一九三四年○又捐款十萬○在香港仔建造一兒童工藝學院○復捐款建一盲生收養所○以贈本港之某盲童生會○香港自開復○

○爵士熱心輸助○史無戒倦○於皇仁大書院○曾捐巨款之獎勵金○前後輸捐○逹二十六萬○其他捐巨款之獎勵金○於港大學堂初立○史大解義○獎抵後進○孜孜不倦○於皇仁大書院○曾捐恰於公益事業○熱心輸助○史無戒倦○

之敎○非其德无不足以致之也○爵士曾任溫重銀行買辦○故行籌有規定○華人供職其中者○須勷臣資保証○宋門下户○抱有長才○每有尚賜

港中精其成績之學校○多案其伙助○所捐分學類○獎品○及基金三挂○但貧窮子弟○殊少進校機會○逆出巨金○遊設義務夜學於香港及九龍兩地○以謀敎育之普及○又以歐重於九龍地境○苦無相當敎育○乃剷設學校○伴西方學序○弦編其中○其不吝遐

行金婚典禮時○復慨然捐贊二十萬圓○以乎數在新界建築兄童幸福會一所○以乎數身充本港貧女敎育費○一九三四年○又捐款十萬○在香

原設東華醫院○房宰狹小○病者恆以擁滿見遣○果萬○紫標黃榜○責行倉庫○非其才不足以清生計○擬令輟學○政習英文○師定其材○嗣免所費○仍俟留讀於墊中者數載○故爵士於漢學朋具洞源○十二歲將入中央學校○（即今皇仁

○西醫割空史復開如○遇有求治之人○苦留醫
院之無所○時抱缺憾○又以港例遇有疫發生○
勒速入西人分隔所○於華俗起居飲食○每感不
便○爵士時在任東華總理○憨爲愛之○引爲己
任○籌建東華東院○創設疫局○捷政疫局○四
方奔走○竭力提倡○卒賴蓋舉○本港米荒○
到於今受其賜○十餘年前○運米拖俐○以拯飢祭○幾瀕亂
事○乃首捐助萬圓○賴以維持○鞏夫爭東洪波
心大定○地方秩序○均以義衆仁慈○撥助救
爲虐○華北旱魃告災○則仁人之利溥矣○一九一五年
濟○存活至衆○暴德恩快續權○征服世界○英與
○歐洲風雲○以維持人道故○起而應戰○爵士義形
約國○捐飛機二衆○及救傷汽車數柄○不惜廠
於色○以維公道○同時港府因籌助軍需○特頌
巨費○增設差餉○租值凡百抽七○令由住戶繳
新例○爵士爲香港最大之業主○本其好義之心○
納○將名下租出及批出房屋○所有加
爲摩施之舉○概歸其繳納○共數凡二萬五千金○港
抽之款○一九二二年○香港海員以加薪問
人稱頌弗至○招舉罷業○風潮亟道○比附益衆○市象凑
題○踏○群情惶駭○幹中英兩政府派員協助調停○

會長○經濟調查局分任委員會長○一九二四至
首總理○保良局會長○華商總會主席○東華醫院
○中外名公臣卿○碩德道儔○雅相倚重○想望丰采○以後
不貴也○爵士禮貴牛士○斯次爲王成褒舉○所捐亦
持國交○調護商業○尤工人給四罷工期內半辭○以難
紛排難之責○尤工人給四罷工期內半辭○以難
公壽辰○獻機以實國防○爵士斥金十萬○捐獻
一機○其對於祖國之熱忱○尤足稱式○一九一五
士最先之一人○亦爲本港太平紳士之先進○曾
年○將英國爵位獎章○一九二二年○將葡萄牙一等獎
等大綬嘉禾章○一九二五年○將英京聖約翰教
傷限爵位獎章○一九三零年○得葡萄牙一等獎
章○一九三二年○將法國大勳章○及德國一等
全國紅十字大勳章○一九三三年○得悉國爵位
勳章○及比利時爵位勳章○一九三六年○得安
南皇佐治五世銀牌大典○港府均批之爲籌
備委員○我國亦於歐時○派克赴美調查商務○
委員○後又委爲太平洋會議代表團關問○現仍
○葡英皇佐治五世銀牌大典○港府均批之爲籌
○英皇佐治五世銀牌大典○派克赴美調查商務
烈地方○爵士親赴大會○充任香港區名譽副監
一九二五年間○英國舉行全國博覽大會於溫殿
會長○經濟調查局分任委員會長○一九二四至

副金氏一致之要求○然一九三六年後之我國奧
正統一○實基於此○客歲我國人擬祝罕委長籌
讓起宏○當其三十歲時○已爲海關百萬財東○智
過遍全球各地○及我國各省○故眼光遠大○智
三十八歲後○蔚爲港中巨業保險鉅務及出入口
各行商業之領袖○其營業範圍○且遠至華北及
南洋爪哇菲律濱等地○現港中最大商行○舉之
任童事或主席者○凡十有八○足微其爲最著名
發起中國和平統一會議○一九二五年○我國內戰甚
舟國府高等顧問號○曾奔走南北○呼顧和平○
委員○後又委爲太平洋會議代表團顧問○現仍

悲天憫人之情○至屬可敬○惟當時未克實現○
國來會議○爵士居中作爲仲達○其愛國傷時○
夫人殊有賢德○樂善好施○曾獲英京聖約翰教
業及財力之人也○爵士於一八零年受室○其
卷及財力之人也○
傷限榮耀獎章○

SIR ROBERT HO TUNG, Kt. J. P.

Sir Robert Ho Tung (widely known as the "Grand Old Man" of Hongkong) was born in a humble home in Hongkong in 1862. As the eldest child of a family of seven, he early acquired and developed those qualities of organization and leadership which paved the way for his brilliant career later on. Being poor, he learned from his childhood days the lesson of frugality and wise employment of limited resources.

Young Robert showed signs of promise from the very first. At the age of seven he was such an adept pupil in Chinese that when his mother had to withdraw him from school on account of poverty, the teacher offered to continue teaching the child without fees. This teacher became so attached to his pupil that when the little boy had to commence his English studies at the Central School (now Queen's College) there was a reluctant parting. As an English student at the age of twelve Sir Robert quickly showed his ability, for after only six years of study he was chosen as a pupil teacher of the School. Then after a year of teaching (that is in 1878) he sat for a competitive examination for a post in the Chinese Maritime Customs at Canton under Sir Robert Hart's regime. Though he was the youngest candidate at that examination Sir Robert easily secured the post. After two years at the Customs young Ho Tung resigned. He then commenced his association with Messrs. Jardine, Matheson & Co., Ltd., which has now lasted over 50 years. His business abilities and his energising will soon became apparent and in two years he was promoted from a junior position to become the Manager of the Chinese department of the leading business firm in the Far East as Compradore of Jardine's. Sir Robert soon multiplied the business returns and connexions of the firm.

A Millionaire before he was 30 years of age, the once poor struggling youth soon became associated with practically every important business enterprise in the Colony. When he resigned his compradoreship in 1900 (at the early age of 38) Sir Robert Ho Tung was already known as the leading expert and merchant in Hongkong in property, insurance, shipping, and import and export business, with agencies in Java and the Philippines. From 1900 and onwards one company after another invited him to serve on its Board of Directors, until to-day he is a Director of 18 of the leading companies in Hongkong & Shanghai as well as being Chairman and largest shareholder of a number of them. A genius in all matters touching finance Sir Robert Ho Tung's opinion has been constantly sought after not only by the Government of Hongkong but also by the Chinese Republic whose High Adviser he is. In Hongkong he has served on many of the leading Committees and Commissions dealing with the economic life on the Colony. In particular he, as Chairman, was mainly responsible for producing the report of a Sub-Committee on the economic resources of Hong Kong and its Dependences in 1920. In 1922 he contributed much towards the settlement of the Seamen's Strike.

Sir Robert Ho Tung also takes a keen interest in the welfare of the Colony. Education in all its forms receives unstinted support from him. He has given $260,000. to the Hongkong University and defrayed the cost of building the old Kowloon British School. Many free evening schools on the island and the mainland are being maintained by him, while almost every school of importance in the Colony for both boys and girls has received something from him either in the form of scholarships or prizes or donations.

The poor and needy also have always had his sympathetic support. Sir Robert was the Chairman of the Tung Wah Hospital as far back as 1898, and during his term of office he was responsible for extending the hospital structurally, by raising funds for a new building as an Extension and Plague Hospital. In 1931 Sir Robert celebrated his Golden Wedding, and announced a donation of $200,000 to mark that occasion. Half this sum was applied to the building of a Children's Welfare Centre in the New Territories and the other half was devoted to the free education of poor girls in Hongkong. In 1934 he defrayed the entire cost of erecting a home for abandoned dumb animals and presenting it to the S.P.C.A. Thus from dumb animals to needy human beings, Sir Robert has held out the helping hand. In the same year he gave $100,000 towards the cost of an erection of an Industrial School for boys at aberdeen so that the poor children of Hongkong may learn a craft as well as the three Rs.

During the Great War he presented two aeroplanes and a number of motor ambulances to the British Government. Among some of the best known of Sir Robert's many public and social activities mention must be made of his efforts to end Civil Warfare in China by setting up a Round Table Conference between the various warlords. Though his efforts were not immediately successful they stimulated a demand for national unification which became an established fact in 1936. He also personally interviewed famine and flood Sufferers in China on various occasions. Another prominent part played by Sir Robert Ho Tung was at the British Empire Exhibition at Wembley in 1924 and 1925, which he attended as the Honorary Associate Commissioner of the Hongkong Section.

Sir Robert was a member of the Committee which organized the Reception to Duke of Connaught, and the then Prince of Wales as well as the celebrations in honour of Queen Victoria's Diamond Jubilee and the King George V Silver Jubilee.

In 1936 Sir Robert presented the Chinese Government an aeroplane costing $100,000 to mark the Fiftieth Birthday of the Generalissimo Chiang Kai Shek. Honours have been heaped upon Sir Robert from many countries. In 1915 he was knighted by His Majesty the King. He has been a Justice of the Peace since 1889, being the senior one on the list, and received several honours from the Chinese Government. To-day his imposing list of honours includes the following:—Knight of Grace of St. John of Jerusalem (1925), Knight Grand of Officer of the Order of Christ of Portugal (promoted Grand Officer in 1930), First Class Order of the Excellent Crop with Sash of China 1922, Knight Commander of the Legion of Honour 1932, First Class National Red Cross of Germany 1932, Knight Commander of the Crown of Italy 1933, Knight Commander of the Crown of Leopold of Belgium 1933, Knight Commander of the Imperial Dragon of Annam 1936. He is also Senior Honorary LL.D. of the University of Hongkong as well as the Colony's Senior Justice of the Peace. Sir Robert has travelled extensively throughout the world and his visits to Europe, U.S.A. and North China have been frequent in recent years. Many local societies claim him either as their Patron or President or Hon. Vice President.

In 1880 Sir Robert married Lady Ho Tung who is a Lady of Grace of the order of St. John of Jerusalem and assisted Sir Robert at the Wembley Exhibition in 1924 and 1925.

周壽臣爵士

SIR SHOU SON CHOW

周壽臣爵士〇名長齡〇以字行〇廣東省寶安縣人〇現年七十七歲〇乃香港爵、德、齒、三者兼備之人也〇清同治十三年（一八七四）〇由南洋大臣曾國藩〇北洋大臣李鴻章〇退充官費學生〇赴美留學〇修業於紐約哥林比亞學校〇光緒七年（一八八一）〇囘國〇由北洋大臣李鴻章奏派往朝鮮幫辦海關稅務〇光緒二十年（一八九四）〇署理朝鮮仁川領事〇光緒二十九年（一九〇三）〇由北洋大臣袁世凱委充天津招商局總辦〇光緒三十三年（一九〇七）〇委充京奉鐵路總辦〇賞戴花翎〇欽加二品頂戴〇因辦理日俄交戰中立事宜〇由日本帝國拱賜四等旭日勳章〇光緒三十四年（一九〇八）〇宣統元年（一九〇九）〇欽命署山海關道〇進加按察使街〇兼山海關監督〇奏改充錦新營口汛兵備道〇因籌鉤出力〇議敘加一級〇又因防疫出力〇傳旨加獎〇凡在任四年〇皆平所屬各府各州縣〇熟理民事、刑事，外交，稅務〇勤政愛民〇去任之日〇各商民鎗造萬民傘〇萬民牌匾〇口碑載道〇旋經外務部奏調以外務部參議上行走〇民國元年（一九一二）〇大總統袁世凱〇給予三等嘉禾章〇民國七年（一九一八）〇晉授二等嘉禾章〇民國八年（一九一九）〇大總統徐世昌頒給紀念章〇晉授二等大綬寶光嘉禾章〇由民國六年起（一九一七）〇充香港太平紳士〇民國十年（一九二一）〇充香港大學堂童事〇民國十一年（一九二二）〇旋奉英政府委充香港定例局議員〇民國十二年（一九二三）〇委赴英京賽會監督〇民國十五年（一九二六）〇奏建賞賜爵士榮銜〇民國十六年（一九二七）〇委充香港議政局員〇民國二十二年（一九三三）〇香港大學堂頒贈博士學位〇民國二十四年（一九三五）〇英皇賞贈銀禧紀念章〇在港凡廿餘年〇由香港政府委派者〇如國防局〇研究財政分任值理〇研究兒童院值理〇東華醫院永遠顧問〇公立醫局顧問〇定例局工務分任值理〇財政分任值理〇文員加薪委員〇保護兒童會會長〇其屬於社團者〇如華商總會顧問〇華人體育會會長〇南華體育會〇中華體育會等名譽會長〇中華全國體育協進會名譽會長〇屬於商業者〇則南洋兄弟煙草公司，香港土地信託公司，香港電話公司，香港電燈公司，香港電車公司，屈臣氏藥房等董事，中華娛樂實業公司，中華百貨公司，及東亞銀行等董事局主席〇勳業彪炳〇楊壽兼備〇香港華人中〇洵與其匹〇元配葉氏〇兄振菩泉

SIR SHOU-SON CHOW, Kt. J.P.

One of the most distinguished personages in Hongkong is Sir Shou-son Chow. He is a native of the Po On District, Kwongtung Province, but he was born in Hongkong and is now seventy-seven years of age. Having attained a good knowledge in Chinese literature he was then selected as a free scholar by the Chinese Government to study in the Columbia University, N.Y., U.S.A., in 1874. He returned to China in 1881, and held an important post in the Chinese Customs in Korea. Three years later, he was transferred to be consul-general in an important city in that country. In 1903, he was appointed president of the Chinese Merchants Steamship Navigation Co., Tientsin, and in 1907, president of the Peking Mukden Railway. During the Ruso Japanese War, he was presented by the Japanese Emperor with the Medal of Brilliancy, and since then, he was in the position of various Mandarins in Northern China and his excellent reputation was spread far and abroad.

After the Republic of China was founded, he was honoured by the late President Yuan Shih-kai with conferring of the Order of the Chia Ho (Excellent Crop) Third Class. The Second Class of the same Order was given him in 1918, while the Second Class Medal of Brilliancy was bestowed on him by president Hsu Shih-chang in the following year.

Since 1917, he became Justice of the Peace of Hongkong and besides this, he has the chair in the Directorate of many important firms and Public Utility concerns such as the Bank of East Asia; the China Entertainment and Land Investment Co., The China Emporium., The Hongkong Telephone Co., The Hongkong Electric Co., The Hongkong Tramway, The International Assurance, A. S. Watson, The Hongkong China Realty and Trust Co., The Nanyang Brothers Tobacco Co., Ltd., and many others.

Sir Shou-son Chow was a member of the Sanitary Board since 1922 and in the same year, became member of the Legislative Council. The Honour of Knighthood was conferred upon him by His Late Majesty King George V in 1926. In the following year, he became member of the Hongkong Executive Council, and in 1933, he was conferred by the Hongkong University with the Degree of LL.D. Another Honour bestowed upon him by His late Majesty King George V is the Order of the Silver Jubilee in 1935.

Sir Shou-son has been noted to be publicly and privately connected with various branches of philantrophic activities and is the president of the Hongkong Society for the Protection of Children and Patron of the Chinese Mission to Lepers as well as being in the Committee of various charitable associations. He is a member of the District Watchmen Committee, Permanent Adviser of the Tung Wah Hospital, Public Dispensaries and the Po Leung Kuk. Though he advances in age, his spirit is vigorous and kind; for he takes as great delight in sports as in business. He is adviser to the Chinese General Chamber of Commerce and Hon. President of the South China Athletic Assiciation and the Chinese Recreation Club.

Sir Shou-son was married in his youth and has many sons and plenty of grand and great-grand sons.

羅旭龢博士

DR. R. H. KOTEWALL

羅旭龢博士。現任奇港行政局華人代表議員。生於香港。先世業商。現年五十有七。幼齡辭業於香港皇仁。拔萃兩書院。攻詩英文。復從游宿儒。研求國學。其他日逐語。於其他日益語。羅公不特學貫中西。而且資賦穎敏。器宇依宏。攬辭令。各屆文。兼愛藝術。養通性靈。於全港。居恒覽群籍。初呂四等文員供職於香港警察已學能效用。初呂四等文員供職於香港警察縣。竣呂長才為上游實踐。於一九一三年。破

坤董。工務局工務局委員。工程繪圖師委員會委員。公冒局委員會委員。研究庄宇委宜委員會委員。定例局法制委員會委員。中缸代理行政局議員七次。而任定例局議員亦歷三屆之多。閱時凡十二年。而其於公益言。以能可貴。在公益言。尤為奇致能可貴。在公益言。尤為奇博士乃力根衛利害。不避勞險。慨助前例。尤為奇博士乃力根衛利害。不避勞險。慨助前例。監督。圓輯分會會長。在慈善言。則歷任奇港童軍總會長。兒童游樂管理會會長。兼主席。則歷任奇港紅十字會副會長。東華醫院顧問。保良局顧問。鐘聲慈善社名譽社長。維持風化會顧問。聖約翰救傷隊名譽社長。在教育言。

值理。聖約翰救傷隊名譽社長。在教育言。則歷任奇港大學董事會董事。香港大學漢文考試委事。香港大學文科會董事。西商會華語學務監督。西商會華語學名譽監督。香港大學學名譽學位。一九二六年香港大學特授校長名譽學位。一九二七年。英廷復授校長勳位。譯義『聖寵耳及聖佐治勳位』此皆崇德勒功。直特致與。一九三一年呂選減收差誤。取銷前例。卒開蘇區奇博士資格。坚請每居博士連任由政府减收差誤。取銷前例。卒開蘇區奇博士連任由政府送詞彙編一書。一九二一年曾編撰呂送詞彙編一書。并纂輯演舞君歡之英國。之滿。一九二二年。英廷有搬劇散迎君之英國。我國莱劇政編『煤嬈學』校之。表演。情殷劭人。座為博士即將並編演籌助人之座為博士即將演。情殷劭人。座為博士即將演六年底仙遊。其高賢之嵐實鳥奇女九人。僑愛庭訓。現業厲於香港旭龢道。

格推為裁判司署前席文案。故選為太平紳士。一九一六年。旋游推為布政司署前席文案。復呂勞約。後呂立志向商業發展。越即本歡。席文案。復呂勞約。後呂立志向商業發展。越即本歡。年服務警界。食呂為龍。成政容敗。于順機謬寄。及服任香港和聲唱片公司總理。華人星音公司。電話有限公司。九龍汽車公司。南洋兄弟姻草公司。中華汽車公司。九龍汽車公司。南洋兄弟姻草公司。中華汽車公司。九司。香港油蘇地小輪有限公司。凡此歡務。均能兼顧。至開於贊助社會義務。則約可區別為政事。公益。慈善。教育。體育。工商等六項。在政言。則歷任香港定例局前席華人代表議員。國防局

員長。一切委員。又曾厲廣东徐省長呂聘為高等顧問。未就。又得厲廣东徐省長顧問。未就。徐不勝枚舉矣。長一切委員。年服務警界。奇才稱之。而峰亦呂眼相看。舉世呂服刃有餘。故務緊囑。時人遂呂法呂稱之。而峰亦呂眼相看。舉世呂服刃有餘。署推升布政司署前席文案。尤見精密。其才其手。尤見精密。港府資為助預算。又機升布政司署前席文案。尤見精密。院大臣所稱許。解級之外。尤見精密。院大臣所稱許。解級之外。尤見精密。相恭頌。港府叠率畫謝其勳勞。褒崇備至。時

Dr. R. H. KOTEWALL, C.M.G., LL.D.

Dr. R. H. Kotewall is a member of the Hongkong Executive and Legislative Councils. He was born in Hongkong in 1880. He obtained his early education at the Diocesan Boy's School and the Queen's College. He takes pride in the fact that he has risen to the present position without a college diploma. What was deprived of him in the University halls he made up with books. What he missed in the college rooms he learned in the school of hard knocks. At home he has his own library where he spends two or three hours every day to read books, newspapers and magazines. He is a typical Chinese leader, modern and modest.

Dr. Kotewall was appointed as a 4th clerk in the Police Headquarters at the age of sixteen. Young in age but old in experience, he was promoted as the first clerk in the Magistrates' Court, Victoria, in 1913. In 1916 he was appointed as chief clerk in the Colonial Secretrate and at the same year he was made a Justice of the Peace, an appointment never before, nor since, given to a Chinese civil servant of Hongkong. Dr. Kotewall resigned the civil service in 1916, to start business. He was officially thanked by the government for his efficient and trustworthy services.

He has been nominated as a Chinese member of the Legislative Council in 1924, and of the Executive Council in 1936. The Hon. degree of LL.D. was conferred on him by the University of Hongkong in 1926. His late Majesty King George V decorated him with the insignia of C.M.G. in 1927.

Besides being an extremely capable Government official, Dr. Kotewall is connected with various social and commercial organizations either in the capacity of a president or a director. He is the principal of the R. H. Kotewall & Co., Ltd.; director of Hongkong Telephone Co., Ltd., director of Wo Shing Co., Ltd.; Hon. Vice-president of Hongkong University Union; Vice-president of Hongkong branch of the English Association; Vice-patron of St. John Ambulance Association; school committee of Diocesan Boys' School; Hon. Member of the Hongkong University Law & Commerce Society; Hon. president of South China Athletic Association; Hon. President of Chung Shing Benevolent Association.

Dr. Kotewall spends a lot of his time for Public Welfares. He has even not forgotten the Street Urchins. There is now a club for Boot-blacks and Newspaper Sellers Street Urchins sho would have otherwise no means of recreation or free tuition for a better future. Dr. R. H. Kotewall is one of the sponsors of the Club which has as its patron-His Excellency the Governor.

Though he is always busy yet he likes art and literature very much. His writings include "Forestry", and "Government in its relation to national welfare", which were written both in Chinese and English. In 1921 he wrote and personally produced a play entitled "Uncle Kim" in aid of charity, which was a great success. He also adapted a play named "The Maid of the Hills" from an old Chinese play, which he produced in honour of H.R.H. the then prince of Wales during the latter visit to Hongkong in 1922.

曹善允博士

DR. TS'O SEEN WAN

曹博士善允。粤之中山縣人。於遜清同治七年，（公元一八六八）誕於澳門。現年七十歲。先德渭泉公。濠江服賈。令聞久彰。以龍致力地方公益。為華僑晉校葡立勸學之第一人。用是見知于清廷。獲欽賜二品榮銜。頂戴花翎之賞。○博士生富裕家。無驕奢習。幼已聰慧好學。頴角崢嶸。超華十四。便于馬貧笈玫讀國學於晉華文人革蕃之德濱。四年面壁。可謂功深。○兩成之卷。遊學英國。以益新知。及秋玫進率周歐威大書院請業。四載學成。即與旅地名家繼尼君訂約為練習生。○期滿。史在英京裏馳。卷之律師樓實習。迨光緒二二年，（一八九六）應英國律師撿定試。以成績優異。獲領執業文憑。得出席英京高等法庭以成績優異。旋年進歸。開業香江。○獨力經營。凡三十載。至民一○六始與其人學洵君合辦。遂以兩人之名。顏其律師樓馬地君和之。○尤獨力捐資與建校舍。故香港大學之庇生。寶胎胚於此校。今藏校學移日形發達。○素徐辦理社會各種事業。恒惟卓越港隹寄是。從西華僑所學府馬。○博士此為辦科人之一。迄今常董其事

○博士善允。粤之中山縣人。○於遜清同治七年。初，作古開人何啓爵士乎。欲與博士叛辨一程度較高之學府。厥貴港地英才。俾貴港青才。快筹素復。可遂進英京大學。免浪柳寶貴光陰。與有用金錢。慇至善也。惜預故障。功敗垂成。未幾已。○納牧師。偷偹尼士他副主教。熱心勷學。尤計劃忙。邁献讓由公乎領衡之。如公乎中西南洋各地華僑。兩廣總督。亦曹予以助力馬。泊一九一一年。

初，作古開人何啓爵士乎。○今先就教育言。（一）聖士提反男校。柚何啓爵士通力合作。○遂建不朽之功。學及幼稚園。以俾將來設立女校之種乎。○同人建其議。故一九一一年。乃開創於卑巴形發達。○且使生平志趣高尚。數十年來。無日不與博士抱持亲為己任。為人類追步與康健踴躍而來。因地點不適中。運於堅道。殞十餘年發展。斯時披提園校舍寶廣不數。○少艾亦聯關停止。○至一九二二年。遷在列提咖道自建之橞金也。○先是英籍富紳毛地君献之前。博士致謝詞者。為已納副主教與博士。逆一九二六年。孜其中之一。（三）香港大學。香港大學之緣起。○辟有廷辦學之基。

應英國律師撿定試。以成績優異。獲領執業文聖士提反男校也。成立時期。為一九〇三年。至一九〇七年冬。而該校肯屆畢業。○景制畢提識。本港應有一大學。故蔣富神毛地君和之。○尤獨力捐資與建校舍。故香港大學之庇生。寶胎胚於此校。今藏校學移日形發達。○遊赤柱者。均獲覩此宏偉之桃李過趕南中。○博士此為叛科人之一。○迄今常董其事。○（二）聖士提反女校。當商辦爵士提反女之際。博士曹提讓應問時與辦一衆牧男女堂之種乎。○校舍寶廣不數。至一九〇四年。遷於堅道。殞十餘年發展。斯時披提園校舍寶廣不數。○少艾亦聯關停止。○斷時披提園主教與博士。逆一九二六年。孜其中之一。○主其基祖馬。○時值英籍君毛地君之贊財。未偹辦學之基。

兩廣總督。亦曹予以助力馬。泊一九一一年。即當時

故大學為完裕基金。舉行賣物會。名譽秘書一
席。亦屬之博士。同年故大學規例選准港府通
過。以博士曾與起草之列。被聘為委員。博士
因辭不獲。至一九一四年而始就。同時兼故校
內之聖約翰，登摩羅士，兩禮科堂之管理委員
。一九二九年，史晉任故大學立例，及董事。
兩局董事。（四）至保羅男書院。博士充任堅保
羅男書院董事。

讚憲為秘書。重行興築。繼就慈善院
讚選為芳原址。
教育者也。
本港教育部成立於一九二零年。博士被
再度勸捐。
院。雅利氏及邪打素醫院，在本港具有悠久歷
史。且為敬完其之慈善機關，係由倫敦教會管
理者。一九零三年博士被選為芳生醫院。博士
其後故院籌款附設接生醫院。及看護學校。博
建之何妙於接生醫院。亦附庸故院。故司庫
重責。亦須博士負之。迨一九二三年，院章重
訂。將財政委員會之權。改為中央委員會。當時
退為該會主席。迨任故院執行委員會之非官式主
席。一九三五年，邪打素醫院来因紐四十
年之久而改造。向外募捐。博士與有力焉。
（二）公立醫局

公立醫局董事。翌年，被推為西環公立醫局
董事會主席。（三）讚育醫院。西環為貧民住
宅區。婦孺為貧民。充宜故立。一九二二年以前
未有注意及之者。故屬疏急。自博士為主席公
立醫局於斯。乃叛辦讚育醫院。特聘香港大學
之婦科及接生科教校宪醫院主任。副後西區婦
孺。復益良多。至一九三四年。以紀常不緩。安
巧婦致為無米之炊。再作同樣財種。博士以港
種牛痘。一九一六年冬。本港西區發生痘症。
其教莫起。華民政務司特名集博士。與衞生
局醫官共同討論。建議應即舉行昔編之微求之
做者凡三十六萬人。於是經恵告息。後三年
為防乾未然。又伍延芳夫人捐
用舉其譽舉大者。（甲）填築九龍灣。當我國民
元革命時。政局未定。各省同胞來港作客者
甚眾。博士約同何啓，區德，張心湖等。發起
填築九龍灣。以展拓民居。歷有年所。始於一
九一四年四月選港府核准。而何竟先於五月奉
世。博士不得不獨任鉅艱。第一期計劃。于一
九二零年功竣。並科啓德汽車公司。以利九龍

（五）潔淨局（即今之市政衞生局）一
九一八年，博士被委潔淨局局紳。服務幾十
一載。功績殊偉。至一九二九年。始自行告退
。（六）東華醫院。一九二五年。被聘為東華醫
院顧問。以其助于慈善者也。至
（乙）改良香港水遶填地之交通。迨一九二七年，第二期完成
。方進行第三期之際。一九二五年，本港工潮
。港督以博士幸勞。頒賜聖約翰
一九一一年，內港府求撥
華人墓地。以及其他。一九一三年管理華人
永遶墳場之董事會。博士均厠其中讚助。港
一九年。復兼環境特別警察。及迴街革命組
教傷保也。童子軍會也。咸有不能助力。或董
事也。一九一八年，任太平局紳。一九二五年。
此止。一九三三年。任香港扶輪分會會長等職。
及兒童遊樂場副會長。同年一月十七日起。任定
例局紳。蟬聯兩屆。至一九三七年一月十七
名譽法科博士街。再於一九三五年錫英
二八年，校以OBE勳章。最近本港諸人赴英祝英
名譽法科博士。英廷賞其歷年勞勣之于一九
人所歡譽吳。夫人陳氏。有賢德。尤熱心服務
以OBE勳章。官方倚重人退。代表亦勞博士任之
則博士之為人。不僅為僑胞所愛戴。抑亦為外
于社會。公子數人。均飽受教育。

（一）雅利氏合衆醫
院。亦附庸故院。故乃
為防乾未燃。再作同樣財種
巧婦致為無米之炊。再作
安。臨時組織特別警察，及迴街革命組織
泉為。委科啓德汽車會。政府以為維持治
之力也。（五）潔淨局
其教莫起。華民政務司特名
港人警察後備隊。而任名譽總救焉。（兩）為華人
軍會也。咸有不能助力。或董
教傷保也。童子軍會也。咸有不能助力。

（二）公立醫局

一九一零年，博士被選為華人
九二零年功竣。並科啓德汽車公司。以利九龍
于社會。公子數人。均飽受教育。

香港華人名人史略（一九三七）

Dr. TS'O SEEN WAN, C.B.E., LL.D., J.P.

The Honourable Mr. Ts'o Seen Wan, C.B.E., LL.D. J.P., was born in Macao on the 10th November, 1868. He is the son of the late Mr. Ts'o Yau alias Ts'o Wai Chuen, a well-known merchant of Macao who was the first Chinese in Macao decorated by the King of Portugal with the Insignia of "Commenda De Nossa Senhora Da Conceicao" (Padroeira Do Reino) and had the Honorary title of the 2nd Degree with the Red Button and Peacock's Feather conferred on him by the Emperor of China Kwang Hsu in the year 1880.

Dr. Ts'o went to Shanghai for his Chinese education in 1881 and returned to Macao in 1885 when arrangements were made for him to go to England for his English education. He left Hongkong for England at the end of February of 1886 and entered Cheltenham College in September of the same year. After passing his Law Entrance Examination he left College after the Mid-Summer term in 1890. He was articled to Mr. W. G. Gurney of Messrs. Winterbotham and Gurney, a well-known firm of Solicitors in Cheltenham and served the last year of his articles at the office of Messrs. Waterhouse, Winterbotham and Harrison in London. He passed his final law examination in April 1896 and was enrolled as a solicitor of the Supreme Court of Judicature of England. He came to Hongkong and set up in practice on his own account as a solicitor in 1897; was subsequently joined by Mr. P. M. Hodgson in 1927 and thereafter has practiced with him under the firm name of Messrs. Ts'o and Hodgson.

Although Dr. Ts'o's ancestral home was in Macao, his family had many friends, business connections and interests in Hongkong. On his return to the Colony he at once associated himself with the late Sir Kai Ho Kai and the late Sir Boshan Wei Yuk, two leading members of the Chinese community, and assisted them, unostentatiously, in various matters of public interest; Sir Boshan Wei Yuk being the gentleman who was responsible for his going to England, and looked after his welfare during the whole period of his sojourn there. His chief interest seemed to have been directed towards education and medical work among the Chinese; holding, no doubt, the principle that sound knowledge and good health are essentials to human beings for progress and happiness. He possesses a quiet disposition and unobstrusive manners and much dislikes coming forward into the limelight. And yet, by the weight of his public services, he was forced to the front and recognized as a leading member of the Chinese community in Hong Kong. His services to the Chinese community have been many and varied and it may be said that they cover the whole expanse of a human life from birth to death as the following list of institutions with which he was and is still connected will show.

EDUCATIONAL

St. Stephen's Boys' College.

This College was opened in 1903. Dr. Ts'o was one of its founders and has taken interest in its affairs since its opening. The object of founding this College was to give Chinese students a higher standard of education so that any one of them who may desire to go to England for a University course of education may enter a University without much further preparation for entrance and thereby save himself from longer residence there and the expense attendant thereto. An attempt to establish such a College for the Chinese was made by the late Sir Kai Ho Kai, Dr. Ts'o and other leading members of the Chinese community a few years previously. But for certain reasons, the scheme was not proceeded with, until the Rev. Mr. (afterwards Archdeacon) E. J. Barnett came to Hongkong in 1902 when he and Archdeacon (Afterwards Bishop) Bannister approached Sir Kai on the subject and undertook to start such a school if the Chinese would promise to support. This promise was readily given by Sir Kai Ho Kai and his associate. One of the two houses known as "Ball's Court" situated between Bonham Road and Western Street was then taken as a start for the school. Under the Wardenship of Mr. Barnett the school flourished. The other house at Ball's Court was also taken the next year. In 1905 it was found that further accomodation was required for the school and a 21 years' lease of Ball's Court with its extensive ground was taken with the object of adding a new wing to the existing buildings; the Chinese supporters of the school provided a sum of $80,000 for the purpose. It was not until January 2, 1910, that a Board of Advice was founded of which Dr. Ts'o was an original member. This Board was changed to a College Council of which Dr. Ts'o was also an original member. The College has now its own school building at Stanley situated on a beautiful site with every facility and ample ground for games and sport. It was at a Prize-giving Day at St. Stephen's College (December 1907) that Sir Frederick (now Lord) Lugard the then Governor of Hongkong suggested that Hongkong itself should possess a University. His suggestion was taken up at once by the late Sir (then Mr.) H. N. Mody, who offered to erect entirely at his own expense the necessary buildings for a Hong Kong University. The idea of founding a Hongkong University, it may be said, originated from St. Stephen's College.

St. Stephen's Girls' College.

When discussing the establishment of the Boys' College, Dr. Ts'o suggested that a kindergarten school for Chinese boys and girls should also be opened as a nucleus for a girls' college. A kindergarten and girls' school was started in 1904 in a building at Breezy Point but only a few very young girls attended. It was subsequently found that the parents of grown-up girls objected to the locality as being too far from the centre of the town and it was, therefore, removed to No. 59 Caine Road the next year 1905. Many grown-up girls then came and the school prospered. It may be said that St. Stephen's Girls' College was founded in that year.

Dr. Ts'o took great interest in the College from its start and it was not until 1922 that the present College building at Lyttleton Road was erected, the foundation stone of which was laid by His Royal Highness, the Prince of Wales in that year; Archdeacon Barnett and Dr. Ts'o as representatives of the College, had the honour of presenting to His Royal Highness, and address of welcome and thanks. The College Council was not instituted until 1926 and Dr. Ts'o has been a member of the Council since that year.

Hongkong University.

When Mr. Mody offered to erect the necessary buildings for the Hongkong University, a committee was appointed by His Excellency, Sir Frederick Lugard, to consider the matter and it was decided that, before accepting the offer, an Endowment Fund of at least $1,000,000 should be raised. The leading Chinese in Hongkong were asked to form a Sub-Committee to assist in raising the Endowment and at a meeting held at Government House in 1909 on the invitation of His Excellency Sir Frederick Lugard, a Chinese Sub-Committee was formed; the late Sir Kai Ho Kai was elected Chairman, and Dr. Ts'o the Honorary Secretary thereof. Appeals were made not only to Chinese in Hongkong, but also in China and abroad. The Viceroy of Canton was approached who took special interest in the scheme and gave substantial help to the Endowment Fund. A University Bazaar of which Dr. Ts'o was the Honorary Secretary was held in 1911 to raise more funds. This Committee continued to function for a few years after the opening of the University collecting further funds for various objects for the University such as for the playground, the union, etc.; and particularly in obtaining funds for starting an Arts Faculty. When the University Ordinance was passed in 1911, Dr. Ts'o was appointed a member of the Court; but he resigned to seat in favour of another gentleman, and was not until 1914, appointed a member thereof. Since 1929, Dr. Ts'o has been (ex officio) a member of the Court as well as the University Council. He was also a member both of the University Sharp and the University Gollan Commissions.

University Hostels.

Dr. Ts'o has been a member of the Board of Control of St. John's Hall since April 1914; and also a member of the Board of Control of Morrison Hall since 1914.

St. Paul's College.

When St. Paul's College was re-established, an extension to the old College building was required. A Committee was appointed in 1914 to raise the necessary funds for the extension. Dr. Ts'o was appointed Secretary to the Committee. He was also a member of the Committee for raising funds to build a hostel in 1918 and a member of the College Council since 1914.

Board of Education.
Dr. Ts'o has been a member of the Board since it was instituted in April 1920.

Munsang College.
The establishment of this College was part of a scheme for the development of the Kai Tack Reclamation. The late Mr. Au Chak Mun left by his will a sum of 10,000 for the purpose and Mr. Mok Kon Sang, a shareholder of the Kai Tack Co., also contributed another sum of $10,000 for the same purpose. When the first section of the reclamation was completed and houses were built thereon, the need for educational facilities seemed apparent and in 1926 the College was first started Dr. Ts'o was elected Chairman of the College Council.

MEDICAL

Alice Memorial and Affiliated Hospitals.
Dr. Ts'o became a member of the Finance Committee of the Alice Memorial and the Nethersole Hospitals in 1903. He took part in raising funds for the building of the Maternity Hospital and the Institute for the Training of Nurses. When Madam Wu Ting Fang presented the funds for the building of the Ho Miu Ling Hospital, Dr. Ts'o was Treasurer of that fund. The last mentioned institutions were affiliated to the Alice Memorial and Nethersole Hospitals all of which were under the management and control of the London Missionary Society. In 1923, a new Constitution (for the draft of which Dr. Ts'o was responsible) was adopted. The Finance Committee was then changed into a General Committee. Dr. Ts'o was appointed Chairman of the Committee in 1930 and (ex officio) he was also Chairman of the Executive Committee. The Nethersole Hospital Building after forty years of useful work was pulled down in May 1935. Dr. Ts'o is making every effort to raise funds for its rebuilding.

Chinese Public Dispensaries.
He was a Member of the Chinese Public Dispensaries Committee in 1910 and became a Chairman of the Western Public Dispensary in 1911.

Tsan Yuk Hospital.
This is a Maternity Hospital in the Western district built in 1922. As Chairman of the Western Public Dispensary, the Tsan Yuk Hospital was under his management and control. As the district was a poor one, the need of a clinic for women's diseases and one for babies became urgent. The Professor of Gynaecology and Obstetrics of the Hongkong University was invited to take charge of these clinics. This Hospital was, for financial reasons handed over to the Government in January 1934 for management.

Vaccination Campaign (1916—1917)
When an epidemic of small-pox broke out in the Western District of Hongkong towards the end of 1916, Dr. Ts'o was requested by the Secretary for Chinese Affairs and the Medical Officer of Health to consider the best means of preventing the spreading of the disease. Dr. Ts'o suggested universal vaccination. He guaranteed that the Chinese would not go against vaccination if certain concessions be given to them when a case occurred in their house. The concession was agreed to by the Medical Officer of Health, Dr. Woodman, subject to the approval of His Excellency, the Governor. His Excellency gave full power to Dr. Woodman to adopt, at his discretion, any suggestion Dr. Ts'o might make during the campaign. The campaign was successful from the very beginning. It commenced in November 1916 and ended in March 1917. No less than 360,000 children and grown-ups were vaccinated during that period. A second campaign took place three years afterwards in which Dr. Ts'o also assisted.

Sanitary Board (now Urban Council)
Dr. Ts'o was appointed a Chinese member of the Board in the year 1918. He served on the Board from that year until he resigned his seat in 1929.

Tung Wah Hospital.
Dr. Ts'o has been a member of the Advisory Board since September 1925. Apart from the great interest he takes in the educational and medical works, Dr. Ts'o has also taken great interest in the general question of over-crowding in Hongkong. Many Chinese came to Hongkong to reside when the revolution took place in China. The late Sir Kai Ho Kai, Dr. Ts'o and Messrs. Au Tack and Cheung Sum Woo formulated a scheme for the reclamation of Kowloon Bay foreshore. Sir Kai Ho Kai was requested to negotiate with the Hongkong Government for a concession to reclaim Kowloon Bay. After long negotiations, the concession was ultimately granted by the Hongkong Government in April. Unfortunately, Sir Kai died in May of the same year and Dr. Ts'o was left to carry out the scheme. A private company was formed to take up the concession and the name of "Kai Tack" was taken in honour of Sir Kai and Mr. Au Tack. War broke out in August 1914 which caused many obstacles in the progress of the reclamation work. However, the first section of the scheme was completed in 1920 and buildings were erected on that section. The Kai Tak Bus Company was specially instituted to give facilities to residents of Kowloon City and the reclamation, and formed part of the scheme for the development of the reclamation. However, after the second section had been fully completed, the Government required the whole reclamation, except the first section, for air service. The remaining area was surrendered to the Government in 1927 and it is now known as the Kai Tack Aerodrome.

During the emergency in 1925 on account of labour trouble, Dr. Ts'o was appointed Chinese Labour Controller by the Government. While engaged in this task, he organized a Chinese company of special constables and also a number of street guards to meet the threat of incendiarism. After the experience of 1925, it was thought by the Hon. Inspector General of Police that a police reserve force should be formed. Dr. Ts'o was requested to organized a Chinese Company and was made Hon. Commissioner of the Police Reserve Force.

In 1925, he was appointed a member of the District Watch Committee and a visiting Justice of the Po Leung Kuk and has been a member of the Permanent Board of Direction of the Po Leung Kuk since 1929.

He has been connected both with the Hongkong Society for the Protection of Children's Playground Association since their foundations in the capacity of a Vice-president.

He was one of the original members of the Committee to apply for a Permanent Cemetery for the Chinese in 1911, and a member of the Board of Management of the Permanent Cemetery when the Board was formed in 1913. He became the Honorary Secretary of the Permanent Cemetery in 1919.

He is also associated in various ways with many other organizations in public life including the movements of St. John's Brigade, Boy Scouts & etc.

The Rotary Club of Hongkong appointed him their President for the year 1933.

He was nominated as a Chinese member of the Legislative Council on 17th January 1929 and is serving his second term which will expire on the 17th January 1937.

He was made a Justice of the Peace in 1918. The Hon. Degree of LL.D. was conferred on him by the University of Hongkong in 1924.

He was created an Officer of the Order of the British Empire by His late Majesty King George VI in 1923 and Commander of the same Order in 1935.

He is being invited by the Hongkong Government to represent the Chinese in Hongkong at the Coronation of his Majesty King George VI on the 12th May 1937 to which invitation he has accepted and will proceed to England next April.

周埈年大律師

法家埈年先生○原籍廣東東莞縣○而生長於香港○乃前本港華人代表周爵少岐之公子○而現任之香港華人代表也○幼秀慧○十七歲已畢業於香港聖士提反書院○越年○赴英留學○習律於牛津大學○及西曆一九一四年○學成歸國○得大律師及文學士榮銜○在港中社會服務多年○曾任東華醫院總理○保良局紳○西曆一九二三年任太平局紳○華商總會名譽董事○一九二九年○任濬海局紳○物業報持會主席○內河輪船商會主席○保○前程無限量○

埈年兼司理○一九三一年英政府以先生服務精忠○委充定例局議員○先生更勢勵盡職○對於港政府法例方面○貢獻良多○而對於華人利益○尤能某劃及保障○一九三五年○第一任期滿○政府不計辭退○故現連任斯職○先生現年四十四歲○

護兒童會司理○整理港口會委員○東黨商會主席○華人核數員試官○中華體育會正會長○中華體育會名譽會董○華人體育協進會名譽會董○童子軍港分會長○華人聖約翰救傷隊名譽會董，兼財政委員○華商會所主席○防範海盜會委員○電話會委員○英荃會司理○內河輪船會委員○救濟水荒會委員○又任慈幼會司○大司庫○港庫○籌辦大學女宿舍司

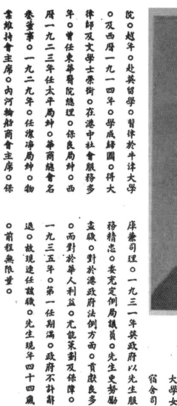

師律大年埈周

Hon. Mr. CHAU TSUN NIN, J.P.
BARRISTER-AT-LAW.

Mr. Chau is one of the most influential social magnates of Hongkong. He is a native of the Tungkoon District, Kwongtung Province, but was born in Hongkong is 1893. When he was but seventeen years old, he was graduated from the St. Stephen's College and in the following year, he set sail to England to continue his studies and to attain a thorough education. He was graduated with the B.A. degree and the title of Barrister-at-law from Oxford University England in 1914 and ever since, he practices his profession in the Colony. Bright and smart as Mr. Chau is, he has rendered himself to the commercial world. He is general manager and director of the Yuen On Steamship Co., Ltd.; The China Emporium, Ltd.; the Chun On Fire Insurance Co.; manager of the Hongkong & Kowloon Land & Loan Co., Ltd.; director of the Wo Shing Co., Ltd.; committee of the Fire Insurance Association of Hong Kong, Marine Insurance Association of Hongkong & Canton. Besides these, Mr. Chau is partner or stockholder of many firms in Hongkong.

Though he is always busy with his own work, Mr. Chau is, very attentive in social affairs. He is a member of the Legislative Council, which he began consumation since 1931; and member of the Sanitary Board. He was appointed Justice of the Peace of Hongkong since 1923 and has been holding important positions in different public-welfare organizations. The most note-worthy ones are finance committee of the St. John Ambulance Association; Hon. president of the Chung Sing Benevolent Society; college council of the St. Stephen's College; Hon. Vice-president of the Hong Kong University Union; Hon. President of the South China Athletic Association; Vice-president of the Boy Scouts Association; Hon. Director of the Chinese General Chamber of Commerce; Ex-president of the Tung Wah Hospital; Justice of the Po Leung Kuk; ex-president of the Inland Steamship Association; and director of the Hongkong Society for the Protection of Children.

Speaking generally, Mr. Chau has done, a great deal to the Hongkong Government as well as to the Chinese population living in the Colony.

羅文錦大律師

師律大錦文羅

文錦律師羅文錦先生者。紳坤長肇會之長公子也。生於西曆一八九三年港寓。賦性溫和。容貌英偉。自少精敏。學貫中英。詳屬風發。新聲英頭角。泉謂羅氏有子矣。及長。資兼英倫。銳

力於商業也。則任香港中華電力公司。香港大酒店。省港澳物船公司等董事。此不過先生半生服務之大畧情形耳。其俗猶或投委於官廳。或見重於社團。聘書疊匯。更僕難數。然最顯著而為僑胞頹手稱慶者。則英提議撤銷華報檢查若干。蓋言論自由。為文明國之公例。而民之喉舌。豈容久遭掊擊。先生激於大義所在。提議撤銷。雖不辛竟遭否決。而正義所在。中外咸欽。淘不愧為華人之代表也。誰日不宜。今先生方年富力強。正大有為之候。其造福于人羣者。寧有艾耶。羅代表。羅先生。吾將鞠。片言立折。故嬰攀大振。於若爭聘。追一九二一年。英政府以其原明精幹。委充太平紳士。一九三二年。又委為團防局紳。先後並充公子。賢夫良婦。相得益彰。現有子女五人云。

清濟衛生等局議員。去歲復委為定例局議員。兼香港大學校董及參事。孔子所謂學而優則仕者。先生以之。其服務於社會也。則充華商總會。東華醫院顧問。保良局永遠議員。兒童保護會等主席。香港扶幼會。歐美留學生聯合會等會長。其致

會。東華醫院顧問。保良局永遠議員。兒童保護會等主席。香港扶輪會。歐美留學生聯合會等會長。其致

志法律。一九一五年畢所業。迄應英京律師檢定。名譽等試。初已及第。爛則名冠全班。此因羅君之美譽。抑亦我國留學生之光榮也。旋即束裝歸港。行其所學。兼執律師。辯訟累奇。卒以案業定。迺遠

士。一九三二年。又委為團防局紳。先後並充公子。賢夫良婦。相得益彰。現有子女五人云。

Hon. Mr. LO MAN-KAM, J.P.
Solicitor

Mr. Lo was born in Hong Kong in 1893. He was bestowed with such talents that he was usually highly commended even when he was a youth. Having graduated from Hong Kong, he went to England for higher education. He passed the Solicitors' Final and the Solicitors' Honour Examinations in 1915 and came first in the First Class in the latter case which was considered to be one of the glories among the Chinese students who studied there.

He returned to Hong Kong in the same year and since then he practises his profession in the colony gaining most recommendation and praise of his line.

Mr. Lo is an influential factor in social affairs. He was appointed Justice of Peace in 1921, Member of District Watchmen Committee since 1932, Member of the Legislative Council in 1935 and Member of the Sanitary Board and afterwards Urban Council from 1932 to 1936. Besides these, Mr. Lo has usually been appointed important positions in various social and commercial organizations. The most note worthy ones are Director of the Hong Kong and Shanghai Hotel Ltd., Hong Kong Canton and Macao Steamboat Co., Ltd., China Light & Power Co., Ltd., Member of the Hong Kong University Law & Commerce Society, Committee of the Law Society, Hon. Vice-president of the Hong Kong University Union, Vice-president of the Hong Kong Branch of the English Association, Ex-officio and former president of the Rotary Club of Hong Kong, Vice-president of the Hong Kong Football Association, Vice-president of the Hong Kong Lawn Tennis Association, Hon. President of the South China Athletic Association, Committee of the Hong Kong Chinese Recreation Club and Legal Adviser of the New Territories Agricultural Association of Hong Kong. He is also Member of the Advisory Board of the Tung Wah Hospital, Permanent Member of the Committee of the Po Leung Kuk, and Hon. Legal Adviser to the Chinese Chamber of Commerce.

Mr. Lo married in 1918 to Ho Kam Chi. They have five children.

Speaking in general, Mr. Lo is one of the most prominent Chinese in Hong Kong and has wrought wonderfully for the good of Chinese Community. One example for which the fame and name of Mr. Lo shall never be faded is the protest against the censorship of Chinese news papers.

李樹芬醫博士

DR. LI SHU FAN

李樹芬醫博士。原籍廣東台山人。而生長於香港。現年五十三歲。久著名香港之華人西醫生新就職之華人代表也。少時。肄業於港中拔萃書院。稍長。隨父兄到美國之波士頓埠。肄業於英國中學。既弱冠。玫進香港西醫學堂。攻習醫科。西曆一九零八年畢業。領有該校執照士之銜頭。旋將清廷資送到英國愛丁堡大學無官費生。攻內外全科。一九一零年畢業。獲科授大學內外科醫學士學位。越年。又榮膺故大學熱帶病學兼衛生學碩士。遂由英返港。時為西曆一九一一年。即民國元年也。當時我國共和政府始初成立。首都暫設廣州。博士被委充新政府廣東衛生部長。未幾我國首都遷於南京。博士仍枕職返港。○遂送往港中自行開設醫務所。一九一三年。○

○曆一九二二年。博士再赴英國。追愛丁堡大學外科學院攻讀。卒膺該學院外科博士銜。一九二五年。博士由英返港時。正為香港大罷工風潮最烈之候。港督金文泰爵士。以博士曾為中國政府官史。托任調人。博士遂奔走省港間。以進行調停工作。卒不辱使命。俾罷工風潮。

九二四及一九二五兩年。○博士曾被聘再到廣州。○參加廣東公醫學校政組大學事宜。及廣東公醫醫科大學成立後。○即被聘為故大學校長兼外科大教授。當時國父孫中山正在廣州組織軍政府。聘博士為大元帥府醫官。○西

從此結束。○至今港人猶稱道之。○於罷工風潮停息後。○博士以跑馬地養和醫院。乃華人所設立之唯一療養院。理應完善。遂從事將故院改組材。擴築五層樓院所。添置最新式醫科用具。○○增設附醫部。及設看護學校。以訓練看護人煥然一新。因對於故院勞役對甚大。故屢被舉為故醫院董事長凡十年之久。於此之外。○博士為港中各機關團體所住職務至多。計歷任遠東熱帶病學會副會長。中華醫學總會會長。中華醫學會香港分會會長。香港大學醫學會會長○香港大學董事。○華商總會名譽幹事。東華醫局議員。非官派太平局紳。○潔淨局議員。市政衛生局議員。○聖約翰救傷會醫官。○墾永遠會員。保護兒童會淨局及衛生條例審查會會員。一九三五年香港歷屆審查會會員。香港孔聖會名譽會長。歐美同學會會長。廣東銀行董事。我國國民經濟建設運動委員會廣東省分會委員。今年史秋委本港定例局議員（華人代表）。博士生平最喜行善。○公餘報等一樓一物。徵於對卹之外。三十年如一日。故獲報甚精。而體魄亦甚壯。

Dr. LI SHU FAN,

J.P., M.B., Ch. B., D.T.M. & H., F.R.C.S. (Edinburgh)

Dr. Li was born in Hongkong in 1885. He received his early education at the Diocesan School and later in Boston, U.S.A. In 1908 he graduated from the Hongkong College of Medicine with the degree of L.M. & S. Thereafter, he proceeded to Europe under a Chinese Government Scholarship and enrolled himself at the University of Edinburgh, where in 1910 he obtained the degree of Bachelor of Medicine and Surgery and in the following year a special Diploma in Tropical Medicine and Hygiene. After several years of medical practice in Hongkong he returned to Edinburgh in 1922 where after a course of post-graduate work, he was elected a Fellow of the Royal College of Surgeons.

Upon his return to China in 1911, the year of the foundation of the Chinese Republic, when Canton was the Capital of China, he was appointed Minister of Health and Later when the seat of the Government was removed to Nanking, he continued to serve in Canton as Commissioner of Health for the province of Kwangtung. Being the first Minister and Commissioner of Health in the history of the country, he had undertaken studpendous pioneering legislative and organization work.

Returning to the Colony in 1913, he commenced the practice of his profession up to the present time. From 1924 to 1925, however, he had served a two years' contract in Canton, being engaged in the reorganization of the Kung Yee Medical College, with the object of bringing it up to the University Status. On the completion of that work, he was appointed President of the Kung Yee University Medical School as well as Professor of Surgery. This school is now incorporated with the Sun Yat Sen University.

During his stay in Canton, a signal honour was bestowed upon him by the Chinese Government in appointing him Medical Officer to the Generalissimo and President of the Republic, Dr. Sun Yat Sen.

During the big strike of 1925 he again returned to the Colony, and in this connection he acted as one of the intermediaries between the Hongkong and Canton Governments, at the special request of the then Governor of Hongkong, Sir Cecil Clementi. His work had helped in no measure towards the settlement of that strike.

Having been back in the Colony, he was primarily responsible for the reorganization of the Yeung Wo Hospital at Happy Valley, now known as the Hongkong Sanatorium and Hospital. This, he completely reorganized, adding thereto a charity department and a training school for nurses and midwives, and in 1932 the present magnificent new hospital building of five stories was completed, designed on up-to-date lines, and equipped with modern appliances. He has now served the Hospital continuously as Chairman of Directors for ten years.

He had been elected as Vice-president of the Far Eastern Association of Tropical Medicine, Vice-president of the National Chinese Medical Association, President of the Hongkong Chinese Medical Association, and Vice-president of the Hongkong University Medical Society. He is also member of the Court of the University of Hongkong.

He is an Honorary Director of the Chinese Chamber of Commerce, a member of the Tung Wah Hospital Advisory Board, member of the Medical Board, as well as a member of the Sanitary Board. In 1935 he was re-elected to serve a second term as member of the Sanitary Board, which is now the Urban Council. He is a non-official Justice of the Peace. He has been nominated as a Chinese member of the Legislative Council 1937.

In addition, he is a member of the Executive Committee of Society for the Protection of Children, for twenty years he was as active member as well as life member and Corps Surgeon to the St. John Ambulance Brigade and Association. He served as member of the Sanitary Legislation Committee, in connection with the Scheme for the Reorganization of the Medical and Sanitary Services of the Colony. At present he is a member of the Hongkong Housing Commission of 1935. He is director of the Bank of Canton.

Incidentally it may be mentioned that he is Honorary president of the Confucian Society of Hongkong, was President of the Chinese Euro-American Returned Students' Union, and in connection with the Canton Government he is a member of the Reconstruction Council of Kwangtung Province.

Dr. Li's hobby is game shooting, spending most of his weekends in the company of his gun and dogs. For close on thirty years he had been shooting in various parts of the Colony, and knows practically every nook and ravine where game is to be had.

香港華人名人史略（一九三七）

何甘棠先生

MR. HO KOM TONG

粵之寶安縣人。現年七十二歲。髫齡肄業於奇
棣生。行五。舜坤晚生之介弟也。謳於奇
棠之富仁不讓。遇事出財兼出力者鮮矣。先生諱
言哉。然開港以來。辦開人造出。興開人造出。
自古非常之人。然後能建非常之業。然後龍立非常之功。是則非常之人。宜易

港皇家英文大書院。又喜研國學。博覽羣想。
既冠畢業。即能隨父洋行。背誦渡旬洋行。經
迎燕梳。叢科糖索。新硎初試。游刃有徐。復
於廣州。汕頭。九江。燕湖。宜昌。鎮江。南京。上
海。寧波。煙台。青島。天津。漢口。復
牛莊。各內地商埠。及澳門。經營金融。伊勢。始
渡華。各外人市場。造訪商號。經營金融。糖
業。花紗。煤炭。什貨等業。及年剛學息。
將渡旬職務言辭。追鈞屆耳順。復教各地商業

方能同鄉研官陳伯陶。尹應舉。諸師恭侶。早
已避敷後桑玉田。一面迎知彼等卒備南岡。一
面讀求得相借箪。兼照商局鄭君陶葡商洽。
造返港江。興招商局鄭君陶葡商洽。放射三
舶。前往沽沽接應。是役救援同鄉造千人。恵
及外省亦二千徐人。至今中江廣慶公所猶紀念
之。(二)戊申。(西一九〇八年。)廣東水患。蜒却空前。
州四年。)廣東水惠。蜒却空前。先生親覩為
懷。忱捐五萬圓。在港倡賣物眼哭。是為賣物

結束。夫人之慈惰。既廣嘗留貽。
為兄張作馬牛。而本次是之。大部輸將。均
作福人羣之舉。五十年來。擇善不下百萬。以
己倡而眾和者。其數又復倍之。用特分述之。以
紀賣勞。併光呼號。為敵民請命協力。計是次勤
後人籍資觀感馬。(一)庚子。(西一九〇〇年)伴
捐造賣物舉款所得。與莆氏請命益力。計是次勤
○於閏八月望日。電港之廣榮公所求援於
我邦恭匯之象。吾粵同鄉官眷。時值

冰河。交通將絕。精事遠起。
卒由先生解索以倡。會員數十人。倡電港
粵協助。共為一萬五千圓。隨電港水
乃於米間京索。精事重覓。
立以某金浣華造勝銀行電
淮。(時派驳仵領。經先生
向旅行討情。後且斜免溫水
)芳鵬米石二千包。斜泵
招局局廣齊物押運。既抵搪
沽。辛間車抵。民食賴宅。
乃於九月初二勤程。水凝地凍。送
舶行跟幸。至初九始入都

救富笑及○公道客申江
参斯讓席。赴會造款者數十人。時值
窮當其乏。○廷時月徐
聯同抵帑路礎。時計行商
倍之。先生尚義忠公。斗命卽赴。自勤各行
會。○踪跟輸將。夕造東華醫院。審查賬戶
其次共賽金六十萬。合港府楠助共壹百二十萬
○除分給賑戶外。仍存六十三萬徐圓。撥呈港
府。以倡助與張油蘇地避風搪之用。(故搪工
程。共費二百五十徐萬。)至今繼最最風。而西
海面招失。較前大減。○(五)西一九〇四年。(
卽甲午。)本港疫症登生。造乎四境。港例為社

民政務司鵝倫浩君。聯同抵帑路礎。膝時月徐
泉。○翰艦作存者等於農。○港府万商諸先生與馮
公華川。出面教濟。並許先生勸捐若干。照數
倍之。先生尚義忠公。斗命卽赴。自勤各行
其雨之歎者。○已厭作期○午夜吉歸。有此者○
鳴而起。○已厭作期○在州逗影躯。無日而不報。此無
是次共賽金六十萬。合港府楠助共壹百二十萬
一九〇六年。(卽丙午。)本港颱風肆虐。慘狀
為開華以來所報見。○脊斜黃薄其工作與馮
公華川。○出面教濟。並許先生勸捐若干。照數
倍之。○斗命卽赴。自勤各行
會。○踪跟輸將。夕造東華醫院。審查賬戶

等款第一人。卽馮公華川協力同心。○卒等四十
萬金之巨。○以眼哭徐。○(三)庚戌。(西一九一
〇年。卽造清宣統二年。)淡水又復兩笑。○均
生乃再捐五萬圓。並向港府求簽五萬圓。以助
善舉。○斗死呼號。為敵民請命益力。計是次勤
捐造賣物款所得。○與莆氏請命益力。○時與先生
○分給賑戶○為倡重計。○故向港方自
○於閏八月望日。電港之廣榮公所求援於

等候。○恤捐五萬圓。在港倡賣物眼哭。是為賣物
程。○共費二百五十徐萬。西一九四年。(
海面招失。較前大減。○(五)西一九〇四年。(
卽甲午。)本港疫症登生。造乎四境。港例為社
紀傳染起見。凡惠此病者。須送往西環之壓趀(
俗傳者)。輒留置。家人團樂陷去。同居亦歡免馬。
○人曾視疾急歸。付諸天命。○因是病目以深
竟告不治。○復恨株造。○業庸造間。
日兄歌百。○先生以政令之嚴峻。乃聯合各紳
翻請。○始殷撤銷此例。○進由個人捐五萬徐金。
撤。○忱捐五萬圓。○在港倡賣物眼哭。○是為賣物

香港華人名人史略（一九三七）

○以贈醫施藥○且廣送治疫藥水數年○樂善不倦○萬家生佛○（六）約西一九〇四年○疫症盛行○卜港賢與先生及劉鑄伯馮華川諸公○在西環第一二三街○割出地段○自行治療○不許將西環之疫局○改為疫局○本港醫生參預○黃洗病人房廄○亦由彼等自理○不受港醫生干涉○人感稱頌○後華民政務司蒲君○以其辦理妥善也○又○整頓馮兩翁報捐公立醫局○不受港府分文○俾或身故○又給紙証明○退往官廳報案○現建對海○共有公立醫局凡九○飲水思源○當飲水思源○富翁寄捐建港仔華陀廟街局址一所○另勸泉捐建港仔華陀廟街局址一所○共致

三問○受理各症○不分晝夜○病重殘時起寤到家診治○藥水不需分文○倘或身故○又（七）痘疹之病○華人視等如界○歐俗醫院見染斯病○其待遇極力防疫務同○不知習尚既殊○感覺自異○若治校之西醫○實非行政長官所能過問○○（八）港例見華人代有路○欲証其言之不謬○大可登報週知貧民○如死後之屍○非獨畏事○且恐累事○泰明華人九死而一生○○余聞情財○實乃民事○非富詳死○與青廄道旁○象例見之交換意見○亦健以也○此公道稅序然○○計在本港從事救傷○遞年增設新界分處共有九

○先生大功告成○猶為為德不卒○誠以竹細慈○乃立宏願以救濟○首輸五千圓○勸捐五萬金○並將自呈之平島廟街樓宇十間○以四萬圓原價讓出○俾蓋業生息○以壹其力○港府初以基金未裕○祇龍分惠三數十人○後值產業漲價○又將東華醫院址○改為疫局○乃右泉君賢勒○將此業售與○計逾二十萬圓○除獲利七萬圓○速歷年粗值贏餘○及最近慕捐所得○計逾二十萬圓○蒲公仁壽比款是乃（十一）本港公共墳地○楚歷七年之久○仍不能安○蓋歎尚由先生與富任華民政務司之於均處○乃因增加隊員問○另長洲一地○救傷員外○兼建技遞電告○知救傷與看護人員○均廄不多數○故會一赴申○往返一九三二年○上海一二八之役○即派隊技遞拼○女看護四十二○男女醫生名○畏暑○以二千磅敦立免費病床乙張○（故會特刊甘業佐助數字以記念之○）以一千磅存放生息○俾作增益敦傷時○概捐英金三十八百磅數○而無容色○速陳救傷私○共當六萬圓○先生任其平上義○○速陳救傷私○亦無吝惜之分○本港梅夫人女青古木雕院型乙座○（三百年前○有良工拙其紀技○皇叔康樂公○駙馬拿士利○收復既失之希用本為故會聯一細徵院型○已遭甘業佐助數字以記念之

○（十）蒲公壽賢○三十年前本港之蒲氏政務司也○（即選出發救援之所○以三百磅聯同其儲君○俾作增益○○（十二）先生與婦人解救傷○遞年增設新界分處共有九

（十三）富西一九二四年游與英金三千八百磅數○以五百磅市一汽車○為

○（九）西一九一五年○港府給地膽廣張○再求港府給地膽廣張○用增加隊員及對海居民○尤易跋涉○故會技遞電告○一九二七年○因增加隊員三百○經費日繁○遞年增設新界分處共有九○均由個人解囊○始行向外募捐○用補不足○英人回國將設立格於成例○不知之何○先生寄其地址○乃委東華權理○剛令今華民政務司○遠百六十人○計逾二十萬圓○莫捐建築新界○蒲公仁壽比款是乃

○（十一）本港公共墳地○楚歷七年之久○仍不能安○蓋歎尚由先生與富任華民政務司之於均處○乃因增加隊員問○另長洲一地○救傷員外○兼建技遞電告○知救傷與看護人員○均廄不多數○故會一赴申○往返一九三二年○上海一二八之役○即派隊技遞拼○女看護四十二○男女醫生名○畏暑○以二千磅敦立免費病床乙張○（故會特刊甘業佐助數字以記念之○）以一千磅存放生息○俾作增益敦傷時○概捐英金三十八百磅數○而無容色○速陳救傷私○共當六萬圓○先生任其平上義○○速陳救傷私○亦無吝惜之分○本港梅夫人女青古木雕院型乙座○（三百年前○有良工拙其紀技○皇叔康樂公○駙馬拿士利○收復既失之希用本為故會聯一細徵院型○已遭散失○後憑流落西班牙○惟索例四百磅○始許珠還，先生乃與三人凑足蔚同，故會起其事，特

五萬有哥。）亞氏無以報○卒尤其請○先生既為我華人爭回自理症症之權○一面亟報製○歡宣得○及俣座同慶戲演語○以安人心○一面在西環立建巨棚○聘中醫主其事○統計是年醫象總率○為百之八六○明廄績料○皆全愈焉

資助也○（自時厥後○先生拖棺給救○費金乃民事○非獨畏事○且恐累事○泰明華人立場○忌醫詳死○與青廄道旁○象例見之交換意見○亦健以也○此公道稅序然○○計在本港從事救傷○遞年增設新界分處共有九

民慎而給以五金○懲之使去○○復念全港貧乏孤苦無依，及修飛發疾之人○

懸一小銀牌，勒四人名於其間，）為簽趙亞力山大宜后女出有護骨院。及捐歸慈善演劇廂房。各英金五百磅。可望能實踐大同主義者也。先生貢獻於政事，公益，慈善。已見上述。而贊勒乎教育，工，商，及其他者。有如下文。（甲）為孔聖會報料人之一。曾捐巨款。（乙）振幼樣育才書院。自捐萬圓。（丙）念徐十餘萬金。（乙）倡建香港大學擬建考查熱務病症館。獨力捐資五萬五千圓。呂戾於成。（丁）本港倡商會所。皆非正式成游息地點。乃與同志先瓶華商會所。健存數十年。追念吉制單皆緒伯。主席道為劉君緒伯。即今之綠輔道廣東銀行六樓是。（戊）再與陳君厚廈發起組織粵理商務之華商公局。名下先捐一千圓。再復勤資十數萬圓。為外基十餘萬金。樹其基礎。時各行會所。皆非正式成畫兩問。圖素具熱忱。繁榮市場。尤不遺立。追念吉制單皆緒伯。始獲准予註冊。乃全體參加。政組為華商總會。且將前盈調業愛賣。為易康樂道中之現有會。先生擬再捐千圓。今會內佈置堂皇。並設關書館。規模日臻廣大矣。至先生與陳君革創之功。及劉君紳煌之力。島克此。（己）光西一九二五年。英儲君（即遜皇）過港。三個夜景恭賀。西一九一八年，世界漸呈不景。前倡魚浩港巡遊。西一九〇七年，歐我尚恭祝會景。實無役而不勞。授夜景歡迎。西一九三五年，銀禧（英先皇）大典。五僑三畫連宵盛會恭祝。西一九三七年，英皇加冕。六僑三畫夜恭祝會景。賢無多勞而不領斯益信。史無時而不忠力以赴。史有三事。能人其言。皆為科服。先生畫精英語。西一九二四

之所不能者。一則力爭國體。一則解紛排難。年歐游時。與英外刊悟譚香港情形，及萬國集烟事。屢三問靜而始舉。惟閉居則靜政審言。位草其精力於國醫。提典等書。三十年來。中西名。時景畀態。請撥款十萬。給地一段者。港府已准之矣。先生知彼等欺世盜名之故。斷為不治之症。往往有于成春。故西醫學會勤聘先生為名譽會員。屢聘先生為名譽會員。致謝不已。亦榮幸也。彼剩痕在抱。匯特不可。且財金抱負。為公道甚為私恨。享受。似公濟私。何能服象。據此力爭為私怨。（丑）十年前。沙滕行之皇仁建值。（寅）再與其鎮。復現遊諸人之門。表明為公道而爭。（卯）本港移司爵馬。（辰）湖跑馬會之故。遠在六十年前。賽馬員。己逾五百人。而甘棠第號。乃臂掬元之遺。共馬念一。而甘棠第號。乃臂掬元之遺。（辰）尤增我華人光榮不小。先生有大志。尤遺憾。西一九二九年，一度賽勝打皮。乃臂掬元之遺。華人光榮不小。先生有大志。真名山。（己）以養其浩然之氣。復新其學問知讖。故發擇拒絕。久爭無效。追西一九二七年，全文泰皆港府給地緒建。原一視同仁。諸我華僑。言論。迦具流俗。嘗有侍道某西人菩勤先生信。生主持正義。始依復與賽之權。至今故莆上海黃浦瀦公園。尚不准我華人參觀。今廣西馬念一。而甘棠第號。乃臂掬元之遺。州沙面公園。亦不計我華人列生。似此吾人生存。華邦各省。以養其浩然之氣。故發擇遊歐美二洲。履名山大川。真名山。（己）尤增我

年歐游時。與英外刊悟譚香港情形，及萬國集一則力爭國體。尤害樂為之記。（子）遜清光緒廿年，即西一九〇四年。有捨科賢買學府之美草其精力於國醫。提典等書。三十年來。中西人士惠病。超其治愈者。不知凡幾。問遊西醫府已准之矣。特為浙�)。先生知彼等欺世盜名之故。屢聘先生為名譽會員。致謝不已。亦榮幸也。彼剩痕在抱。匯特不可。且財金抱負。為公道甚為私恨。（丑）十年前。沙滕行之皇仁建值。乃臂道往調處。卒頼以和。迄今和約。獨存政移司爵馬。（辰）（寅）湖跑馬會之故。遠在六十年前。賽將研求所得。為其慈慈一住城於西界居庖賓員。己逾五百人。而甘棠第號。乃臂掬元之遺。港府給地緒建。原一視同仁。諸我華僑。表拒絕。久爭無效。追西一九二七年，全文泰皆生主持正義。始依復與賽之權。至今故言論。迦具流俗。嘗有侍道某西人菩勤先生信莆上海黃浦瀦公園。尚不准我華人參觀。今廣州沙面公園。亦不計我華人列生。似此吾人人生存。君等尚肯登諸天堂乎。其人乃叛頏頑丁外人數象。與先生期論色象之濃淡。左視人之頭愛。孝服尚黑。必其為最深之色也。抑由黑而白耶。竟何尚尚白。由白而黑耶。敦淡敦深。髮。皆為科服。先生畫精英語。西一九二四其言。皆為科服。先生畫精英語。西一九二四

年歐游時。與英外刊悟譚香港情形。佩戴。西一九二四年，英京銀禧獎章。及慈善銀獎章。及慈善銀獎章。是年六月念四十字會章赤頒於獎章。由廣東莆省長朱慶瀾羽為佩戴。西一九二四年，英京銀禧獎章。保良局以辭位獎章。國防局總辦。盡述。西一九二二年，及一九二四年，港富局擬微為定倒局員。均有島英。均為定倒局員。我國歷任總統。為期友考之。代舉吉穴。安碑為船親為之卜葬。定緣。安碑為船親為之居。馮頭瓊時。實給二等大綏島水章。中國紅十字會赤頒以獎章。由廣東莆省長朱慶瀾羽為佩戴。西一九二四年，英京銀禧獎章。及慈善銀獎章。是年六月念四錫以爵位獎章。及慈善銀獎章。盡述。西一九二二年，及一九二四年，港富局日校勤。統由英廷叙尊代表。且兩度賜安於北歲宮御園。將與識之皇親國武。一一鉤為赴超。又一九二八年，英廷貨給〇B上勤象為介紹。其非常人。其銀回不宜。男女八〇男女八八。男女一五君子曾妹兵西北園遼此榮竉耶。粹之畫非常人。何能生淑配挑抧氏。于男十四。于女八。男女十五生淑配挑氏。南京軍政部。獨子曾妹兵西北園防區。少男現任職南京軍政部。淘可謂鵬趾呈科。周毛涛美矣。

Mr. HO KOM TONG,

O.B.E.; J.P.; Kt. of Grace. Ven.; Order of St. John of Jerusalem

There are two kinds of philanthropist recognisable in the world. The first kind is a person who is always generous in giving money to the poor, while the second kind is a person who is always busy in making his personal efford in charity besides giving his money. The story of Mr. Ho Kom Tong will show one of the second case.

Mr. Ho Kom Tong, the younger brother of Sir Robert Ho Tung, was born in Hongkong in 1866. He received his early education at the Central English school (Now Queen's College), and concurrently he was taught Chinese literature under private tuitors.

Starting his commercial career at the age of twenty, Mr. Ho's first occupation was Chinese agent of the Insurance department of the Jardine Matheson Co., Ltd., Hongkong. He was successful in business because of his hard efford in social affairs. He invested a large capital in sugar enterprise, so his business extended throughout China, Manila, Iloilo and Java. He resigned from the Jardine Matheson Co., at the age of fifty, and concluded all his business to led a retired life at seventy. Mr. Ho is always considered as the most influential figure in benevolent affairs in the Chinese community. Most of his money and time were spent for the poor sufferers. The followings will show his natural humanity and bigness of beneficence.

Upon the uprising of the boxers in 1900, the whole city of Peking, the then Capital of China, was in a chaos. The Cantonese inhabitants therein cabled to the Cantonese in Shanghai for relief. Mr. Ho, who was in Shanghai at that time, immediately held a meeting in the Cantonese guild to discuss that matter and gave his contribution to lead the others. At the same time he sent a telegram to Canton and Hongkong for assistance. Finally, a sum of $15,000 was raised. $10,000 of the money was remitted to Peking while the rest amount was used in purchasing two thousand bags of rice for the sufferers there. Through much difficulty, more than a thousand Cantonese and nearly two thousand people of other provinces were saved.

In 1908, when Kwangtung was in a terrible flood, Mr. Ho contributed $50,000 and at the same time he held a Relief Fund Bazaar to raise money for the purpose. Consequently, more than $400,000 were raised.

The flood came again in 1910 and Mr. Ho contributed another $50,000. Besides, he made an appeal to the Hongkong Government to sue relief. At the conclusion, nearly $400,000 were raised, and aside from the necessary sum for relief, the remainder was used to build dykes and embankments to prevent further misfortune.

The story of the typhoon of 1906 is a sorrowful page in the history of Hongkong. Especially those who lived on the sea suffered the worst. Mr. Ho, with the aid of the Hongkong Government, raised $1,800,000 in a short time. Besides the relief work, a remainder of $630,000 was submitted to the Hongkong Government for the use in the construction of the Yaumati Breakwater. (The whole expense of the construction amounted to $2,500,000).

When the pleague visited Hongkong in 1894, Mr. Ho contributed $50,000, and at the same time distributed medicine and medical mixture to the inhabitants of the Colony.

In 1904, the pleague was again in action, and the plan of establishing public dispensaries was suggested by Mr. Ho. After the pleague was entirely cleared, Mr. Ho established the Kau-U-Fong public Dispensary, the late Mr. Lau Chu Par established the West Point Public Dispensary; and Mr. Ho induced the Chinese community to build the Wan Chai Public Dispensary. At present, there are altogether nine public dispensaries in Hongkong and Kowloon.

Small-pox is a disease which is considered by Westerners as bad as leprosy. When an epidemic of small-pox broke out in Hongkong towards the end of 1908, Mr. Ho, after the frequent and fruitless petitions of the late Sir Ho Kai and the late Sir Boshan Wei Yuk to the Hongkong Government for improving the treatment of the disease, supplicated the favour of Dr. Atkinson, who was then president of the Medical Board of Hongkong, to allow the disease to be healed by Chinese medical doctors. The supplication was granted and in that year more than eighty-six percent of the sufferers were cured.

As the inhabitants in Hongkong and Kowloon increased rapidly, Mr. Ho realized the urgent need of a public hospital besides the Tung Wah Hospital. With the aid of his colleagues, he founded the Kwong Wah Hospital in Kowloon.

In 1915, Mr. Ho organized the St. John Ambulance Brigade in Hongkong. For twelve years he was sole supporter of the organization, and within that period, not less than $150,000 of his money were spent. Till 1928, when members increased to a number of three hundred and expenditures became too big, Mr. Ho suggested that Endowment Fund should be subscribed from the public to maintain the institute. At present, there are nine plants in the New Territory and one in Cheung Chau.

Mr. Ho is one of the original member of the "Brewin's Fund" and hitherto, hundreds of poor people have been bestowed with this beneficence.

The rule of the Chinese Public Cemetery in Hongkong is that seven years after the burial, the remain should be removed and buried in somewhere else. In 1911 Mr. Ho was one of the original members of the Committee to apply for a Permanent Cemetery for the Chinese.

Mr. Ho is one of the founders of the Hongkong Confucian Society; a committee in the re-construction of Ellis Kadoorie School; and one of the founders of the Hongkong Chinese General Chamber of Commerce.

Mr. Ho is a Justice of the Peace of Hongkong. The honour of O.B.E. was conferred upon him by His late Majesty King George V in 1928. He is also the proud possessor of several Chinese decorations. By the late President Yuen Shih-kai he was honoured with the Order of the Chia Ho (Excellent Crop), Third Class; the second class of the same Order was given by President Fung Kwok Chang; while the Second Class of the Order with brilliancy came to him from President Hsu Shih-chang. The Red-Cross Association of China honoured him with a Medal. The Order of St. John of Jerusalem was given him by the St. John Ambulance Brigade, England, in 1924.

李右泉先生

李右泉先生

李榮源先生○號右泉○粵之南邑瀝滘表鄉人○現年七十有六○醫齡居鄉尚學○未冠來港習商○平生勇於自奮○而頗能靈於待人○屏絕不良嗜好○愛惜有用金錢○故能壽享延齡○夫人生七十○古已云稀○現先生年將杖國○精神矍鑠○老當益壯○彌覺可珍○又況善營商業○資庫豐○

右泉先生○本節今代表大英皇帝○頒國勳章○甚為欣幸○右泉先生○於西一九二九年七月十二日香港總督金文泰校勳位之演詞○及英皇上諭足呂航之○茲分錄於後○

總督張人駿○表表嘉獎○奉旨實給鹽運使○加四級三代從一品封典○遠及民國○眷眼三江水災○慨然在抱○絀瀚為懷○乃企家國府三等嘉禾勳章○及二等嘉禾勳章之錫○其在港中服務社會之經過情形○觀於西一九二九年七月十二日香港總督金文泰校勳位之演詞○及英皇上諭足呂航之○茲分錄於後○

右泉先生○本節今代表大英皇帝○頒國勳章○甚為欣幸○英國勳章○甚為欣幸○湖足下在港居五十餘年○所辦公益事宜○贊勞昭著○始於一八九七年○為東華醫院總理○又由一九〇六年為故院顧問○且至今日○又為廣華醫院有委○又為廣華醫院總理○又自公立醫局開辦理○又克任保良局倡建總理○團防局紳○又一九一四年○歷任團防局紳○又一九一二年○充華商總會主席○數年來○董事至今○足下又克華商總會主席○數又為天水運大英國○阿爾蘭○及海外屬土皇帝○宗教保護主○印度皇帝○兼統全國佐治第五○諭於足下之大英國三等勳章○侔爾保持永享榮典○特諮○

近立乎香江○且創辦廣東窖廠○鹽步機器製紙廠○皮革廠○呂雖持工業○不可謂非人瑞而兼人傑也○先生不特獨善其身○亦能急公尚義○樂善好施○於遜清光緒念六年○在家鄉捐田百人○迨於足下之忠實勤苦者○奉天承運大英國○阿爾蘭○及海外屬土皇帝○宗教保護主，印度皇帝○兼統全國佐治第五○諭於足下之大英國三等勳章○侔爾保持永享榮典，特諮○

故○粵故免費高小兩等學校○其鄉靈育才之基故也○為百年樹人之計○畢凡購地建築校舍公眥等費○俱由一己解囊○復恐經常不充○歲練善美○保由一己解囊之○光緒卅四年○兩廣○史每年另千餘圓似助之○光緒卅四年○兩廣○

次○此誠任何國得足下為其民者○均莫大之幸○現足下為港中人士所敬仰○足下之指導又為舉世之所推崇○故香港政府○從未侵其他一人○迨於足下之忠實勤苦者○

Mr. LI YAU TSUN C.B.E., J.P.

A native of Kwangtung Province, Mr. Li Yau Tsun was born in 1861. Having obtained a good knowledge in Chinese literature, he came to Hongkong in his "teens" to practise in the commercial sphere.

Starting with but a common position, Mr. Li soon procured a rapid promotion in the community for his activities and confidence.

He was Chairman of the Tung Wah Hospital in 1897 and since 1906 he has become permanent Adviser of that benevolent institution. He was also Chairman of the Committee in the courses of the establishing of Kwong Wah Hospital and Po Leung Kuk, and since 1914 he became a member of the District Watch-Men Committee. As a Director of the Public Dispensary, Mr. Li has performed many distinguished deeds. He had been holding important positions in the Chinese Chamber of Commerce, such as Chairman, Treasurer, and Director. He is Vice-patron of St. John's Ambulance and Hon. President of the South China Athletic Association.

In 1928, he was honoured by the British Government with the Conferring of the C.B.E. title.

During the disastrous floods in China, Mr. Li wrought wonderfully in the relief, so the Third and Second Class Orders of the Chia Ho (Excellent Crop) were conferred to him successively by the Chinese Government.

Mr. Li is very attentive to educational affairs too. In 1905, he contributed a large amount of money to originate a school in his own village and besides this initiation, he supports the institution annually with a regular fund.

簡東浦先生

生先浦東簡

簡東浦先生○廣東順德縣人也○現年五十歲○乃東亞銀行總司理○而香港當代華僑領袖之一也○幼年時已秀外慧中○初肄業於香港皇仁書院○後留學於東瀛○通中○英○日○三國文字○學成致用○遂入商途○曾先後在日本正金銀行及萬國銀行服務○凡十二年○先生以優異之才○而務服於其國○楚材晉用○情非得已○當先生在東瀛時○秀宛遠矚○知世界競爭之焦點○在乎經濟○見外國銀行林立○組織完備○令人羨佩○遂決意回國○創立銀行○此則西曆一九一八年春○香港有東亞銀行之創辦也○該銀行成立後○因先生為創辦人○被選為總司理○現該銀行營業蒸蒸日上○為今日港中華人銀行之泰斗者○則先生起驗策劃有以致之○先生任總司理職○至今已有十八年○於香港中銀業歷史所未曾有○先生服務銀業界前後共三十年○無時不克勤克謹○潔身自愛○平時待人接物和藹可親○富有國家觀念○當九一八當瀋陽之變及一二八上海之戰兩役○先生在港領導銀業界○基款接助○歡迎百萬○而歷年因教育或慈善事業○由其個人解囊輸出之款○已不可勝計○故稱先生為志士出之為仁人○亦無不宜○先生現充香港太平局紳及香港大學董事等職○

Mr. KAN TONG PO, J.P.

Mr. Kan who is a native of Shun Tak District, Kwangtung, is one of the Colony's leading business figures. He received his education at Queen's College and in Japan where he afterwards joined the Yokohama Specie Bank and the National City Bank of New York.

When the Bank of East Asia Ltd. was formed in 1918, he was given the chief managership of the new institution of which he was a founder. Due to his foresight and enterprise, the Bank has made steady progress in the field of finance, and to-day it occupies the proud position of one of the leading Chinese banks in the Colony. Mr. Kan has been the chief manager of the Bank for 18 years which not only constitutes a record in the history of banking in the Colony, but also contributes much towards the future development of the Bank.

Mr. Kan has been in the banking business for 30 years now and despite the fact that he has risen to the topmost position in one of the Colony's leading banks, he still remains a very modest, highly patriotic and unassuming personality that is so rare in the business circles.

Mr. Kan is a Justice of the peace and a member of the Hong Kong University Council.

香港華人名人史略（一九三七）

馬應彪先生

MR. MA YING PIU

馬應彪先生。中山縣沙涌鄉人。生於民國紀元前四十九年。天性穎悟。堅忍持久。其父在明公。乃澳洲華僑。先生幼時。家道清貧。母季氏。訓誨嚴謹。十一二歲。即助父母操作。無論除晴寒暑。自朝至暮。紀無暇晷。稍長。則從事農業。以園蔬鬻之於市。年十四五。兼作生菜鮮魚小販。日入雖微。每年仍有餘積數十員。人多異之。其勤儉之著效如此。此十八九歲已萌遠遊之志。二十歲。遠志益堅。請命於父母曰。男兒志在四方。久居鄉井。余之欲遠遊異國。非徒求利。乃以求志讀也。遂打以三年為歸期。父母壯其志。給以舟資三拾五員。遂整裝赴澳洲之雪梨。

恭興，馬永燦，郭樂等。回國省親。及與牧師宣靜山之女公子結婚後。旅港有暇。郡携幻燈映畫。及洋琴一具。到處演講耶穌教義。或到內地各市鎮宣傳致力。此務義務。有多者。當時先生朝壹歎友。在工商界服膺者。僅得數人。為應。乃聯合教會中人。在港創設華信莊。每股五元。共集資二萬元。尚料出入口貨。懲在聯絡華僑信遵者。發展商業。繼創永昌泰金山庄。每年獲利。可派利息二分至四分之多。但服務六年之久。年俸金。僅受一百二十元。其夥伴薪金。則有年給五六百元者。蓋其志在此而不在金。光緒廿二年。即西曆一九零零年。欣立先施公司。勗行實價不二政策。開設佈公。創設先施開業未久。慘被颱風容摧倒。

祭埠。到澳洲後。且入山裏為礦工。初獲微利。旋遇折閒。轉操農業。勞作逾年。仍無餘積。又改販蘇杭雜貨。或國作各埠水客。留澳十有二載。凡工農商賈。無不閱歷。而智識之廣。忽悟之精遠。倍加奮勉。年廿九。創立永生公司於雪梨正埠。代理各埠土產。及中國貨貨。營業極形發達。隨所生態付托氏。訓誨嚴謹。自朝至暮。紀無暇晷。

摧倒樓房。格於港例。交涉數年。始得重建。各同事多萌退志之勢。有分爾離析之。先生堅持不可。大局始定。迨後生態發展。時只七載。除分官息外。溫利九萬餘元。先生歷任經理道中。溫利史厚。先後增設廣州分行。由資本惟所受月薪亦不過廿元耳。後遷任經理。式萬五千元。遞漸擴充。至一千萬元。史於先地旗下。創設國民銀行。保險置業公司。化粧品公司。人壽保險公司。銀業信託公司。資本各諳一二百萬元。均能平均發展。先生賦性�。勤苦堅忍。遇異常流。注重公益。不計私利。充任大公司董事十六處。充司庫十七處。充司理大公司董事十六處。除先後創設之公司外。國民銀行監督外。挺司理理職者二處。充司庫職貴者二處。偏辦及附設之生態大小共一百號有奇。其在慈善界。教育界。政治界。被舉為董事，值理，委員，參謀者。凡四十八次。充司庫者五次。獨力捐資成立公益之建築物。凡九處。捐出善款約五十餘萬元。敷作人立案者。計有九十餘人。有為各號司理，董事，參事，及商埠鄉長，行政界者。凡所栽培。無不成立。足見其有知人之明也。現年七十餘歲。猶華華矻矻。力於貿業之途。不知老之將至。堪為社會人士之矜式焉。

Mr. MA YING PIU

Mr. Ma is a native of Chungshan District, Kwongtung Province, where he was born in 1862. His father was a Chinese farmer of long residence in Sydney, Australia. He was not born with the proverbial silver spoon in his mouth and had no means to obtain a through education. Yet, with his bestowed talents and by his vigorous struggles, he was able to gain a position in the cosmopolitan society.

When he was but eleven years of age, he helped his father in the fields in order to lighten his heavy burden of the family. Later, he became a dealer of fruits and vegetables and lived many years in his native village.

At twenty, he begged permission of his parents to set sail to Sidney, Australia, in search of better prospects as well as to further his knowledge. When he was there, he was first a laborer in the tin mines. Though the work was hard, he was able to accumulate a little savings by his frugality. Later, he became a farmer there, and then became a merchant of Chinese commodities. For twelve years he remained in Sidney, tendering his service in every line, including commercial, agricultural manufacturing and others.

When he was twenty-nine, in partnership with Mr. Choy Hing he established the Wing Sang Co. in Sydney, dealing in Chinese native products. This soon showed him success, and he returned to China to see his parents and to get married.

Then he established the firm of Wah Sun Hong with some of his friends and he himself became its manager. This shop prospered in such a way that within a year it became one of the most outstanding firms in Hongkong. This firm was later reorganized under the name of Wing Chong Tai & Co.

In 1900, he founded the Sincere & Co., Ltd., an universal provider. This company commenced with a capital of $25,000 and through the perseverance of Mr. Ma, the company grew to be one of most famous department stores in the Far East.

Branches were opened in Canton and Shanghai. At present, its capital is $10,000,000 Hongkong Currency. Later, he founded the Sincere Insurance & Investment Co., the National Bank and many other firms.

He served as managing director of the Sincere Co., Ltd., and the National Bank, and manager of seven other firms at different times. He has been a director of sixteen prominent firms as well as partner and stock holder of numerous firms.

Mr. Ma is an earnest Christain. Whenever there is any campaign concerning charity; he is sure to render his valuable assistance. His advice is often sought in matters concerning social affairs, and he holds important positions in numerous associations and social organizations.

His contributions to public welfare ars totally about half million dollars, and there are nine buildings, the construction of which were entirely at his own expense.

蔡興先生

蔡興先生，字科泰。列字英祥。號禮和。中山縣屬六區外沙鄉人。現年六十八歲。力港粵港先施公司及大新公司創辦人之一。現任該兩公司總理之董事局主席也。少英俊。有大志。曾修業於上海英華書院數年。精長觀熟有遠圖。隨長渡重洋。經商於澳洲之雪梨埠。計然。衆積漸富。率與同鄉組織永生公司。我國三大公司。貿發科於此地。而先生鴻才偉著。

行於港粵。業務益形發達。時人稱之為我國三大百貨公司焉。先生商界稱雄。長袖善舞。曾任充董事兼主席於偉大商行者。計有廣東銀行。圓亮銀行。水生公司。先施公司等。而於貿易提倡。尤為努力。惜環境不良。失敗比比。計有馬玉山餅乾公司。興華製絨廠。中興糖廠。中國郵船公司。中澳航業公司等。先生服務社會。殊為熱心氏二。故舉為前中山區醫察名事。氏三。中山縣歷敘名。

國三大公司。貿發科於此地。而先生鴻才偉著。亦展布於斯特。從此營謀日進。今開愈影。深件異邦人士。與我國同胞信仰。歷時華僑不鮮。況迷于黑府中者。與先生懇懇愛之。作普濟之慈航。既任飛烟會書員。又吹尤力。卒繁富地政府協助。擬禁午收百餘萬之烟稅。以成其其。由是烟毒。遂言蔚清。彼以多年旅外之遊勤鄉思。別報臣堂於奇港。二十五年前。與其昆李等組織大新公司。規模宏偉。與先挑。永安。嘉足並立。炤而設分濟救國之願已償。而教育與邦之願。亦將達矣。

款捐迎萬。報歧光醫院於邑城。反哺於祖國也。如是。貢獻於奇港者尤為由港府委充保良局紳。及國防局紳。中山偏等醫院肯總理。腎內助平夫人。德碩才高。展仁蹈義。老而彌篤。賢任本港保良局首屆婦女總理。聯妗始於四十年前。惜乎其夫人十年前早逝矣。長子束生。現任本大新公司秘書長職。次于天福。方攻讀於滬聖約翰大學。是先生繼模宏偉。

蔡興先生

Mr. CHOY HING

The Chairman of the Board of Directors of both The Sun Company, Ltd., and the Sincere Co., Ltd., two of the well-known department stores in Hong Kong, Shanghai, and Canton, is Mr. Choy Hing. He is a native of Chung Shan District, Kwangtung Province, where he was born in 1869.

He obtained his early education in his native town, and later he proceeded to Shanghai and continued his studies in the Anglo-Chinese School there. After attaining a fair knowledge of both Chinese and English, he set out for Australia, to start a commercial career.

While in Australia, Mr. Choy went through many hardships, but eventually attained success in his line of business. He also interested himself in various philanthropic movements for the welfare of his compatriots.

Returning to Hong Kong in 1912, Mr. Choy founded The Sun Co., Ltd., with his brothers and a few friends, and later established branches of the Company in Canton and Shanghai. To-day The Sun Company, Ltd., shares the distinction with The Sincere Co., Ltd., and Wing On Co., Ltd., of being the three largest department stores in China.

Mr. Choy is a man of broad sympathy and every good cause finds him a willing supporter. He has held many important positions in China, and still holds, amongst others, the posts of Honorary Adviser to the Kwangtung Provincial Government and Honorary Adviser to the Chung Shan District Government.

In the Colony, Mr. Choy has been Vice-Chairman of Tung Wah Hospital, Member of Po Leung Kuk Committee and Member of District Watchmen's Committee. He is now a member of the Chinese Chamber of Commerce Executive Committee and Chairman and Director of numerous banks, companies and public institutions both in Hong Kong and China.

Mr. Choy has two sons. The elder is the Secretary of The Sun Co., Ltd., Hong Kong, while the younger is studying at St. John's University, Shanghai.

生先泉郭

郭泉先生○鳳輝其字○年五十九○模範縣人○富毅力○喜任事○壯有大志○質筱澳洲○以堅忍之精神○勤儉之德性○常晶澳洲僑胞○從事墾殖○販輸果品○水安公司○批銷果品○貿易先生發軔之始○營謀日進○乃於遜清光緒年挺港之○組故水安有限公司○兼任總司理○規

華挺算之餘○復龍贊助社會公益慈善教育各種善學○民十三任保良局總理○民十五任東華院總理○為中山岐光醫院販辦人○曾充中山僑立醫院董事○倡設中山僑商會所義學○中山世光學校○中山良都什秀眉學校○曾任校董職○而中山女子師範學校○歐棠學校等○均加以資助○迩來中山卑子鄉總理起心學董事兼司庫○最近國大初選○香港區為商界冠○居全港亞軍之列○非常業事物臻此○先生克己○○○

坐葛克○非物○臻此○先生克○陀馬燕生○清爽長于淑士女○嶺南大學農科商安學士上海○琳○現任水安

模範具○以況香苦幹○而業務蒸蒸日上○繼而創設上海水安有限公司○水安紗織有限公司○水安水火保險有限公司○水安人壽保險有限公司○及水安銀行○附設雄益威造廠大東酒店等○或兼董事○或任經理○碩劃益爲我國現代有數之大企業家○其他如枕選爲香港中山民泉貿易銀行董事長○國民商業儲蓄銀行○岐關車路公司○利民與國瑊造廠董事等職○故於持○

有限公司總經理○次子琳鍚嶺南大科學士○現任水安銀行總行副司理○三子琳戾○英國文車士打大學工程科學士○現任水安紗織有限公司工程師○四子琳驤嶺南大學商科學士○現任香港水安有限公司追貨部主任○五子琳珊○方在學齡○進嶺南大學攻政治經濟科○則先生不徒營商多偉畧○而教子有義方哭○

Mr. PHILIP GOCKCHIN.

Mr. Gockchin is a native of Chungshan District, Kwangtung Province, where he was born in 1877. He procured his primary education in his own village and stayed there until he was old enough to render his service in the commercial world.

He first set foot in Sydney, Australia, where he founded the Wing On Co., dealing only in fruits and vegetables. At the same time, he encouraged the over-seas Chinese there to take the business of cultivation and plantation.

Returned to Hongkong in 1908, he founded the Wing On Co., Ltd., an universal provider, of which he has been the General manager for a period of about thirty years. His experience and bestowed talents enable him to expand his business in such a way that to-day the Wing On Co., Ltd., is considered to be the biggest and most prosperous department store in China.

During his management, the Wing On & Co., Ltd., Shanghai branch, The Wing On Textile Mfg. Co., Ltd., Shanghai, The Great Eastern Hotels, The Wing On F. & M. Insurance Co., Ltd., The Wing On Life Assurance Co., The Wing On Bank, Ltd., and the Wai Sun Knitting Co., Hongkong, all of which may be considered as train business concerns of the Wing On & Co., Ltd., the main-office, Hongkong are successively established.

Besides the above mentioned, Mr. Gockchin is the president of the board of directors of Chungshan People Real Estate Bank and also of the Hongkong and Yaumati Ferry Co., Ltd., He is the president of the Chungshan Chamber of Commerce, (Hongkong), Director of Chungshan-Macao Auto Bus Co., Ltd.

Mr. Gockchin has often been noted to be privately and publicly, locally and distantly, for his zeal in benevolent and educational affairs. In Hongkong, he is ex-director of the Po Leung Kuk and also of the Tung Wah Hospital. In Chungshan District, his birth place, he is director and treasurer of the Dr. Sun Yat Sen's Memorial School, founder of the Kee Kwong Hospital, ex-director of the Chungshan overseas Chinese Hospital. He is also director of many other schools both in Hongkong and in Chungshan District.

As Mr. Gockchin is very popular in Hongkong and China, so he has been nominated by the Chinese community in Hongkong for the election of delegates for the first Congress of China to be held in the near future.

Married when he was nineteen years of age to Ma Yin Ching, Mr. Gockchin has many children. His eldest son is a graduate from the Ling Nan University and is now manager of the Wing On Co., Ltd., (Shanghai) The second son was also graduated from the same institution and is now assistant manager of the Wing On Bank, Ltd., Hongkong. His third son is a graduate from the Winchester University, England. He is engineer of the Wing On Textile Mfg. Co., Ltd., Shanghai. The fourth son is also a graduate from the Ling Nan University and is now holding an important position in the Wing On & Co., Ltd., Hongkong. The fifth son is pursuing the course of Economic of Commerce in the Ling Nan University.

胡素貞女博士

士博女貞素胡

以一中國女子而能在外人治下。延設宏偉完善之學校。仗桃李成林者。實非易事。以一中國女子。而能足跡遍歐美。且切具族君皇之寶賜。及他邦學府之榮施者。尤屬鮮能。今胡素貞女士。党克兼此。則其才德超泉。志氣過人。至為長。任藏迄今垂二十年矣。女士既熱心於教育。尤致力於基督教務。及公益慈業事業。為中華國內佈造會七位發起人之一。亦香港女青年會五員創辦人之一。創組香港女童軍。歷任香港西人完祓會司庫。現教員會副會長。凡三載蟬聯。香港善會董事。凡十八年。香港保護兒童會董事。中華聖公會會省南華稻境董事。香港中華全國女青年會協會董事。香港聖保羅堂董事會永遠會員。上海全國女分會主席等職。一九二六年英前皇位治第五。頒以 M.B.E. 勳章。開全華女界愛勳之新妃錄。一九三冬年。當女士遊美洲加省大時。溫珠利埠市長。又為我國女界生色不少。而女士為之金飾起。又為我國女盆新知。眾使史向美國哥林比亞大學研究院身修教育科。迨一九三三年。美國南加省大學。錫以教育博士榮街。尤令外國人士。頒政以前輕視吾邦女子之觀念。女士向抱獻身主義。以身獻職。樂育英才。籌建聖保羅女書院新校舍。不惜多年养是。卒能在本港徵集二十萬圓。往新大陸之美國各埠勸捐十五萬金。共得三十五萬元鉅款。以完成其志願。彼才德志氣及毅力。均超人一等。稱之為女中豪傑。不亦宜乎。

吾儕所義佩者吳。女士原籍粵之鶴山。而生長於香港。現年四十六歲。幼時活澄聰明。已具龍眉氣概。稍長改讀於本港安立間女學校畢其業。一九一二年負笈英倫。先遊車士打尼女子學院。繼進牛津大學下帷業載。至一九一六年畢業。且得學士學位。遂雖其。時香港聖保羅女書院。由林護先生甄科。住及一年。原聘英人主校。既聞女士學成返港。遂政聘女士為校

Dr. F. C. WOO, M.B.E., D.Ped.

One of the most prominent ladies in Hongkong is Dr. F. C. Woo. She is a native of Hock-shan District, Kwangtung Province, and was born in 1891. She procured her early education from the Church Missionary Society Girls' High School in Hongkong. Then she proceeded to England and studied in the Chelterham Ladies College and later transferred to Cherwell Hall, Oxford.

Returned to China in 1916, Dr. Woo was appointed head-mistress of St. Paul's Girls' College of Hongkong and hitherto she is still in the post. For a long span of twenty years she has devoted her sole interest and energy on the institution, and to-day it becomes one of the most famous girl schools in the Colony.

Dr. Woo is a faithful Christian and has taken much pain in developing Christianity in China. She is one of the seven founders of the Chinese Home Missionary Society and one of the five original members who organized the Chinese Y.W.C.A. in Hongkong. For eighteen years she has been a member of the Executive Committee of the Ministering Children's League (British Empire) and she was for two years Chairman of the Chinese Y.W.C.A., where she is now treasurer. She was Vice-president of the Hongkong Teachers' Association for three years; member of the standing committee of the Diocesan of the Chinese Episcopal Church of South China; member of the "Church Body" of that organization in Hongkong; life member of the Vestry of St. Paul's Church; member of the committee for the Protection of Children; member of the National committee of the Y.W.C.A. (Shanghai); member of the National Christian Council (Shanghai) Chairman of the Chinese Home Missionary Society of the Hongkong branch; member of the National Committee of the Home Missionary Society (Shanghai).

Dr. Woo determined to establish a good and complete girl school in the colony and she sailed to America in 1928, and two years later she returned to Hongkong with $150,000 which she raised from U.S.A. and Canada. With this money and $200,000 which she raised in Hong Kong, she built a magnificent edifice for the purpose of the school.

When she was in America, she entered the University of Columbia, N.Y., to do research work in American education. In 1930, she was presented by the Mayor of Windsor, Canada, the key to the city. She was conferred the Honorary degree of Doctor of Pedagogy in 1933 by the University of Southern California, U.S.A.

Dr. Woo is the first to start Chinese Girl Guides in Hongkong, and is Vice-president of the Girl Guide Association. She has done a wonderful lot in the cause of education and in promoting religious activities in the Colony.

His late Majesty King George V. decorated her with the insignia of M.B.E. in 1926, and she was presented the Jubilee Medal in 1935.

周錫年醫博士

錫年先生○籍隸粵之東莞○而生長英籍香港○乃名商周卓凡翁之寧醫兄也○本港華人代表周埈年大律師之姻堂弟也○生有鳳鶿○英俊非凡○少時攻讀於聖提反

博士兩榮銜○後赴奧京○再進維安邸大學研究○一九二七年學成囘港○卽自設醫務所○以濟世活人○一九三〇年至一九三五年間○兼充香港大學醫科眼科講師○暨國家醫院眼科主任醫生○學問俊良○信用昭著○甚為社會所推重○歷充

本港市政衛生局議員○香港醫藥局議員○中華醫學會長○香港大學醫學會

學校○西一九一八年而學成○旋致進香港大學○粵修醫科○一九二三年而畢業大學○以求深造○同時在英京皇家眼科且位醫醫學士○乃負笈英京○進倫敦

副會長○兼和醫院董事兼眼科名譽醫生○孔聖名譽會長○東莞商會值理○華商總會名譽值理○南華體育會名譽董事等職○以年僅三十四之人○而有此地位及榮譽○誠不易得矣○先生於一九二七年

腎院○及倫敦耳鼻喉科醫院為助理醫生○達獲專醫眼科博士○及專醫耳鼻喉科

完娶○夫人劉氏○甚有才德○

周錫年醫博士

Dr. S. N. CHAU, M.B., B.S., D.O.M.S., D.L.O. (London)
Eye, Ear, Nose and Throat Specialist.

Dr. S. N. Chau, son of Mr. Chau Cheuk Fan, and cousin of the Hon. Mr. T. N. Chau, is the president of the Chinese Medical Association, Hongkong. Though a native of Tung-Koon, Kwangtung Province, he was born in Hongkong in 1903.

He matriculated from the St. Stephen College in 1918 and proceeded to the Hongkong University where he took up the Medical Course and graduated with the M.B., B.S. degrees in 1923. Then he proceeded to England and joined the London University, specialising in Eyes, Nose, Ear and throat work. He was appointed as Clinical Assistant at Royal London Ophthalmic Hospital and Central London Nose, Ears and Throat Hospital. Later, he qualified for the degrees of D.O.M.S. (eye specialist) and D.L.O. (Nose, Ear and Throat specialist).

With a view to further his studies in the above subjects he went to the State University of Vienna, from where he returned to the Colony in 1927 and started practice.

Dr. Chau is an influential figure in social affairs. He is a willing supporter of public welfare. From 1930 to 1935 he was lecturer in ophthalmology in the Hongkong University and ophthalmologist in charge of the Eye Clinic of the Government Civil Hospital. He is a member of the Urban Council and the Medical Board, Hongkong; Vice-president of Hongkong University, Medical Society; President of Chinese Medical Association, Hongkong; Hon. President of Confucian Society; Director and Hon. Visiting Ophthalmologist of Hongkong Sanatorium and Hospital; Executive Committee of Tung-koon Chamber of Commerce; Hon. member and Executive Committee of General Chamber of Commerce, Hongkong; and Director of South China Athletic Association.

生先坡鑑陳

陳鑑坡先生

陳筱字南山○號鑑坡○五十五歲○廣東省寶安縣人○於前清宣統元年○得美國加利福尼大學農科學士○曾任錦縣郵局局長○安東電報局局長○長春航政局中華農會農林試驗場監督○長泰郵局局長○資安縣參議會議員○廣東省長公署顧問○軍政部警衞軍司

南山小學校董會主席○香港華商總會司庫○駐港寶安商會主席○香港保良局總理，兼司庫○宏發公司總理○寶安嚴口平路有限公司董事長○港安輪船有限公司董事，兼司理○英利行總理○兼董事○廣東銀行觀察委員會主席○兼董事○生平見義勇為○故來因慈善及教育事業輸出之款○不可勝計○其犖犖著者○為在前清光緒二十七年○捐式萬二十四元○萬勤學會會育勤學○倡興學會○提倡人偏寒極佳學故庠○團人來奉○民國五年○捐道台銜○民國七年賞給二等嘉禾章○偏非在國家社會○著有勤勞○何能致此○先宦葉氏○前清光緒二十八年結婚○女士○乃萬智女中學畢業○於民國甲式年結婚○長男水昌二十五歲○得美國紐約大學法學博士○現任江西建設廳身員○長女慧莊三十歲○已嫁○次女慧英○二十歲○在約智女中學校高中畢業○現任廣東民政廳書記○徐尚年幼○

令官○寶安清仰局總料○兼寶安護沙局局長○萬育勸學會會長○文苑中學校校董會副主席○香港東華，廣華，東院，三院統一首屆總理○香港保良局甲式年○各年服屆總理○香港鐘磬慈善社社長○現任保安醫身員，黃○香港南華體育會會長○兼孔聖會高初兩等小學校校長○香港孔聖會會長○港新界展索會常務董事○兼宏得部委員○現任廣東民政廳蓄記○徐尚年幼○

Mr. CHAN KAM PO, B. Agr.

Mr. Chan Kam Po born in Hongkong in 1882, but his native place is the Po On District, Kwangtung Province. He secured the B. Agr. degree from the University of California in 1907 and since his return to China from America in that year, he held important positions under the Chinese Government, including those of postmaster of Chin Hsien, Superintendent of the Telegraphic Administration of An Tung, Harbour Master of Changchun, adviser to the Kwangtung Governor and many others.

Commercially, Mr. Chan has also been prominent and at present holds the following commercial positions, viz., Managing Director of C. Ah Ying & Co., Ltd., Chairman of the Board of Directors of the Po On Nnam - How Motor Road Co., Ltd., Chairman of the Committee of Inspection of the Bank of Canton, Ltd., Chief manager of the Wing Fat & Co., Managing director of the Kong On Steamship Co., Ltd., and Director of the Bank of Canton, Ltd.

In spite of his many duties, Mr. Chan still devotes considerable time to the advancement of education for the Chinese and is chairman of the Nam Shan School, Vice Chairman of the Man Fun College, and the Principal of the Schools (19 in number) subsidiary to the Hongkong Confucian Society. In 1898, Mr Chan subscribed a sum ($20,000.00) to the Man Yuk Educational Society as an endowment fund for the advancement of the aims of that society.

Mr. Chan is also an influential figure in the social circle and semi - social affairs and has been President of the Man Yuk Educational Society, Superintendent of the China Agricultural Society, Director of the Tung Wah, Kwong Wah, and Tung Wah East Hospitals, and committee and Hon. Treasurer of the Po Leung Kuk for several terms. He has also been Chairman of the Chung Sing Benevolent Society, and is at present the popular president of the South China Athletic Association, the President of the Hongkong Confucian Society, An Executive director and the Hon. Treasurer of the Chinese Chamber of Commerce, (Hongkong), Chairman of the Po On Commercial Association and many others.

In 1916, the Chinese Government honoured Mr. Chan by conferring on him the Order of "Chai Choong" (Excellent Good) Third Class and in 1918 conferred on him the further honour of the Second Class of the Order of Chia Ho.

Mr. Chan has many children. All of them are well educated and the eldest of them, Mr. Chan Wing Cheong, deserves special mention for his being secured the D.C.L. degree from the University of New York in 1936. Since his return to China in June, 1936, Mr. Chan Wing Cheong has been appointed Secretary to the Kiang - si Government.

香港・澳門雙城成長經典

42

陳瑞祺先生

陳瑞祺先生○乃當今之仁人志士也○平生樂善好施○並在港設道字總社以改革我國文字為己任○去歲獨捐六萬元○以助賑綏遠○並自組赴綏徵賑眼團○編者以

字腳氣水○施道字荊唯散○客歲赴綏眼災○與最近赴綏散眼等○無一而非本我素志而行○知我者園曰無他○不知我者

既漆總編輯先生大篆○啓者○來書敬悉○弟之所以不欲掛名史冊原因○前函已畧言之○未蒙鑒諒○猶復詳囑再三○弟服務社會○全為良心所驅使○毫無名利於其間○來翰所稱○弟之故道字教育之贈道

其為難得○曾三次徵求其史畧及玉照○以刊之於此書○惟先生謙懷若谷○不允所請○按之編書宗旨○原為表德揚善○不允對於此種慈善人物○焉可付諸闕如○故

○竟婆短淺長○不詣沽名釣譽○則曰別有企圖○卑吾人做事○但求心之所安○然為免招物議計○故對於涉及名巷之記載○概不敢領教○此所以罪貴處三次徵求○而三次卻辭也○諸希見原○不勝厚幸○陳瑞祺敬復○

編者一面○原文發下○

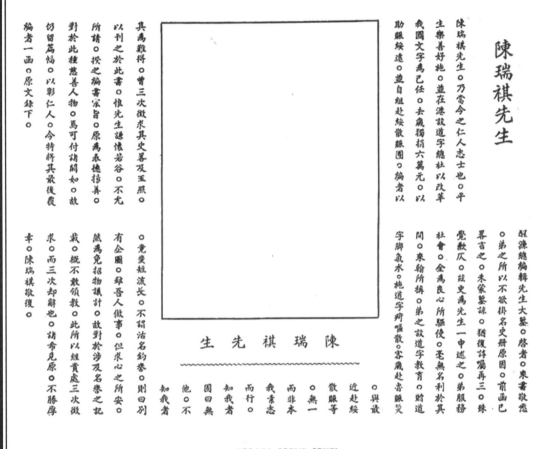

生先祺瑞陳

Mr. CHAN SHUI KEE

It is hard to find one who can sacrifice his thought, money and time for his community to secure a name. It is harder to find one who thus sacrifices but not for name. In spite of his humbly refusal upon our request for his photograph and biography, the story of Mr. Chan Shui Kee is deserved to put in this book because of his broad sympathy and great sacrifice.

Realizing that the Chinese characters and literature are too complicate and difficult to learn, Mr. Chan has concentrated his thought and devoted his time in inventing a new system of Chinese characters named "Toa Tze." It is so plain and simple, that every one can master it in a few months. With the view of promoting his new invention and making it known to the public he has established the "Toa Tze" main Association in Hongkong and many branches in other places. All the students under the Association and branches are free of charge. Prizes are also given to those who can learn hard. In doing so, Mr. Chan has spent a lot of his money within these few years.

The poor people are easily neglected by the rich, but they are never be forgotten by the kind and generous Mr. Chan. He distributes every year thousand bottles of medical liquor for beri-beri and thousand packages of medical powder for vomit to those patients who can not afford to buy these kinds of medicine owing to poverty.

Among all Mr. Chan's charitable deeds, the following two cases should win our special respect. In 1935 he contributed generously a big sum of money to relieve the sufferers in Shantung province and in 1936 he contributed sixty thousand dollars for the relief works in Sui Yuan province. He said that he did these nothing more than to do his own duty.

In short, Mr. Chan is a man of charity and a scholar of ambition besides a merchant of ability.

許地山碩士

許地山先生○福建龍溪人○現年四十二歲○乃近代之著作家○而現任香港大學中國文史學系之主任也○性敏悟○過目問文章○為世所仰○前曾充北平燕京大學教校○國立北京大學講師○國立清華大學講師○孔子謂學而不厭○誨而不倦○先生是也○先生著作甚富○除工屬文外○復精國語○歷充我國教育部國語統一等備委員會委員○北平研究院研究員○

民國二十五年○香港大學○聘其為華○充該大學中國文史學系主任

成福○幼時已以頭角崢嶸○為師友所器重○既弱冠○畢業於北平燕京大學○曾得文學士學位○先生以學問無止境○遂負笈於美國○進哥侖比亞大學○畢業後○得文學碩士學位○先生仍不自滿○遂赴英國○進牛津大學○亦得文學士衔○學成○先生到任之日○全港學界為之歡呼○先生於民國十八年已結婚○夫人周俟松女士○乃北平師範大學理學士○男才女貌○相得益彰○長女梣新○十六歲○現在武昌美術學校肄業○于苓仲八歲○次女燕吉四歲○均在港聖士提反女學肄業○

許地山碩士

Professor HSU TI SHAN, B.A., M.A.

Professor Hsu is a native of Lung-ki District, Fukien Province, where he was born in 1894. He procured his education in the Yenking University. After he obtained the B. A. degree from that institute he continued his studies in the Columbia University, N.Y., U.S.A., where he obtained the M. A. degree. Then he was transferred to the Oxford University, England, and again attained the B. A. degree.

Since he returned to China, he was appointed at different times as professor in the Yenking University; the Peking University; and the Ching Hwa University. In 1936 he was appointed by the Hongkong University to be the dean of the Department of Chinese Literature.

Professor Hsu has written many books regarding Chinese literature, and besides, he is an expert in Mandarin language. He was a member of the Preparatory Committee of Unification of Chinese Dialects in the Board of Education; and a member of the Post Graduate Institute Peking.

Married in 1929, Professor Hsu has three children.

羅仁伯先生

羅仁伯先生

羅仁伯先生，嶺南望族。新會家鄉。誕於廣州。年剛十春。乃久奉港府教育部高級華人學校之視學官也。家風文采。束髮就讀於眾居名儒。世胄書香。引

一九一五年，甫試新硎。即代理漢文視學官。連一九一九年，以名實相副。選任考試委員會委員。及專門學校漢文師範班學監之職。一九二零年，兼除正視學官。兼充港仔官立學校校長。同年至一九二四年，兼任本港教育委員會名卷秘書。一九二二年，調充新界視學官。

一九二五年，內遞代理金港華人學校高級視學官（並教育委員會委員）。至一九二七

齡博通乎我國古學。精長審辭業於育才書院。年甫弱冠。留學英京。攻進金橋。專攻理化。公元一九一二年畢業。且膺學士文銜。返國兩易寒暑。不憚急。且膺學士文銜。

年兩實校高級視學官。任職以迄於今。非先生能協其職。與港府敬才善任。吳能致是耶。先生辦事精明。律身廉潔。對於倫肥辦學。指導勸助。尤為竭力。故極將全港文學界之完善。元配江夏氏。已作古。男女公子數人。俊秀非凡。長女尤亭亭王立。遞前兩展盟運使陳維周之文郎。

於自見。贊醫陳書。以增益其學問。不精窮其錦銘。果也不飛則已。一飛冲天。不鳴則已。一鳴為人。於

Mr. LAW YAN PAK, B.A.

Mr. Y. P. Law is a native of Sunwoi District, Kwangtung Province, and was born in Canton in 1888. He received his early education from private tutors and also attended for a few months at the Ellis Kadoorie School, (or the Honan College) Canton. In 1905 to 1912, he continued his studies in England, where he obtained his B.A. degree in the University of Cambridge in 1912.

In 1915, Mr. Law was appointed assistant master in the Education Department Hongkong. In the following year, he became acting Inspector of Vernacular Schools.

In 1919, he was appointed a member of the Board of Examiners and concurrently Supervisor of the Vernacular Teachers' Classes of the Technical Institute. In the following year, he was appointed Inspector of Vernacular Schools and was acting Head Master of Wanchai Government School.

From 1920 to 1924, he was Honorary Secretary of the Board of Education. From 1922 to 1925, he was Inspector of Vernacular Schools for the New Territtories.

Since 1925, he has been Senior Inspector of Vernacular Schools for Urban Districts, and an Ex-office Member of the Board of Education.

黃炳耀先生

黃炳耀先生

黃先生炳耀○籍廣東台山縣○生於海洋洲烏綠倫島○現年六十二歲○是香江百萬華僑十八領袖之一○當局常資得力○藻倫秦為主集○議傑出之人物也○幼時○已隨父母返港○時為一八八六年也○

其門如市○而先生益自策勵○以期無負眾人屬望○如何能使利保戶也○如何能進益公司也○兼顧統籌○未嘗一日精懈○蓋秋已高○跨寬有子○仍不自逸○常至公司○主持大政○以匡集之不逮馬○其辦事精神○長足欽仰○先生不惟能成偉業○於商戰稱雄○亦極愛護同華○為社會造福○現任太平局紳○市政衛生局員○香港大學校董會董事等○其職尚多○他○不及備述○○夫人伍氏○名貴賢○○內助得賢哲○

卽讀於皇仁書院○中英學識○均甚豐富○一八九二年再赴烏綠倫島肄業於奧梯高書院○一九○六年始畢業返港○因先生具商學天才○對於經濟一科○不假師承○日有心得○故學成後○卽出而就商○實習於多文朗公司○將其國土木工程之經驗○及英國建築工程會○恆為會員○現充工程師於廣州梅菉鐵路○次子兆榮○雙榮本島○亦商界後起之秀○

兩人○長名選○字兆良○畢業香大工程科○一九三○年○肄土木工程學士街○曾任職本港工務局二年○繼陞克城門水塘助理工程師○一九三三年○史求深造○實習於多文朗公司○將其國土木工程之經驗○及英國建築工程會○恆為會員○

且持人接物○謙遜有禮○成遠之也○於是○

Mr. B. WONG TAPE, J.P.

Mr. B. Wong Tape, one of the most prominent merchants in Hong Kong, is a native of Toishan District, Kwangtung Province, and was born in 1875 in Dunedin, Otago, New Zealand.

He came to Hongkong with his parents in 1886 and entered Queen's College, where he passed out Class I in 1892. As there was no University in Hongkong at that time, he proceeded to Dunedin, New Zealand, and completed his education at the Otago Boys High School.

In 1906, he returned once more to the Colony and joined the China Mutual Life Insurance Co., Ltd., where he rose to the position of Secretary in 1909 and became manager of the Hongkong branch in 1919.

Later, the firm was taken over by the Sun Life Assurance Co., of Canada and in turn he became Resident Secretary of the local branch of that company. He became official-in-charge of that firm in 1927 and retired from this executive position in 1934, but retaining his connection with the company as local adviser for South China.

Mr. Wong Tape has been a non-official Justice of the Peace since 1924. He has also been a member of the Po Leung Kuk; Chairman of the Chinese Y.M.C.A.; President of the Chinese Club, the Chinese Recreation Club and the Queen's College Old Boys' Association and Vice-president of the Kowloon Residents' Association. He is at present a member of the Urban Council and a member of the Court of the University of Hongkong.

Married to Ng Kwai Chuen, Mr. Wong Tape has two sons. Mr. Eric Wong Tape, his elder son, obtained his B.Sc. degree from the Hongkong University in 1930. Then he became a staff in the Public Works Department and two years later became assistant engineer in the construction of the Shing Mun Dam and Resevoir. He proceeded to England in 1933 and completed his practical training as an engineer with Messrs. Dorman, Long & Co., where he obtained the degrees of A.M.I.C.E. and A.M.I. Struct. E.

His second son, Mr. Irwin Wong Tape, also obtained a thorough education and possesses a good reputation in the commercial sphere.

范潔朋先生

范潔朋先生

范潔朋先生，粵東南海人。現年中壽晉七○生而不見。少有大志。賦性沉毅勇敢。持躬刻苦耐勞。識見越卓。胸懷磊落。平素對於社會公益事業無不悉力以赴。社應即以傑出之材。受知於兩廣總督。（時值清代，譚公鍾麟總制兩粵）。派赴扶桑。致査商務。新知益進。青朋終續。民元時曾加入中國同盟會。獻身革命。

被舉為廣州市參事。香港出口爆竹商會主席。澳門兵災慈善會主席。現承全國經濟建設運動委員會籌會總會籌會諮詢委員。澳門商會主席。鏡湖醫院主席。香港華商總會值理。鏡湖學校校長。慈德女中校董。聖羅撒女中校董。鏡湖救傷會總理事。鏡湖模士學校校長。民二五因大選舉。澳門華僑區監督。且先生年將花甲。而猶精力迤邐。今待人接物。和藹可親。是以旅澳未及一年。卽週閩澳僑胞愛戴。各大社團。咸推舉為領袖。

五載羈絆○感績昭著○而其能富平忠恕○抱愛圓熱誠○尤為難及也○用分遍之卿以風世○今之捉人者多勞○誠不易得○而其急公好義者多勞○誠不易得○而其概豪懷○亦有求拔○而心始安○先生本實力以赴○立一毫而不為也○古者有德之士○地位者○自視太高○而人想有求拔者○以赴○而心始安○先生○應力以赴○報辦先生○千里而先生向無降級之○交○則敗大夫卒○折節與謙謙○能以好之○報辦先生○時處順境之變○而先生時為國家出力○而故也○古者不拔一毛○不捨一文財賄○而先生時為國家出力○年來為慈善之役○前港陽之○

報臂而起○倡料兵災慈善會○領導全澳華僑合作○救亡之舉○忙捐巨款六千餘圓以為之倡○募集十餘萬全○另各界景應亦數萬圓○義賑所播○舉國同欽○去歲值接自接公葬辰○又偕獻儀餉○以圓接充實國防○聯合同志○戮力勤捐○時值兩遇○款逾三萬○以澳中商務之興○落○偽民之困苦○有此紀錄○堪稱勤能○先生又繼續終遽營開○將士沿血○軍政商學之聞人○可敬哉○

為總理忠實信徒○討龍之役○推勤撫桑○曾女贊軍總部軍需○迭陳匡之役○決策運籌等○又主軍旅部懷慨○時也百粵江河不靖○送糧會料於衛旅保商管○各機關附重長材○復完挞鎮於廣東省長公署○暨滇軍總司令部○此民十一以前先生之建樹也○嗣後摒脫軍政兩浼進厰○從事工商實業○舉其學學大者○在羊石則有五盞公司之組織○其次於社會公益○慈善○教育○工○商○等事業不論居留母，港，澳，三地○均有不鮮贊助○曾受各埠愛國之志士○

范潔朋先生

Mr. FAN KIT PANG.

One of the most prominent Chinese whose name spreads not only in Hongkong but also in Macao is Mr. Fan Kit Pang. He is a native of Nam-hoi District Kwangtung Province, where he was born in 1880.

Owing to his clever thought and exellent conduct, Mr. Fan was sent by the late General Tam Chong Luen, who was a high official of the Ch'ing Dynasty, to go to Japan to investigate commerce.

Later, he returned to China and devoted himself in the commercial sphere. He initiated the Macao Investment Co., Ltd., in Macao and organized the Ah Tung Knitting Co., in Canton. Besides, he is either stock-holder or partner of many business concerns in Hongkong.

Mr. Fang is a man of board sympathy and every good cause finds him a willing supporter. He was Councilor of the Canton Government; Chairman of the Hongkong Firecrackers Exporters' Association; and Chairman of the Society of Charity of Macao. At present, he is one of the committees of the Financial Construction Campaign of China; Committee of the Hongkong Chinese General Chamber of Commerce; Chairman of Macao Chinese Chamber of Commerce; President of the Kiang-Vu Hospital, Macao; Principal of Kiang-Vu School and Kiang Vu Nursing School, Macao; Besides he is director of many outstanding schools in Macao.

In 1936, during a selection of delegates for the national Congress, which is to be held in the nearest future, Mr. Fan was appointed Supervisor of that campaign in macao by the Chinese Government.

Mr. Fan is a faithful nationalist, and was an important member during the building of the Republic of China.

朱汝珍太史

持有之○高山仰止○景行行止○雖不能至○然心嚮往之○余讀朱氏訴○想見其為人○先生名汝珍○字聘三○亦號隘園○嶺南世家也○其高曾綵堂公○逵河公○以結塵司馬○其封翁寶悊公○以軍功擴廳○海岳文衆○久邸家風○陸機詞賦○良多世德○學邃厖訓○素愛名師○芝蘭

素於日本法政大學○列最優等○）歸國○將獎記名總續題賽○任京師法律學堂教校○仿繼續慕修法律○艱時創定民法○先生詢親操承纂兩篇○各國法律○皆可採用於中國○不必採用○應按中國禮俗而制定之○參派赴各國導詢查商事統已○創定商律○創制度言○又以所著各國刑法比較慣○報告凡數十萬言○修律大臣卒從其議○宣十卷里○得獎何諸衙○廣戌首次畢行法官考試○卒前派為貴州省主考○公尋入都○復慕成試○卒回派為貴州省主考○公尋入都○復慕成德宗實錄○入直南書房○（宣卒派編德宗御製詩文○清查內廷書畫圖籍○將獎頒品項戴○紫禁城內騎馬○以迄清祚告終○）先生之德己立○而先生之操守愈整○負以揭時○居家著述○（先生於甲南歸○年已耳順矣○）于十月停讀○廣午○現有清代詞林輯著等書家著述○隨以揭時○居家著述○現有清代詞林輯著等書不求聞達○浮海桑梓○於邯侯○闡發聖言於異域○）卒末○香港大學聘為哲學文詞兩科教習○就孔教學院董事之聘○為故院院長○遵附故中學校長○寢將聖進○嚴功有足多者○循循善誘○香江之學子賴焉○慰慰長征○豫島之悔胞幸矣○又復情欣慕樣○（先生學之清遠縣人○）而總其成○保先逵而期勿失○（封翁之蓋○在羊石束郊塘龍崗○屢被勒遷○力爭而止○圖有獸有起早象堂○至情至性○尤篤孝思○今則謀于昇孫○三年闋卷○富貴非關○帶鄉可期矣○

就秀○薈集泮池○（弱冠縣試冠軍○與其兄汝琦○汝湖○汝璪○次進庠○角逐文理○稱煒廣雅○恥驚藝苑○食餼脞序○丁酉與試選拔○戊戌朝考先登○遠奔祈社○瑩宮祈社○○應順天鄉試○中舉人○）甲辰之歲○雁塔題名○○應會試○聯捷成進士○鸞特逵而校拾遺○○殿試欽定一甲第二○賜進士及第○校敍翰林院編修○先生園足以自豪○○即為我百學增光不淺○○從梅謨博士讀律○三年學成○）命先生○留學束瀛○

○壬申○續聘○而先生乃辭之○於西哲學文詞兩科教習○

○丁午闋卷○富貴非關○帶鄉可期矣○

史太珍汝朱

Dr. CHU U-CHUN.

Dr. Chu was born in 1869 in Ching-yuan District, Kwangtung Province. His predecessors and father were notable mandarins of the Ching Dynasty. He was under tutor at his early age and his destined talents and intelligence in his studies may be seen from the fact that he procured the scholastic title of Hsiu Tsai when he was but twenty years of age.

In 1897, he began to study law in Kiangsu, and after three years when he had a thorough knowledge in the subject, he was promoted judge of the District Court of Kiangsu.

At that time, the emperor of Ching Dynasty realized the urgent need of reforming the administration of government and commanded to retrench those unnecessary staffs of the government organizations by means of a strict examination. More than four hundred candidates were summoned and Doctor Chu was selected first and the result was that he should be promoted to combine law, a post of high dignity.

Dr. Chu is one who loves studies more than anything and he continued his studies with renewed efforts. In 1903 he attained the degree of Chin-Shih, equivalent to Doctor degree, and later was admitted free scholarship to study law in the University of Law and Politics in Japan. Three years later, he graduated and returned to China. Then he became tutor in the law school in Peking. Since then, he had been holding many important posts in the Chinese Government.

In 1931, Dr. Chu was tutor of Chinese philosophy and literature in the Hongkong University. But he resigned the post in the following year.

Since then, he has been president of the Confucian College.

胡惠德醫師

DR. ARTHUR WAI-TAK WOO

惠德先生，籍原廣東鶴山○生於香海○現年四十有九○故名醫胡爾楷翁之哲嗣也○少時肄業於本港拔萃書院○宣畢赴英留學○習法文，及拉丁文○旋進倫敦大學習醫科○以繼父志○一九〇七年，入倫敦醫院實習○初試獲內科臨床醫學優等證書○至一九一三年，而學成○修業期間○一九一一年，中國政府給以駐英華軍上尉軍醫榮銜○同時當地政府復派往倫敦第一師野戰隊第三隊服務凡三載○旋任倫敦醫院眼科醫師○繼充島扶敦醫院駐院醫師○統理該院內外科及X光科各部○時當歐戰○該院房產接收由

其時歐戰延長○醫師缺乏○英政府再委為來修○復及葉斯域醫院高級駐院醫官○及世界和平○先生獲煤油富商駝克利氏之學額○赴美留學○再求深造○首進紐約產科醫院○繼入約翰哈堅大學醫院○歙後實習於美興醫院○該院察路

氏外科剖験用之鏡，及把針器○精神悦力○有具尋常○應付裕如○尚有徐剛○也可知○且同時兼主該院婦科門診部○及倫敦市立花柳醫院間駐局醫官○倫敦邸政總局○一身數職○根

據利華殿氏原理，而發明胡氏外科剖験用之鏡，而登院婦科門診部○及倫敦市立花柳科教授○且報選該院產婦科副教授○厭職尚無異諸國外人者○先生以不同種族之新俊學○竟能任此○其選拔之迢○躬任醫務總監○故院儀器完備○可稱敏○對於惠為之貧苦病人○不少免費治療○可稱三十年來○因研求醫學○遠遊歐美者四○於銃醫療焉○

先生學歷○為倫敦大學內外科醫學士○英國皇立外科學院○及倫敦皇立內科醫學院膺士○英國皇立熱帶病學院會員○美奧外科醫會○及維也納美國醫學會永遠會員○

病療在抱之者也○先生學成○為大都市之醫療機關，如倫敦，紐約，愛丁堡，柏林，巴黎，漢堡關，皆有特別經驗所探討○故能日進新如○馳名中外○復生於一九一六年胡梳谷著「食管膨脹六醫案」○一九一八年「利華殿氏鍼及把針器，對於外科及婦科之功用○」一九二二年「弗拉芬連綠收璃等消毒劑」，對於外科及婦科之功用○」一九二三年「在中國醫生之子宮外孕○」一九二四年「白喉三百醫案」○

法運回傷兵之最前綫，為供先生多量診斷與拖術之良機○任滿○倫敦約造產科醫院聘之當歸國○卸任北平協和醫學院產婦科副教授○兼統理產婦科門診於○育才濟世○兼而有之○是以白宮徵為名譽醫官○外交交通兩部聘為醫事顧問○一九二三年，代表於大總統出席上海

醫師○耳先生治理傷兵之經驗○請先生演講「我時用亞尼林染料治療創傷之觀察」○世界各處醫師

『一九三五年「伊弗啟庇祿樂一百醫案」。一九三七年「武烈血清治療。附一千醫案」等書面世。他如醫學組織。無不熱烈參加。為中華醫學會永遠會員。現任該會監察委員。曾充香港中華醫學會會長。中華醫學會香港分會秘書。復又為會長。英國醫學會員及香港分會理事。港大醫學會歷聯兩屆會長。尤以一九二八年任上海博醫會中華及香港分會理事。港大醫學會歷聯兩屆會長。此為叛舉。翌年。參與上海醫學會長。為我國醫界最光榮之事。誠以華人齒斯職。此為叛舉。翌年。參與上海醫學大會。荷拔為大會主席。博醫會在我國成立。午將半百。至於社會公益慈善會同組織。前會與中華醫學會合併。又獲舉為副會長。連任兩屆。本由中外醫師善商界名事業。贊助尤為熱中。不獨解衣。且肯出力。為中華癩救濟會香港支會值理。華人慈善會籌下武煙兼母嬰指導所義務總醫師。倡故華人慈善會值理。當義務醫官。復任該會副主席。最近政充執委會倡辦。復被聘為聖約翰教傷院義務外科醫官。申江一二八之役。與財委會委員。現史兼該會籌下武煙兼傷隊永遠會員。復任該會醫官。及主考。與聖約翰救傷團。現充史兼該會籌下武煙傷院救傷外科醫官。中江一二八之役。倡組德戰救護團。任主席。計用香港藥專。組從于壽過卒。除分批派送義務醫師護士藥料等往上海紅十字醫院外。並送兩救護醫生大會。前任香港華人青年會副會長。擔任演講及檢驗工作。現充藥學所之用。一千提又光横。造將事告急。乃微將全國同氣。將餘款萬圓撥充中華醫學會建拔革書院醫生值理。聖保羅女書院校醫。及霑街公會華南財政委員。香港扶拔書院醫官顧問。現任值理。中華醫院。醫科大院。數任倫敦各校醫務顧問。聖保羅堂值理。及霑術公會華南區長。一九三六年召集百屆聯合會。任該會主席基督教服務團贊助員。英國海外僑民會永遠會員。華商總會會員。香港全龍酒家永遠值員。華商俱樂部會員。鍵聲慈善社社員。聯育社義務工作。現充義員。一九三五年。本港籤工時期。曾任幹事值理。上海大新公司董事。香港金龍酒家永遠值理。前任香港羅工時期。自告奮勇。肩任義務工作。復得政司組畫函效謝。一九三四年。本港羅工時期。在播音台演講。極荷皇制早嘉獎及海沐。尤省體育。早期創術。春柳。胡珠。泉馬有益運動。現為香港馬會會員。全港學界。德配金月女士。本港股商聚興君之愛姓。曾修業於聖士提反女校。現有子女六人。

Ambulance, Mr. A. Morris, by Dr. Woo from his society. He was first made Vice-president of the Advisory committee, and later became Co-director on the Executive Committee of the new organization. Dr. Woo is a life member of the St. John Ambulance Association and Brigade and besides being a Divisional Surgeon and Examiner for first-aid certificates, he serves on the Finance Committee. His most recent appointment is Honorary Surgeon to the Association's Haw Par Hospital in Cheung Chau Island.

In 1932 during the Sino-Japanese trouble in Shanghai, when an urgent appeal for medical aid came to Hongkong, Dr. Woo was elected Chairman of the Hongkong Medical Relief Committee. The total subscription raised exceeded $40,000, more than half of which was raised by Dr. Woo himself. Besides supplying money to the Red Cross Society in Shanghai, doctors and nurses, medical supplies, two ambulances and a set of portable X-ray were sent up as well. After the trouble was over, through Dr. Woo's influence, the sum of $10,000 was sent to the Chinese Medical Association in aid of the Association Building Fund.

During his student days in England, besides taking part in many sports such as fencing, boxing, tennis and riding, Dr. Woo was also keenly interested in Christian work among Chinese students. In 1908 he founded the Chinese Students' Christian Union of Great Britain and Ireland, which continues its excellent work. He was its Chairman for the first five years of its existence and also served on the Executive Committee of the London Intercollegiate Christian Union. In 1913 he was elected to be one of the Chinese representatives to attend the World Students' Christian Federation Conference held at Lake Mahonk, New York. He was a Vice-president of the Hongkong Chinese Y.M.C.A. and has given many Health Campaign lectures, as well as personal service in examination and guidance for the general health of members. He is a Committee Member of the Diocesan Old Boys' Association and serves as Honorary Medical Advisor to the Diocesan Boys' School, and St. Paul's Girls' College in which connection, with the help of his colleagues, he gives free annual examination to the boarders as well as free vaccination to both schools. He gives also free treatment to the inmates of the Blind Girls' Home. He is a member of the Executive Committee and Hon. Medical Advisor of the Street Sleepers' Shelter Society.

In 1925 during the General Strike in Hongkong Dr. Woo was one of the first to volunteer for service, and later received a letter of appreciation and thanks from the Colonial Secretary.

In 1934 at the request of His Excellency the Governor, Sir William Peel, Dr. Woo broadcasted in Chinese on behalf of the Cancer Campaign and received afterwards a personal letter of thanks from His Excellency.

In 1935, Dr. Woo was honoured by His Majesty, the late King George V with the Jubilee Medal.

Dr. Woo was a member of the Committee of St. Paul's Church and is a member of the Diocesan Board of Finance of the Chung Hwa Sheng Kung Hui (Church of China) for South China. He has also been a member of the Committee of the Mission to Chinese Seamen.

A charter member and Director of the Rotary Club, he is also South China District Governor of the International Association of Y's Men's Clubs. He had the honour of calling and presiding over the first District Conference of Y's Men of South China, which was a great success. He is a builder member of Toc H, a life member of the Overseas League and a Fellow of the Royal Empire Society.

A Member of the Chinese Chamber of Commerce and Chinese Merchants' Club, and past committee member of the latter, Dr. Woo is also a Director of the Sun Company, Shanghai, and a permanent Director of the Kam Loong Restaurant.

Attesting to his interest in and patronage of sport, he is a member of the Hongkong Jockey Club, Hon. President of Interscholastic Athletic Union, and a member of the South China Athletic Association, the Y.M.C.A. and the Chung Sing Benevolent Association. He has been a supporter also of the Chinese Recreation Club, the International Golf Club and the Craigengower Cricket Club. His chief recreations now are gardening and swimming.

香港・澳門雙城成長經典

Dr. ARTHUR WAI-TAK WOO

M.B., B.S. (LOND), M.R.C.S. (ENG), L.R.C.P. (LOND).

Doctor Woo was born in Hongkong in 1887, and received his early education at the Diocesan Boys' School where he had a brilliant scholastic career. In 1905 he went to finish his education in England. Following in the footsteps of his father, Dr. Woo Yee Kai, he chose the medical profession. After passing the necessary French and Latin tests in record time, he matriculated into the London University and entered the London Hospital in 1907. In his first competitive class examination he was awarded the certificate for efficiency in Elementary Clinical Medicine.

In 1911 the Chinese Government granted Dr. Woo an honorary commission as Captain in the Chinese Army Medical Service, and from then to 1913 he was attached to the Third London Field Ambulance, First London Division (T), for training in Army medical work, which served him in good stead during the Great War.

In January 1913, Dr. Woo graduated and his first appointment was that of an Ophthalmic Clinical Assistant at the London Hospital, working under Sir William Lister. His next appointment was that of Resident Medical Officer at the Gravesend General Hospital, having charge of both departments of Medicine and Surgery, including X Cabinet This hospital was one of the first to receive the wounded from France at the beginning of the War. When that commission was completed he became House Physician at the General Lying-in Hospital, York Road, London, and from there took up next the post of Assistant Resident Medical Officer at the London Fever Hospital under the eminent physician Sir John Broadbent. Subsequent to this, he was appointed House Physician at the well-known Brompton Hospital for Consumption and Diseases of the Chest.

Dr. Woo then decided to turn his attention to surgery, and in 1916, after the competitive examination, he became House Surgeon to Lieutenant Colonel Sir Alfred Pearce Gould and Mr. Sampson Handler, at the Middlesex Hospital. After that he became Gynaecological Obstetric House Surgeon under Sir Comyns Berkeley and Mr. Victor Bonney, world famous gynaecologists also at the Middlesex Hospital. Before very long he had the distinction of being asked to take the post of Gynaecological and Obstetric Tutor, Registrar, and Acting Lecturer on Practical Midwifery at the Middlesex Hospital, a post previously held only by a Britisher. At the same time he was in charge of the Gynaecological Out-patients and the Venereal Disease Clinic under the London County Council. In conjunction with this work, and for night duty only, he was performing the functions of Resident Medical Officer to the London General Post Office, thus relieving three men at one time for war service.

It was during this busy period that Dr. Woo invented the "Woo" needle and holder for abdominal surgery—a modification of Reverdin's in principle. Later, because of the further shortage of doctors as the War progressed, he was asked to take up the post of Senior Resident Medical Officer at the East Suffolk and Ipswich General Hospital, having charge of three hundred military and one hundred and fifty civilian beds.

After the Armistice Dr. Woo became a Rockefeller scholar and left England to take up post-graduate work, first at the New York Lying-in Hospital and Post-graduate Medical School, later at the Johns Hopkins University Hospital under Professor Howard Kelly and Dr. Thomas S. Cullen, and lastly at the unique Mayo Clinic in America. Dr. Charles Mayo paid him the compliment of requesting him to address one of the weekly staff meetings which are attended by visiting doctors from all over the world, on his observations of the treatment of wounds with aniline dyes during the War.

Upon his return to China, and for a period of two years, Dr. Woo was, first, Assistant Surgeon to Professor J. Preston Maxwell and later an Associate with him in the Department of Obstetrics and Gynaecology at the Peiping Union Medical College, of the Rockefeller Foundation. At the same time he had full charge of the whole outpatient Gynaecological Clinic. During his stay in Peiping he was made Physician Extraordinary to the President of China, and Medical Adviser to the Ministry of Foreign Affairs and Ministry of Communications, and in 1923 he was asked to be President Li Yuan Hung's personal representative to convey his special message to the Biennial Conference of the China Medical Missionary Association held in Shanghai. Before leaving Peiping he was decorated by the President of China with the Order of the Chia Ho (Excellent Crop) Fifth Class.

Upon his return to Hongkong to take up medical practice, Dr. Woo was appointed lecturer on Gynaecology and Obstetrics at the Hongkong University as well as being Internal Examiner on the same subjects during the period of 1924-1925 prior to the arrival of the University Professor.

On four occasions Dr. Woo returned to Europe and America for post-graduate work, mainly in Radium Therapy and General Surgery. The cities where he made his special studies were London, Edinburgh, Berlin, Paris, Heidelberg, Vienna, New York and Rochester (Mayo Clinic).

Dr. Woo is now a Bachelor of Medicine and Bachelor of Surgery of the University of London, also a Member of the Royal College of Surgeons, England, and a Licentiate of the Royal College of Physicians, London. He has also been a Fellow of the Royal Society of Tropical Medicine. He is a life member of the Mayo Clinic Surgeons' Club, Rochester, and a life member of the American Medical Association, Vienna.

Dr. Woo is now Principal of the Woo Clinic, China Building Hongkong. He opened the Babington Hospital and Sanitarium in 1934 and is its medical director. The Home is fully equipped, even having radium for treatment of cancer cases and many from the poorer classes have been treated there free of charge.

Dr. Woo's medical writings are:—(Co-author, with Dr. Batty Shaw) "Six Cases of Oesophagectasia" (a paper read before the Section of Medicine of the Royal Society of Medicine on November 28. 1916). "Reverdin's Needle-Holder and Needles" (The Lancet, March 23, 1918). "Some Observations on the uses of Flavine, Brilliant Green and Ensol in General Surgery and Gynaecology," 1922. 'Ectopic Gestations in China," (Journal of Obstetrics and Gynaecology, of the British Empire). "Study of three hundred Cases of Leucorrhœa," 1924, Evipan Anaesthesia 100 Cases," 1925 Chinese Medical Journal, and "Auto-serum Treatment for Opium Addicts (Observation on 1000 cases) in January, 1937 Chinese Medical Journal.

As well as performing distinguished medical service and keeping himself abreast of the development of medical science, Dr. Woo has taken a prominent part in matters of medical organization. He is a member of the Supervisory Committee of the Chinese Medical Association, of which he now is a life member. He has been President of the Hongkong Chinese Medical Association, and also Secretary and later President of the National Medical Association of China, (Hongkong Branch) and a Council Member of the British Medical Association, Hongkong and China Branch. He was twice Vice-president of the Hongkong University Medical Society.

In 1928, Dr. Woo received a high Chinese medical honour when he was elected to be the first Chinese President of the China Medical Association. The following year he presided, and delivered his presidential speech, at the 1929 Biennial Conference held in Shanghai. This association was an international medical organization of more than forty years' standing, which later became amalgamated with the National Medical Association of China to form one united organization known as the Chinese Medical Association. In the new organization Dr. Woo was elected to serve for two successive terms as its Vice-president.

Parallel with his medical work, Dr. Woo has taken an active interest in social and other public problems. He has contributed much time, thought and effort to Leprosy, Opium and other evils affecting the Chinese population. He is a Committee Member of the Hongkong Auxiliary of the Chinese Mission to Lepers and a keen worker in the cause of charity.

He is the chief medical officer in charge of the Anti-opium, Ante and postnatal, Birth Control, Sterility, and Child welfare Clinics run under the auspices of the Chinese Benevolent Association, which he founded in 1933 and of which he is now an Executive Committee Member.

Realising the great need for medical service among the villgers in the a New Territories, Dr. Woo organized in November 1930 the first medical clinics in ten different centres, where there were no Government doctors, and later founded the New Territories Medical Benevolent Society. Its total expenditure for doctors, nurses and drugs was over $22,000. At the request of His Excellency the Governor, this society became amalgamated with that of the St. John Ambulance Association to form the New Territories Medical Benevolent Branch of the St. John Ambulance Association. A cheque for $10,000 was handed over to the Director of

林承芬博士

士博芬承林

Dr. SHING FAN LAM, Ph. D.

Dr. Shing Fan Lam was born in Kwangtung Province in 1888. After obtaining a good knowledge in Chinese literature, he went to America to continue his studies in the American Institute of Banking, New York. Many years later, he succeeded to get the Standard Certificate from that institution and there after he was employed by the Anglo-California Trust Company, San Francisco, California, U.S.A., as manager of their Chinese Department. His business ability and wide contact with the Chinese overseas enabled him to be advanced to the position of manager of their Montgomery Street Branch. He was afterwards promoted to be Assistant Cashier, and Assistant Vice-president at the time when he resigned in favour of the Bank of China.

Dr. Lam is a man who is always anxious to learn more, so he made use of his leisure hours and continued with his studies and research work in the Lincoln University, San Francisco, where he procured the degree of Ph. D. in Banking Administration.

The Bank of China, Shanghai, offered an attractive position to Dr. Lam. Knowing that such an experienced technical man is beneficial to a banking concern, the Anglo-California Trust Company, California, where Dr. Lam was working, offered a triple increment of salary in order to make Dr. Lam to stay with their institution. But Dr. Lam is a sort of man who always intends to render himself to serve his own nation, so he refused the American Bank and returned to China where he was appointed sub-manager of the Bank of China, Hongkong.

At present, the bank has established a branch in New York City, U.S.A. and Dr. Lam may be sent to extend service in that direction.

Although Dr. Lam is not a rich man, any occasion that concerns charity he is always doing his best to contribute.

Dr. Lam has four children. All of them obtained a thorough education. His oldest daughter acquired the B.S. degree in Home Economics from the University of Nevada, Reno, Nevada. The second daughter graduated from the University of California, in plant genetics, Berkeley, California. His son is studying mechanical Engineering in U.S.A., and his third daughter expects to study police Administration or Education in U.S.A.

李景康先生

李景康先生

李先生景康○字鳳坡○東粵南海人○現年四十五○學貫中西○才名藉甚○誠我國富有學問之教育家也○幼在珂里松溪鄉私塾肄業○旋貧苦之先生家也○香港聖士提反中學○民國元年○考獲英國牛津大學高等試文憑○中文特著俊異○其時香港大學創辦伊始○乃攻文科○民國四年○以第一屆

畢業○得學士銜○民國六年○朱慶瀾任廣東省長○創辦全省保衛團總局○以維治安○且通民隱○先生被徵為參謀○朱省長去粵○乃就教席○於母校聖士提反中學○逾五歲○民十一年○因受邑內紳商公舉○往廣州任南海中學○兼縣立南海師範學校校長○洎員整頓邑校之責○成績卓著○邑人多之○前後輸將故傷費達五六萬金○民十三年○膺香港政府之聘○任漢文視學官○兼英文視學官○輿論僉然韙拄○民十五年

○本港政府徇紳商之請○亟思提倡我國國學○遂有官立漢文中學之創設○而思司者因胡先生長之○遂使主官立漢文師範學校事○垂歷十載○以迄於茲○能循循善誘○沾溉士林○故本港○聲譽於焉益著○先生凡遇教育設施○多出其門○馨於其難○如民十三○在粵○勤勞其職務○尤樂勷廠事○者也○先生擔任廣東全省教育會計議員○及歷充廣州南海中學校董○偏任香港孔聖堂幹事值理○偏廷香港南海商會董事○創辦南海石門中學董事值理○倡港大中文學會名譽會員○港大歷屆投試委員○皆其尤著者也○先生擅詩文○工

社湖集社員○江蘇吳縣中國國學會社員○香港社湘南長沙南社社員○湖南長沙南社社員○廣社社員○先生擅詩文○工辭章○枕漱江蘇常熙○述甚富○嘗著披雲樓詩○壬申書畫合作社幹事值理○歷恆浯心國學○著理○

草○七言律法舉隅○及與區大典光祖兩太史○陳垣屏退士等合編國文模範讀本三冊○吳張谷維君合編揚芳砂圖考○葉公譽虎為之序○多聲多才○不惟顧南名士也○先生祀鄧夫人○名遂賢○上海啟明女中學生○得款○早卒○顧室蘇夫人○男公子六○曰尚教○尚勇○曰尚治○尚沛○尚平○鮮棠小學○尚信仙○女公子四○曰綺株○已婚○綺煙○則尚幼為○綺樱○均就小學○綺嫻○

官○兼其文視學官○輿論僉然韙拄○民十五年全○民十三年○邑人多之○前後輸將故傷費達五六萬金○膺香港政府之聘○任漢文視學官○兼其文視學

李景康先生生先康景李

Mr. K. H. LI, B.A.

Mr. Li is a native of Nan-hai District, Kwangtung Province, and was born in 1892.

He received his early education from a private school of his native village, and later entered St. Stephen's College, Hongkong, where in 1912 he passed the Oxford Senior Local Examination with distinction in Chinese and the first Hongkong University Matriculation Examination. Thereupon he took an Arts course at the local University and graduated in 1916 with a B.A. degree.

In 1917 when General Ju Hing Lan was Civil Governor of Kwangtung, the Bureau of Provincial Protection was established and Mr. Li was appointed a councilor of this institution.

Mr. Li returned to Hongkong in the following year on being offered a teaching post by St. Stephen's College, his alma mater. He held this post until 1922 when he was appointed Headmaster of the Nan-hai Middle School and the Nan-hai Normal School, Canton, on the recommendation of the gentry and the Chamber of Commerce of his native district.

Appointed Inspector of vernacular Schools and English Private Schools by the Education Department in 1924, he returned to the Colony for a second time. In two years he was transferred to the Headmastership of the Government Vernacular Middle School, and that of the Government Normal School, the former institution was founded in 1926 and the latter in 1921.

Mr. Li is a man of broad sympathy and every good cause finds him a willing supporter. In recognition of his success in educational work he was elected a member of the Advisory Committee of the Kwangtung Provincial Education Association in 1924 before he came back to Hongkong in that year. The various social services he has rendered in Canton and Hongkong may be well signified by the following elections and appointments. He has served as member of the school council of the Nan-hai Middle School, Shek Moon Middle School, Canton, Executive Committe of the Confucius Hall; Hon. member of the Chinese Association of the Hongkong University, and Hon. Treasurer of the Hongkong University Graduates' Association, Hongkong.

In 1928 he was called upon together with Dr. Au Tai Tin and Dr. Lai Chai Hsi to draft the scheme and syllabus for the establishment of the Chinese School of the local University, and has served as member of its Board of Examination.

Mr. Li is an adept of Chinese literature and pictorial art. He is a member of the U-Shia Literary Association at Chang-Han, Kiangsu Province; member of the Nan-Shia Literary Association at Changsha, Hunan Province; and member of the China National Learning Association at Wu Hsien, Kiangsu Province the last two being the leading societies of men of letters in China. He has published three of his many literary works in Chinese, namely, the Pi Yun Lau Poems, a study of Seven-Word-Line Poems, and a set of three books entitled Model Readers on the Diction and Styles of Chinese Essayists. For the last work he is a joint editor. Being a connoisseur of Chinese painting he was responsible for the organization of the Chinese Pictorial Art Section of the China Exhibition held in the local City Hall in 1931.

Mr. Li has six sons and four daughters; except those who are still young, the others are receiving their education in local schools.

杜其章先生

MR. TOH KEE CHENG

提起「杜其章」三個字○可謂「天下誰人不識君」○其愛國愛鄉○名聞寰宇矣○先生字嶸文○原籍福建泉州清蒙鄉○入閩堂族○世代簪纓○杜「少陵」「祁公」之遠裔也○其先君柏森公○梁進士○文武兼資○有上馬殺賊○下馬草露布之才○當清之世○排滿最力○丁亥前後○赴越南○隱於商○與劉將軍永福抵抗法軍於諒山高平等省○不受清廷命令○西保全粵南關逃防要隘○人至於今稱之○先生生而歧嶷○少年靖書破萬卷○最俠有乃父風○博愛為懷○有我不入地獄○誰入地獄之志○且天縱多能○如文學家,書畫家,美術家,藝術家,教育家,政治家,慈善家,音樂家,泰術家○均兼而有之○年未及壯○憤清政之綱○參與庚戌,辛亥,兩役○浮海而有之○民國建立○功成不居○以跳房已餘○乃退近祖國○來港經商○市塵混跡○垂廿餘年○年來對於國事○常有杜甫傷時之感○海隅之變○宋港之役○愴懷國難○開廣州書畫展覽會○為宣傳,香港,澳門等埠○抗敵救國最力之一人○現仍報效不絕○所謂愛國之忱○與日俱積也○先生不徒熱血滿腔○有澄清當世○而天性孝友○亦篤於時誼○且屏絕不良嗜好○有倜儻橫溢○尚無間飢割分○倡平民化○尤愛護文人學士○有安排廣厦千萬間○普歡顏之宏願○生平提倡文化○宣揚國粹○舉辦教育慈善事業○不遺餘力○是以海內外友京滬杭平粵杜汕厦書畫名流○如高劍父,黃賓虹,徐悲鴻,劉海粟,馬萬里,黃墈磨,孫福熙,黃曼庭,陳天嘯,洪毅,至蘭亭○一到香港等閒美展○必先訪詢先生○蓋以先生為書畫文藝界領袖○一呼百應○萬山響應○其號召力之偉○足以左右一切○故遇人歸之○先生以本港為世界交通樞紐○宣揚文化○此地適宜○乃於民國十六年組織書畫文學社○以保存國粹為宗旨○社友近海內外○泉仰先生尚義粹財○乃舉為永遠社長○成立迄茲○十餘年矣○其他國內外各機關社團倚重先生○而以委辦相煩者○亦夥○現任香港裕茂行東主○旅港杜氏宗親會主席○福建義學主席○書畫文化事業社董事長○非非畫報社社長○留港學生公立菜茹義學顧問○梅芳中學美術顧問○現任香港書畫文學社主席○香港文化事業社董事長○中華學術院會顧問○領島男女中學童事○廣州廣大女子中學童事○香港華商總會會董○福建商會董事○廣東革命紀念會董事○烈士遺裔學校董事○培德中學永遠顧問○大中女子中學童事○全港小型足球進會正會長○全國小型足球協會董事○廣州城西方便醫院名譽董事等職○對於桑梓○在其故里○力為事提倡開學校,建醫院,開公路,築公圖○為鄉黨父老所敬重○舉為鄉中紳士○而港中各界○史推之為求衆醫院總理,保良公局總理馬○先生雅愛音樂○善操古琴○而於攝影一

繳舉。尤稱屁譬。饉期未遇。素不自炫。前歲
青年會為籌款事。徵求先生登臺報効。始獲階
其第一次雅奏。音額緞紬。有統樓三日之槩。
至先生之書法。均臻妙境。雄健清秀。有如鐵畫銀鈎。真
草籀篆。均臻妙境。雄健清秀。有如鐵畫銀鈎。真
對此造。發鑽追三十年。而楷書尤為壓倒一切。欲
○其書學案大字。筆力之雄。不可忍議。編者
於午前參觀廣東全省市展會。得覩先生浪地一格
爽狀。「相率中原豪傑還我河山」一氣呵成。有
觀眾棠聲如雷。致為觀止。
其俗如「國破家何在」等聯。其讓饯澉昻之氣。躍於字裏
行間。善書之名大眾。求者遠紛至香來。惟先
生個性特奇。遇聲氣相投者。則連紙墨亦樂贈
之。倘雰有未愜。錐萬金亦不能將其隻字。蓋
慕其名者。恭求墨寶。戶限為穿。於時堤岸一
埠。頗成洛陽紙賞之地。至先生之春街造詣
先生之墨頭。不能以全錢而代償之也。前年先
閗濄內功甚深。向秘不示人。編者客冬遇諸警
務。方悉先生前夕曾客退身于。追獲兩匪於松
秀束街。交警署查出。曾遮解出境十年期尚未
滿之摹魋也。足微其懷有妃技。與奮不顧身之
膽量。現先生年緧四十餘。而才名籍甚。馨巻
崇隆。來日方長。為國家社會人羣謀幸福。正
未可限量。于四女四。均是秀出班行。淵源家
學。盛德者福大。積厚者流光。理固昭然不爽
也。

Mr. TOH KEE CHEUNG

Mr. Toh Kee Cheung is a native of Chuanchiufo, Fukien Province, and was born in 1897.

His fore-fathers were famous officials of the Ch'ing Dynasty, and Mr. Toh, being came from a high stock, is well bred and educated.

He is a member of the Nationalists Party and rendered great assistance to the Chinese Revolution. After the establishment of the Chinese Republic, he declined every position offered to him, but came to Hongkong and mingled himself in the business field.

He organized the Association of Arts and Literature in the Colony and was appointed Permanent President of the organization. During the Sino-Japanese Conflict of 1932, he held an exhibition of painting works in order to raise money to relieve that calamity.

Mr. Toh is very attentive to public weals. He is a member of the Prosperity-scheming Committee of the Chinese General Chamber of Commerce, Hongkong; Director of the Fukien Chamber of Commerce, Hongkong; Chairman of the Fukien Free School; Chairman of the Board of Directors of the Hongkong Literary Enterprise Association; Adviser of many local schools; President of the Tung Wah Hospital; Committee of the Po Leung Kuk; and Hon. Director of the Western Public Hospital, Canton.

Mr. Toh has eight children and all of them are well educated.

容子名先生

生先名子容

容子名先生〇原籍中山南屏鄉〇而世居於香港〇祖諱良〇充本港渣打銀行首任買辦〇父諱寬邦〇繼之而為第二任買辦〇

〇忽丁父艱〇先生極孝〇遭此大變〇哀痛欲絕〇蓋銀行以先生才德遒茂〇且在行中服務多年〇勞績甚鉅〇遂亦聘充買辦〇俾繼父職〇先生自任職以來〇孜孜十餘年〇無日不忠克誠〇以勤以謹〇益現已成為港中巨商之一矣〇

〇先生性情豪爽仁俠〇向能熱心社會事業〇故港政府委充太平紳士〇並歷任華商總會幹事值理〇東華三院及保良局董事〇香港銀行買辦房團主席〇

〇祖興父均能積善儲德〇無怪乎先生能為孝子賢孫矣〇先生幼已聰明好學〇見稱於師友〇稍長〇致進香港皇仁大書院〇孜孜求學〇成績屢冠儕輩〇首鴯冠〇使以最優等事業〇離校後〇即任職於渣打銀行〇膺助乃父〇以學識優長〇其明精幹〇極為該銀行總理所器重〇年三十

〇先生於十七歲時已娶親〇原配余氏〇繼室陳氏〇均有賢德〇子名次蕊〇年方二十八〇曾畢業於皇仁書院〇現亦在渣打銀行任職〇先生齡高五十有四〇然生平慎起居〇節飲食〇不喜徵逐於酒色之場〇故身健康〇容貌豐潤〇絕視之〇實似三十餘歲之人〇

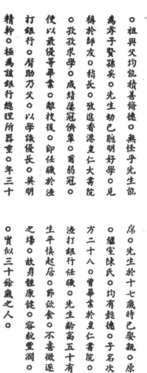

Mr. YUNG TSZE MING, J.P.

One of the most important figure in Hongkong is Mr. Yung Tsze Ming, compradore of the Hongkong Charter Bank of India Australia & China.

His grandfather was the first Chinese Compradore who worked in that Bank since its inauguration, and his father was the second to succeed. Mr. Yung Tsze Ming was born in Hongkong in 1883 and was educated in Queen's College. After his graduation, he worked in the Charter Bank, helping his father.

His intellegence and his ability soon came to be understood by the president of the Bank, who made him compradore of the same bank after the death of his father. Since then he assisted greatly in flourishing the business of this outstanding firm.

Mr. Yung is a Justice of Peace of Hongkong and an influential figure in the Chinese community. He held important positions in the Chinese Chamber of Commerce, Hongkong, and was in the Directorate of the Tung Wah Hospital, the Kwong Wah Hospital, the Tung Wah East Hospital and the Po Leung Kuk. Chairman of the Banking Compradore Association. Besides these, Mr. Yung is very popular for his bigness of heart in dealing with charity and social matters.

At present, Mr. Yung's son Yung Chi Yim is also working in the Charter Bank.

馬叙朝先生

馬叙朝先生

生先朝叙馬

馬叙朝先生○廣東省台山縣白沙塘口村人○現年五十九歲○容貌温良○壯情致

一九二四年○充保良局總理○一九二五年○充東華醫院主席○及太平局紳○一九二六年充團防局紳○一九二八年○充

保良局首席總理○一九二九年○又任團防局紳○其在華人團體所任名譽職務○

歷充華
商總會
紳事
四邑商
工總局
，及台
山商會
董事
現任中
國經濟
建設運

厚○乃香港享有佳譽之縉紳○而現任公有源綢莊之總司理也○先生諌悦壮成○

熱心國家社會事業○民國三年○我國大總統為酬報勤勞起見○曾頒給以四等嘉禾章○其在港府所任名譽職務○西历

勤會廣東省分會委員○其在商場所任職務○除今任公有源綢莊總司理之外○現尚充四邑輪船公司○及新寧鐵路等董事○一生忠厚○人多敬之○十八歲時已

結婚○現有兄孫及尾矣○

Mr. MA TSUI CHIU, J.P.

Mr. Ma is a native of Toishan District, Kwangtung Province and was born in 1878. Having acquired a good knowledge in Chinese literature, he came to Hongkong in his early age to obtain commercial knowledge. At present, he is the General Manager of the Kung Yau Yuen silk piece store which is dealing with piece goods and silk commodities.

Mr. Ma was Chairman of the Po Leung Kuk in 1924 and 1928, and in 1925 he was appointed Chairman of the Tung Wah Hospital and Justice of the Peace, Hongkong. He was appointed member of the District Watchmen Committee in 1926 and 1929 respectively.

Mr. Ma is also a commanding figure in his own community. For many times he was member of the Board of committees of the Chinese Chamber of Commerce, Hongkong.

He is also Director of the Sze Yap Commercial and Industrial Association, and Chamber of Commerce, Toishan.

In 1924, he was honoured by the Chinese Government with the Order of the Chia Ho (Excellent Crop) Fourth Class.

Besides his vast interest in the Kung Yau Yuen Store he is also Director of Sze Yap Steamship Co., and the Sun Ning Railway.

盧仲雲先生

盧仲雲先生〇名家裕〇以字行〇粵之中山縣上柯鄉人〇現年五十八歲〇乃本港早已成名之鉅商也〇生有風鑒〇未弱冠〇已畢業於香港皇仁書院〇因成績優異〇遂將受該書院之聘〇充任

盧仲雲先生

盛大宴會〇過這中外鐘商〇以誠先生〇銀行總理〇即席贈與先生以一最古而最有價值之時辰鐘〇稱先生以確實之商業報告及悠久之服務〇以贊助該銀行〇其功用極似此古時辰鐘云〇同時駐港荷蘭領事〇亦即席讚揚先生〇並代表荷蘭女皇〇頒賜先生以實星一枚〇故先生不特名溢於香港〇而在荷蘭國〇及不哇羣島各地之人莫不景仰先生之名卷也〇先生歷充東華醫院及保良局董事〇香港政府於西曆一九二五年〇曾派充郵政檢查員〇職位更要〇偏非為公家服務〇尚稱努力〇實不易得此

教員〇惟先生向有志於商業〇故未幾〇即辭教職〇就本港德華銀行之聘〇活動於金融界〇歐戰發生〇德華銀行停閉〇遂轉就我國北方京奉鐵路要職〇二十五年前〇再返港〇遂就荷蘭銀行充任華經理(即俗稱買辦)〇當先生服務於該銀行已滿二十五年之日〇該銀行以先生忠誠勤敏〇二十五年如一日〇為酬勞獎勵起見〇特設

至於其在商業方面〇歷充大新公司〇嚴口長途汽車公司〇廣安輪船公司〇國民銀行〇及永安人壽保險公司等董事〇裕興豆業有限公司永遠監督〇現被舉充華商總會值理〇香港銀行辦房團主席〇港仔公立醫局副主席〇發重人歸〇令人羨慕〇而生平見義勇為〇當仁不讓〇尤為當世所敬仰也〇

Mr. LO CHUNG-WAN.

Mr. Lo Chung-wan is the Compradore of the Netherlands Trading Society, and a very prominent figure associated with the commerce of Hongkong, Holland and the Dutch East Indies.

Born in Chungshan District, Kwangtung Province, he was educated at the Queen's College. Upon completing his education, he was offered a position in that College as a Member of the Teaching Staffs.

His vocation, however, proved to be mercantile, so he resigned from the College and entered the Commercial Circle.

About twenty - five years ago, he joined the Netherlands Trading Society and has become the Compradore of that very large and respectable Banking Institution.

Upon his completion of a quarter century of meritorious service, he was invited to a large reception tendered by the Bank and which was attended by many prominent people of Hongkong.

In a speach made by the Chief Official of the Bank, Mr. Lo Chung - wan's services were very highly eulogized and he was presented with a very antique and costly Dutch Clock. The high official of the bank remarked that Mr. Lo Chung Wan's good qualities were very identical to that of the clock for in as much as the clock had for a long period given very accurate reports of the time and positions of the moon etc., Mr. Lo Chung - wan likewise had been very useful to the officials and clients of the bank by his supply of very useful trade informations and assistances. The Consul for the Netherlands Mr. M. H. van Schreven spoke very highly of Mr. Lo Chung - wan in his speech, remarking to the gathering that in connection with most excellent services rendered by Mr. Lo Chung - wan, Her Majesty the Queen of the Netherlands was most graciously pleased in awarding him with the very coveted and most Excellent Order of the Orange of Nassau.

Mr. Lo Chung - wan was also in the Directorate of the Tung Wah Hospital and the Po Leung Kuk and also enjoyed the confidence of the Hongkong Government in 1925 when appointed to the important position of Postal Censor which position he very capably held and was suitably thanked by the Hongkong Government.

Besides his many important activities, Mr. Lo Chung - wan is in the Directorate of the internationally known firm of Department Stores, The Sun Co., Ltd., operating Chain Store in China and the huge building in Nanking Road, Shanghai. Director of Ngan How Motor Bus, The Kong On S. S. Co., the National Commercial & Savings Bank, and The Wing On Life Insurance Co., Ltd., and is in the Committee of the Chinese General Chamber of Commerce. Mr. Lo Chung - wan is also the Chairman of the Bank Compradores' Association of Hongkong, a very important and potential financial association in Hongkong.

香港・澳門雙城成長經典

58

陸靄雲先生

生先雲靄陸

陸靄雲先生〇廣東肇慶府高要縣人〇現年五十五歲〇容貌秀俊〇體貌壯健〇壯

該校第一班學生〇西曆一九〇〇年畢業離校〇二十一歲應日本橫濱烏恩倫燕梳公司之聘〇充任要職〇繼調充港行華組理〇服務三十餘年〇其恆心與毅力〇殊非他人所可及〇在社會亦有盛譽〇西曆

一九三六枚〇充委太平局紳〇一九三七〇充保良局紳〇歷任南華體育會主席

情誼〇乃烏恩倫燕梳公司港行之華組理〇亦新任本港之太平局紳也〇幼年時〇已受良好家庭教育〇精長〇進培英學校〇捷政進皇仁大書院〇攻讀英文〇勤蓄學勤業

〇現任該會會長〇生平樂善好施〇忠誠坦直〇賢近代不可多得之人物也〇長女麗婷姑娘曾在嶺南大學,及北平燕京大學畢業〇現正留學美國柯力近大學,及求深造〇其餘子女〇亦受良好教育〇

守規〇最為師友所嘉許〇年十八已升為

Mr. O. W. LUKE, J.P.

Mr. Luke is a native of Kwangtung Province and was born in 1882. He was born in a well-to-do family which can afford him to obtain a thorough education. He procured his early studies in the Phui Ying School and later he enrolled in the Queen's College, where he left in 1900.

He started his commercial career in 1903 in the New Zealand Insurance Co., Ltd., Yokohama Branch. He did not remain there long, and a few years later he returned to Hongkong and became compradore of the same company. For thirty three years he was employed under the same firm, and his experience, consciousness and ability are valuable assets to the company. His honesty and innate courtesy endear him to all his business associates and friends.

In different times he has been member of the Financial Committee of the St. John's Ambulance and of many other local educational institutions and Chairman of the South China Athletic Association for a number of years. He was appointed a Justice of the Peace in 1936, and Member Committee of Po Leung Kuk in 1937.

Mr. Luke has many children. His eldest daughter is a graduate from the Yenking University and Ling Nam University and she is advancing her studies in the Oregan University, and Merril-Palmer School, Detroit, U.S.A.

何華生先生

何華生先生○廣東省順德縣人○現年六拾五歲○非特為港地名人○亦南洋巨賈也○君少時○家非素豐○而能奮志創業○成今日之聲望者○實非偶然○憶前清庚子年間○君創設瑞昌號於本港水藥街○僅經營銅綢疋頭耳○繼而代售中西藥品○為在港華人藥業之前輩○浸假而營業日進○發行鸚鵡牌各種經驗良藥○至今亦三拾七年○久已風行於廣東，廣西及夫南洋群島，及荷屬之爪吐各埠○瑞昌之名○逾不脛而走○於是努力邁進○故立老威普威藥房於廣州○又創五洲藥房於廣西之南寧，梧州，桂林，柳州○廣東之韶開等埠○又於潮安，汕頭，厦也○

門，設立會豐商店○國內之通商大埠○皆有何君之商業○旋由國內而推行於國外○於是創會豐商店於星州○開設三十餘家○營業中西粗驗良藥○數年間生意進展，遂分枝會豐分號於嘔龍，頒灑○中國之上海等埠○又在江門，佛山，及遷羅○設立中法藥房○繼復發展營業於尽吐○設三昌公司於沥水埠○三益公司於五嘉錫埠○及大世界公司於八打威等埠○營業西藥○旁及入口土洋什貨生意○亦蓮勃非常○何君一生馳騁南北○策劃經營○舜年逾耳順○猶復精神突奕○於經營商業餘暇○努力於社會公益事業○本港之慈善機關如東華醫院則為總理○於保良局則屢任值理○在精武會則為會長○在華商總會則為值理○又為何君本邑之順德商務局主席○及連任三屆司庫之職○其熱心公益○造福社會○久為港地人士所推崇○其哲嗣耿中君○年少英偉○亦曾任東華醫院總理○及保良局董事○實後起之秀也○

何華生先生

Mr. HO WAH SANG.

Mr. Ho Wah Sang is one of the most prominent business men in Hongkong. He is a native of the Kwangtung Province and was born in 1872. He was not born in a family which could provide him with a thorough education and yet with his vigorous struggles and unwearying labors, he was able to gain a good position in this commercial sphere.

Thirty-seven years ago, he established the Sui Cheong Co., in Wing Lok Street. It was dealing with piece-goods and later it dealt in retailing of drugs and medical products. For many decades, under the able management of Mr. Ho, it becomes to-day one of the most outstanding business house in Hongkong.

The chief manufacturings are the famous different kinds of "Parrot" branch medicines, which are welcome not only in South China but also throughout the Malayan Peninsula and the Dutch East Indies. Branches were established in different important ports to represent its products.

Mr. Ho is not only a prominent business man, but also a social magnate. He has been the chairman of the Tung Wah Hospital: a member on the board of Committee of the Po Leung Kuk, and the Chinese Chamber of Commerce: Chairman of the Chin Wu Athletic Association and many others.

Mr. Ho has many children. His eldest son, Mr. Kung Chong, is a smart young man who has been chairman of the Tung Wah Hospital and director of the Po Leung Kuk.

馮先生伯燎，字耀卿。廣東鶴山縣人。現年中壽晉七。前香江皇仁書院之畢業生。性聰頴，勤讀書，試輒前列。曾考授故院免費生厚利臣學額。今粵港利豐出入口莊之總教事也。生而岐嶷。少有大志。當慨我國商戰不競。基於故少自人一等。觀其能改良雜貨中之什器。橤器。草器等。以博取優厚之代價。從而嘉惠國際出之材也。先生個性喜遠行。歷横過太平洋。今

一九一五年。美國三藩市已金馬世界博覽會開幕。先生充我國粵省出品委員。既沐其雨。復斯歐風。從而接近各地廠商。用謀鎔國發展。果能如願以償。依為擴張海外營業起見。乃分設支莊於香島。業務進展。史一日千里。抑先生不徒想達有術。而眼光與思想。均邁起

馮耀卿先生

封。倘弗急起直追。將受天演淘汰。乃慨念以商業救國。遠學成而廣州寶興破莊器其材。廷主出口部事。時公元一九零四年也。越二年。先生念寶興佳營破器一案。未足以應外人需求。乃與李君道明另組利豐號。以承其乏。營謀大綱。凡三。漢杜，漢興，漢邦，漢彥。女公子偉，漢杜，漢興，漢邦，漢彥。女公子凡三。漢芘華，芘素，芘鸞。均受相當教育。長男漢偉，次男老成。兩君之佐父分任粵港要緘。年少老成。才矢貿。○虎父無犬子。將門無弱兵。信然。

蜂非少壯超華。獨領故男償償長征。遠遊歐美各國。則其志趣之有異乎人。已可想見。其賢內助林蕙貞女士。知書能文。四德俱全。現有男公子凡五。名漢

Mr. FUNG PAK-LIU.

Mr. Fung Pak-liu is a native of Hok-shan, Kwangtung Province, and he was born in Canton fifty six years ago. He was educated at Queen's College, Hongkong, and after graduation joined the Po Hing Co., in Canton in 1904, as manager in the export department. This firm dealt mainly in porcelain and earthen wares. Under his able management for twelve years, he considerably advanced the prosperity of the firm.

An opportunity was given to him in 1915, when he was appointed as a Committee Member in charge of the products of Kwangtung Province to be exhibited at the Panama Exposition. It was during this period that he visited many famous American and European factories.

On his return to China, he established an Export and Import firm under the name of Li & Fung in Canton, in partnership with Mr. Li To-Ming. A Hongkong Branch was opened not many years after the establishment of the Canton Head Office. This firm proved a success and before long it became and still is one of the most famous business houses in Canton and the Colony.

Married to Lam Wai Ching, Mr. Fung was blessed with eight children. Two of the older sons are holding important positions in the firm, and the others are receiving their education at various schools.

劉德譜先生

德譜先生○廣東省寶安縣人○年四十有九○為作古閒人雙壁香島之劉公鑄伯哲嗣○現本港油蔴地物船有限公司之總理也○生於豐厚家○而無紈紛習○其弟器之大才○不屑屑於章句○以為我國積弱

退也可知○吾慕其人○嘉其志○尤慶我國商界有此卑鄙奇才○故樂為之記○先生忠孝景子天姓○早年服勞盡瘁○曹獲中央政府寵錫三等嘉禾章○對於貢獻本港社會○史能善體婆心○亲承遺教○前任保良公局值理○港府特委電報檢查員○華商總會值理○現充寶安商會值理○孔聖會值理○中華聖教總會值理○佛學會

理○佛學會會長○中南中學校董○西南女子中學校董○養中女子中學校董○華商俱樂部會員○華商會員○五陵會會員○平湖紀劭螢學校董事長○

生先譜德劉

平湖念賢醫院董事長○至商業經營○舉其大者○除主油蔴地物船公司事外○且任德信銀號董事○平湖銀興公司總理馬○夫人曾文儀女士○蓬於國學○系出名門○男公子鎮國○年念七畢業於拔萃男書院○女公子慕儀○年十七○攻讀於拔萃女學校○

○在乎惠寶○惠洽其棟○商業是尚○故佳舉案於育才書社○卻出而角逐於遠東第二市場○富香港英教育代理物業銀兩有限公司司理○耀乃周旋於我國唯一商埠○充上海成洋行司理○中間服務於宗邦革命發源地之廣東○任全省酒稅局總辦○少壯時期○已展長才○恥盈榮，於港滬粵○則今日有此地位○其能遠

Mr. LAU TAK PO.

Mr. Lau Tak Po is the eldest son of the late Hon. Mr. Lau Chu Pak, C.M.G.

Born in 1887 he was educated in Hong Kong and on graduation commenced his business career as manager of the Anglo-Chinese Educational Co., Ltd.

He subsequently became Shanghai manager of the Hong Kong Mercantile Co., Ltd., where his ability and business acumen greatly assisted the prosperity of the firm.

On appointment as Superintendent of the Kwangtung Provincial Wine-Tax Bureau he returned to Canton.

In 1923 he promoted the Hongkong & Yaumati Ferry Co., Ltd., and became managing director of this important concern.

Married to Miss Tsang Man Yee he has a son and a daughter.

Mr. Lau who is the recipient of the 3rd class Chai Ho, Order of the Excellent Crop is an important member of the Community and amongst other position he is President of the Buddhist Association, Vice-President of the Chinese Confucian Association, the committee of the Tak Shun Bank, the managing director of the Chun Hing Co. in Ping-woo, the committee of the Sai Nam Boy & Girl School and the Yeung Chung Girl School, the chairman of the committee of the Ki Kui Loo School and Nim Fu Yin Hospital in Ping-woo, member of the Chinese Club, the Sports Club and Chinese Merchants Club, a former Committee member of the Po Leung Kuk, Chinese Chamber of Commerce, former Hon. Censor and a committee member of the Po On Chamber of Commerce.

羅文顯先生

生 先 顯 文 羅

羅文顯先生〇粵人〇於西曆一八九六年〇生於奇港〇父諱長榮〇乃己故著名港紳〇家庭富裕〇故先生得受教育機會較多〇未弱冠〇已畢業於奇港皇仁書院〇即致進奇港大學〇攻讀三年〇於西曆一九一八年畢業〇且屢學士榮銜〇學問文章〇奕然可觀〇畢業後〇歷年馳驅商場〇懋遷有無〇馨巻信用俱佳〇一九三四年〇升任渣甸洋行華經理之職〇生平品格清高〇誅恜性成〇熱心社會事業〇歷克奇港太平局紳士〇華商總會值理〇五陵會值理〇洋行買房聯合會主席〇及廷公

新公〇引童〇事〇平時〇喜運〇勤〇尤擅〇網球〇故〇健晩〇壯健

於西曆一九二七年己結婚〇夫人林恩姬女士〇甚有淑德〇現已有子女三人〇長女佩馼〇次女佩琦〇均肄業於梅芳女枝〇予名德政〇年纔三齡〇

Mr. M. H. LO, J.P., B.A.

Mr. M. H. Lo is one of the commanding figures in the commercial sphere of Hong Kong.

A native of the Kwangtung Province, and born in 1896, Mr. Lo is a member of a very well known Chinese family in Hongkong, his father being the late Mr. Lo Cheung Shiu, J.P., a prominent and well respected resident.

Mr. Lo was educated at Queen's College and in 1915 entered the commercial Course of the Hongkong University, and left in 1918.

In 1934 Mr. Lo was appointed Compradore of the Princely Hong of Jardine Matheson and Company, Limited. His experience, conscientiousness and natural ability are valuable assets to the firm, whilst his transparent honesty and integrity, and innate courtesy endear him to all his business associates and friends. He is a member of the Committee of the Chinese General Chamber of Commerce and the Sports Club, Director of the Hongkong Engineering and Construction Co., Ltd., and Chairman of the Compradore Association. He was appointed a Justice of the Peace in 1936.

Mr. Lo's favorite sport is tennis. Married in 1927 he has two daughters and one son.

陳鏡湖先生

生先湖鏡陳

陳鏡湖先生。廣東番縣河南寶岡鄉人。現年三十有八。少懷大志。氣宇不凡。幼甞肄業於廣州宏英中學。試必冠其曹。深得校長教員之贊許。而以高材生目之。在平當被子之自下。為此尤見於師友。如是四年。乃畢其業。自下。為此尤見於師友。如是四年。乃畢其業。先生滿擬負笈來港。以求深造之。而居於信先生之者。尤其。先生深造之。而居於信用昭影之際日記珠寶辭馬。陳日記者。

經營偉大。為同業所推重。時輩中之人。統其其環。以軟筆者環請主任。先生自忖年少。難勝其成。且英港之關心求學者。何待賣儒乃。乃軟筆者國請。以先人創業。其大義相責。就卻之不敢。未敢自信。試新鄉。誠以先生之持己以信。汲汲。先生之退慇學。商初。先生祖武。寧知近悅遠來。若錮。若兄相責。以先生之無華。貿易盛大倍。五玉。過卻立判珠石出納。以珠石出納。玉。過卻立判。本港為辭罷聯二。中珠石出納至鈍。先生既富天賢。參加間。人以是盛稱先生之能。而交易洋幣。

為義學。為造就色育有用之才而故。又在任人辟風夜在公。不遠庭之故。惡先生一身業主席。以上委員事繁。史任校觀。以上委員長之。在恆人辟風夜在公。不遠庭之故。惡先生一身業主席。以上委員事繁。復舉為建故會員委任。碩劃鴻獻。

龍棐劉周詳。多所與革。摩波厚霭。更褆聘之。暨語請如處。善公益等事業。如修葺和館。更史不路躄勞。善語請如慈。好許。州閩塞士也。與廣州之聞。好許女校畢業生。劉少史蓮生結婚。現有子女。德洪。請於廣州南武中學。二人。長及鳳儀。請於晉江惠大利醫堂。次子于。

則以大會主席。具忍久之歷史之偉大人物。不忝其歷任之中華民國。乃請育界主席焉。深為體育界各名人慶。全港體育界一致。深為體育界各名人慶。全港體育界一致。亦有重大之關係。奇寄務之臨。與整個中華民族。服務。弄之奇寄務之臨。與整個中華民族。全世界之。關像。武會。其忍久之歷史之偉大人物。不忝其歷任之中華民國。乃請育界主席焉。深為體育界各名人慶。全港體育界一致。亦有重大之關係。

服。晉而考察金石鋪底。亦能億則優中。平甫創辦源五金鏢務有限公司。以先生之營盤陰重。故拒務為該公司董事長。及總經理之職。支持且上。同事深慶得人。牽氛天賦多能。委亦先生奏勁敏。對此一道。尤刻苦研求平日于不釋卷。已深領此中三昧。故乎人無一之。常在校時之。已當領此中三昧。故乎人無一之。體魄。不可以捨當大事。而國家多難外侮。彼於中教育界者。倡請全港。學界聯合運動會。風仰先生熱心體育。致請為該會會長。而中南中國健兒之辯育界者。亦為南中國辯育界之名譽會長。史為南中國辯育界之名譽會長。史為南中國辯育界之名譽會長。生熱心體育。致請為該會會長。而中南國健兒之辯育界者。

Mr. CHAN KENG WOO.

Mr. Chan Keng Woo, general manager of Yat Kee in 4, Lyndhurst Street, is a native of Poon-U District, Kwangtung Province, and was born in 1899.

He acquired his education from the Wang Ying College, Canton, and after his graduation he came to Hongkong and was appointed as General manager of the Yat Kee, a dealer in curios, pearls, jewellery and head ornaments. His business acumen and his ability to distinguish the true jewellery from the false have allowed him to further his business, and to-day Yat Kee possesses a good reputation amongst its line.

Mr. Chan pays an immense interest in sports and athletic affairs. He is Hon. President of the Inter-schools Sports Association, Hong Kong; Chairman of Chong Nam Athletic Associaton; Chairman of the Advisory Board of Chin Wu Athletic Association; and committee of the Poon-U Chamber of Commerce, Hongkong.

Married in 1920 to Lau Ling Sang, Mr. Chan has two children.

香港・澳門雙城成長經典

64

顏成坤先生

顏成坤先生○籍廣東潮陽○年三十有七○美丰儀○優品格○具冰雪聰明○富國家思想○持躬尚道○萬學早見于髫齡○建業有方○從商已始於弱冠○香華之傑出人物也○從早歲曾致力敎國工作○追隨孫總理有年○後以革命將屆成功之港別發展○時九龍方面○交通事業○尚未普及○為造福僑胞計○公元一九二三年○創組中華汽車公司於半島○十載服務○人咸稱便○至一九三三年○再向香港方面努力建設○改組為香港中華汽車有限公司○與電車公司分道揚鑣○同人島其勞於任事○公推為董事主席兼監理○而荀行商誼○與商業機關○各方眼熱○猶翰為懷○殫數萬四十餘萬○分濟以勷大章者○遂孚相延攬○故歷任大光報館董事主席○遠孚相延攬○嘉華人壽保險公司董事主席○新亞酒店董事○華商總會值理○潮州八邑商會會董○米業商會顧問○潮洲同鄉會顧問等等○其他利慶堂華僑孕生○素有賢名○

廉不以英雄相加○蓋仰慕先生之為人○而莫肯錯過者也○彼性豪爽○當仁不讓○計前後所肩繁劇○約有如下列○且其中不鮮屬於歷任後所肩

（一）體育○華人體育協進會主席○南華體育會副會長○兼主席○學界運動聯合會會長○兼名譽會長○第六屆中華全國運動大會名譽顧問○參香港區代表團總領隊○第十一屆世界運動大會○中國代表團足球隊教練○

（二）教育○英華女校校董○英華男校校董○民生書院校董○廣州濟時中學名校董○汕頭港商義校董○

（三）教會○中華基督教第六區會主席○香港基督教青年會副會長○中華基督教合一堂主席○

（四）慈善○東華○廣華○東院三院統一首屆主席○廣華醫院院主席○東華醫院籌建委員○東華東院籌建員○雅麗氏醫院兄童保護會幹事值理○優生會值理○聖約翰救傷隊值理○

（五）公益○華人後備警察財政委員○尚有值得表揚者○則當其主席東華三院之○統一○院務交集○復遇粵省及華北各地水災○救民救溺千萬○敖敖待哺○情實可憫○先生病瘼在抱○慷慨為懷○立籌巨款四十餘萬○分濟各方眼熱○至今稱頌四方○殘教災黎○堪資倚界○特委盡瘁國事○亦能孟亨勤剿匪○寧非淑配黃女士亦梅○恐大

生先坤成顏

Mr. NGAN SHING-KWAN, J.P.

Mr. Ngan Shing-Kwan is one of the most prominent personages in Hong Kong. He is a native of Tsao-Yang District, Kwongtung Province, and was born thirty seven years ago.

He obtained a thorough education from a local college, and after he was graduated, he became a faithful follower of the late Dr. Sun Yat Sen and his service was highly appreciated.

In 1923 Mr. Ngan initiated the China Motor Bus Company in Kowloon, and a decade later he secured the bus franchise from the Hong Kong Government for the whole Island of Hong Kong, and the Company was then re-organized under the name of the China Motor Bus Company, Limited. Since then Mr. Ngan has been the managing director of the Company, and beyond doubt, as long as it is managed by Mr. Ngan, its prosperity reached the apex.

Mr. Ngan is an influential figure in social affairs. He is the chairman of the board of directors of the Tai Kwong Newspaper and Printing Co., Ltd., Committee of the Chinese General Chamber of Commerce, Hongkong; Director of the Chiu Chow Chamber of Commerce, Hongkong; and adviser of the Rice Merchants' Association and the Chiu Chow Residents' Association. He was also the Chairman of the Ka Wah Life Assurance Co., Ltd., and Director of the New Asia Hotel Ltd., in 1934.

Mr. Ngan is also very attentive to the athletic and educational world and the followings are posts which he has held or is holding.

Athletic.
Chairman of the Hongkong Chinese Amateur Athletic Federation, Vice-president and Chairman of the South China National Athletic Association, Hon. President of the Hong Kong Inter-Scholastic Athletic Union, Hon. Adviser of the 6th Chinese Sports Meet and Chief Delegate of the representatives of Hong Kong and Coach of the Foot-Ball team which represented China in the 11th World Olympiad.

Educational.
Committee of the Ying Wah Boys' College, the Ying Wah Girls' School, the Mun Sang College, the Hong Kong Merchants' Free School in Swatow and Hon. Director of the Chai Sze College in Canton.

Religious.
Chairman of the Sixth District of the Kwong Tung Synod of the Church of Christ in China, Vice-president of the Chinese Y.M.C.A., Hong Kong; and Chairman of the Hop Yat Tong Christian Church, Hong Kong.

Public Welfares.
First Chairman of the Tung Wah, Kwong Wah and Tung Wah Eastern Hospitals; Adviser of the Tung Wah Hospital; Chairman of the Kwong Wah Hospital; Member of the Tung Wah Eastern Hospital Building Fund Committee; Committee of Alice Memorial Affiliated Hospitals; General and Executive Committee of the Society for the Protection of Children; Executive Committee of the Hong Kong Eugenic League; Vice-patron of the St. John Ambulance Association; and Member of the Financial Committee of the Hong Kong Police Reserve (Chinese Company).

Moreover Mr. Ngan is a Justice of Peace, Hong Kong; and Member of the District Watchman Committee in 1932.

陳符祥先生

生先祥符陳

陳符祥先生。粵之台山水南鄉人。幼讀於鄉。身修國學。年十八。業備智商。來港三年。自覺學歷尚淺。為求深造。念一歲覺申江。考進南洋公學。修業任一年。四粵轉考入嶺南學堂。肄業四載。粗學成後。再來港經商。料理近

館。陸海通飯店。陸海通銀行。以次成立。向港府註冊。營業獨立。各有專司。纜西開設六國飯店。及彌敦酒店。以上諸事業。均賴先生益華碩劃。方底於成。非可多得之材也。

廣東銀行。新寧鐵路公司。四邑輪船公司。平安公司等董事。其對於社團。各學校。亦肯貢獻。前任東華醫院總理。香港華商總會。

四邑商工總局。旅港台山商會。香港基督教育年會。董事或值理。現任廣州嶺南大學。梅芳中學。香港嶺南分校。歷年助公益慈善事業。其他伙索計。當逾萬餘。用是富國籌恩想。有乃父風。後之七千餘圓之捐輸。先生贊助革命之

名滿國中。前廣東省長公署。廣西省長公署。台山縣皆。咸重其人。禮聘之為參議。先生年

先又出入口貨。前後凡五歷宋著。初由四邑輪船公司。選派出赴日本。檀香山，美國，古巴，墨西哥，秘魯，智利，柯根廷，巴西，及西

印度等處各大都會。考察商務及航務。歷時十三閱月。返港後。遂隨李公煜堂艦線上海聯保水火險有限公司。任總利理。遠兹二十有二年。

民十三。倡設陸海通有限公司。任總司理。而陸海通人壽保險公司。陸海通旅中學。四女梅芳。讀於飛利學校。

十六時。聖譚氏女為室。開三年。譚氏去世。年念三續娶朱氏。生三女五男。現共男女九人。長女齊華。次女齊華。均嫁華校高材生。一適張。一適梅。長于伯純。次于伯宏。前督修業與皇學校。現已就商。三女梅性。讀於嶺南大學。三子伯銘。讀於華仁書院。四子伯昌。讀於嶺南大學附中。五子伯聯。讀於西南昌。廣西省長公署。先生年

Mr. CHAN FU CHEUNG.

Mr. Chan Fu Cheung is a native of Toishan District, Kwangtung Province, born fifty-eight years ago.

He was educated in his native village till he was eighteen years old and then he came to Hongkong to practice business. Finding it is difficult to look for a high prospect in this complicate society without a thorough education, he proceeded to Shanghai in 1900 and continued his studies in the Nanyang College (now University of Communication). He returned to Kwangtung in the following year and entered the Ling Nan College, Canton. Four years later, when he left the college, he came to the Colony again and mingled himself in the commercial sphere. He transacted imports and exports and concurrently dealing in exchange business. For five years he was in the position until he was chosen by the Sze Yap Steamship Co., to investigate navigation in the Western countries. A year and a month later, Mr. Chan returned to the Colony and with the co-operation of Mr. Leo Yok Tong, one of the local prominent merchants, he established the Shanghai Fire & Marine Insurance Co., Ltd., where he holds the position of manager up to the present time.

In 1924, Mr. Chan organized the Luk Hoi Tung Co., Ltd., and after its inauguration, he established the following business in successive order:— The Luk Hoi Tung Life Assurance Co., Ltd., The Luk Hoi Tung Hotel and Restaurant; The Luk Hoi Tung Dispensary; The Luk Kwok Hotel and the Nathan Hotel.

Besides the above mentioned, Mr. Chan has been in the capacity of either director or committee of the following organizations:— The China Navigation Co., Ltd., (defuncted); The Bank of Canton, Ltd; The Sun Ning Railway Co.; The Sze Yap Steamship Co.; The Ping On Co.; The Tung Wah Hospital; The Chinese General Chamber of Commerce, Hongkong; The Sze Yap Commercial and Industrial Association; The Toishan Chamber of Commerce, Hongkong; and the Chinese Y.M.C.A., Hongkong. At present, he is director of the Ling Nan University, Canton, and its branch school in Hongkong; the Mui Fong College and the Sze Nan College.

Mr. Chan is an enthusiastic nationalist. He has contributed not less than seven thousand dollars to assist the Chinese revolution, and large amount has been contributed by him to accomplish philantropic and charitable affairs. He is so popular that he has been appointed counsellor by the Kwangtung Government and the Kwangsi Government.

Married when he was sixteen, Mr. Chan has nine children. All of them have obtained good education, and his eldest son is at present practising business in Hongkong.

生先重自李

Mr. LEE CHI CHUNG.

Mr. Lee Che Chung is the oldest son of the late Mr. Lee Yok Tong, one of the most prominent personages of Hongkong. He is a native of Toishan District, Kwangtung Province, born in 1882.

He was taught in a school in his native village till he was seventeen years old, and then he went to Canton and acquired practical knowledge in the Electrical Power Co., Ltd., which was initiated by his father.

He proceeded to Japan in the following year and learned the craft of military - training.

At the end of the Ch'ing Dynasty when the late Dr. Sun Yat Sen started revolution, Mr. Lee, who is an enthusiastic nationalist joined into the party. In 1901, he became a member of the Kwangtung Independent Federal Association, Yokohama, which was organized by Dr. C. W. Wang. Two years later, when the late Dr. Sun Yat Sen established the Revolutionary Military Training School in Tokyo, Japan, Mr. Lee was one of the members of that institution.

He was under the instruction of Dr. Sun, and returned to Hongkong in 1905 to ally with those revolutionary members in Canton and Macao.

By that time, Mr. Lee established the Kwong Hon School in Kowloon with the main object to furnish the students with, high education and military training. His object was favorably appreciated by the Chinese community and many schools such as the Tai Yok School, the Yok Ying School, the Chi Yung School, the Ho Kut Po School, the Mok Lai Che School, the Lai Chi School, and the Ellis Kadoorie School, by which he was offered respectively the position of a teaching staff. Mr. Lee returned to Canton and became a student in the Public Medical College, when he was twenty four.

After the Chinese Republic was established, Mr. Lee returned to the Colony and set himself in the business field. He was Treasurer of the Bank of Canton, and later promoted to the position of assistant manager. He was connected with this bank for twenty - four years until it was re - organized in 1936. At present, he is general manager of the Shanghai Fire & Marine Insurance Co., Ltd. Besides this, he has been president and treasurer of the South China Athletic Association; director of the Shui Fung Cotton Co., Hankow; the On Lok Yuen Co., Ltd., Hongkong; and the Hong Lin Life Assurance Co., Ltd.

During the famous Sino - Japanese Conflict in 1932, Mr. Lee contributed a great amount of money to relieve the calamity.

Mr. Lee has many children and all of them have obtained a good education.

聞申嶽先生

聞裕先生，字申嶽○浙江寧波府鄞縣人○現年五十有六○少時讀書家鄉○繼而學習商業○念一歲來香島○創設恆興成分莊○經營川漢參桑南北雜貨生意○逐

○其倫德羅洋行港行華經理○曾承辦建蔡中環救火會大樓，及昂船洲火藥庫山洞榴背前後兩水塘○城門石等處工程○此在本港之建樹也○其於星加坡○廣州○汕頭○各方面○亦有不鮮貢獻○在星洲任丕當華經理○迎曾承辦建築當地郵政局○工務局，及新山水塘工程○故星洲海軍港塢工捄之為總代表焉○香港自有華商總會○為僑港浙江商會出席代表○現任江浙商會主席

聞申嶽先生

今三十又三年矣○前幾以本港為交通樞紐○史自立順記字號○專辦出入口貨○業務蒸蒸○大有進展○先生信用昭彰○長袖善舞○歷年所幹偉大事業○卓然可觀○如上海美華銀行港政府膠東註冊人○駐港浙江銀行副理○兼理廣東官錢局○超營順記銀事○

香港分局○德園地亞士洋行軍裝代理人○

旅港寧波象商公會會長○廣州寧波會館主席○汕頭寧波同鄉會名譽會長○星加城三江會館名譽會長○香港各省客邦聯合會代表○其他等等○不及備述○淑配伶氏○公子二人○長友謨○字昭俊○從事銀業○次友麟○字徽明○從事銀業○均頭角崢嶸○有聲香海也○

Mr. WEN SYN YOAH.

Mr. Wen Syn Yoah, proprietor of Messrs. Shun Kee and Hang Hing Sing, prominent business houses of the Colony, is a native of Ningpo, Chekiang Province, and was born fifty-six years ago.

He received his early education in his own town. When he was twenty-one years of age, he came to Hongkong and established himself in the business field. He initiated the Hang Hing Sing, dealing in drugs and general merchandise. Later, he operated the Shun Kee, dealing in the same particles and imports and exports in addition. Through his perseverance and hard-working, the firms advance to the climax of success.

Through his business career, Mr. Wen has come into close contact with many other lines. He is a representative for the shareholders of the Mei Hua Bank, Shanghai, to register in the Hongkong Government; Assistant manager of the Chekiang Bank, Hongkong branch, Contractor in the construction of the Central Fire Brigade Building; the Peninsula Hotel, the Reservoirs in Sek-lau, Shing Mun, and the tunnel of Ngon-shuen-chow; Compradore of the P. Louis Co., Singapore; Contractor in the construction of the main building of the General Post Office, and the Public Works Department, Singapore; and the construction of the reservoirs in Johore Bahru.

Mr. Wen has been elected as representative for Shanghai laborers in Singapore during the construction of the Naval Base there. He has been a committee of the Chinese General Chamber of Commerce, Hongkong; and delegate for the Kiang-Che Chamber of Commerce, Hongkong, of which he is at present chairman; He is president of the Ningpo Association, Hongkong; Hon. president of the Ningpo Association, Swatow; and Hon. president of the three Kaings Association, Singapore.

Mr. Wen has two sons, Mr. Wen Ching Ming, his elder son, is now managing the Shun Kee, and Mr. Wen Chao Chin, his second son, possesses a good reputation in the commercial field of Hongkong.

生先三省黃

我國自絶海禁○門戶洞開○趨新慕外之徒○厭不舶來是尚○懷械物質○挹彼注茲○猶可説也○文化藝術○舍短從長○

中題楚也○彼箱廣東番禺○現年五十六歲○品清高○志淡泊○學宗孔孟○日以趨史自娛○衛紹岐黃○惟期醫學濟世○古人所謂不為良相○亦作良醫○先生讀書得閒○殆己三復斯言○抱負不凡○慨然以活國自任○其期許也深○其用功也

苦○故卒咸富代良醫○咃名港母○與做譽京滬之陸氏仲安○南北辉映○名重公卿鳥

亦住事也○若辭心異族文明○舉數千年來先民怡留可貴可珍之國粹○如固有之醫學○如土産之藥材○亦不加愛護○任受摧殘○良足惜己○我國懸壺問世者○縱多不學無術之流○宣乎讀書破萬卷○而後從事三指活人者○黃省三先生，此

○且先生宅心慈善○對求醫者○雅重情廠○不較酬勞○特徇介自持○不隨流俗○非富貴所能淫○威武所能屈○重視氣節○老而益駐○惟讀書人○能存本色○是真名士○別樹高風○先生之醫術○固值表揚○先生之節操○尤當效法也○

Mr. WONG SING SAM.

Mr. Wong Sing Sam is one of the well-known Medical Doctors with Chinese method in the Colony and in South China

He is a native of Poon-U District, Kwangtung Province, and was born fifty-six years ago.

He had obtained an excellent knowledge of Chinese literature before he began to pursue the Chinese medical course. His high talent and great learning have made him very successful in practice of medicine. He has earned a good reputation not only in Hongkong but also in many places.

Mr. Wong is a quiet and wonderful man. He is a man of emotion and generosity. He cannot be possibly hired by money; but his kindness has always made him to give free service to many poor patients. Unlike other Chinese medical doctors, he does not advertise and not even putting on a sign-board. His office is exactly a common residence and no passers-by can know that it is the office of a famous medical doctor.

曾寶琦先生

曾寶琦先生○廣東寶安縣人○現年四十九歲○乃本港安和商號之總理也○父諱展材○原為安南華僑名商○先生幼曾隨

故祖濟克裕○信用昭彰○歷任本港華商總會值理○寶安商會委藏一九三三年副主席○又因熱心好義○服務社會○故一九三二年秋推充任東華醫院總理○一九三三年起港府委充保良局紳○一九三六年秋推充任孔聖會副主席○於一二八滬變時先生慨捐鉅款○其愛國之心○至為熱烈○而平時為慈善公益○解囊輸出之款

父南渡○精長○四鄉攻讀漢文○十四歲來港○卽在堂叔所設之安和號○肩助乃叔營業○克勤克謹○極為各方所信仰○民國三年○乃叔棄世○先生遂任總理之職○除安和之外○另有合股生意多處○

○己不可勝計○廿六歲時○已結婚○夫人文氏○生三子四女○長于鏡坤○十五歲○次拉興○十三歲○三洪光○才四歲○長女愛枝○已適陳氏為室○次棠枝○三煥枝○四靈枝○均在港中僑校肄業○

曾寶琦先生

Mr. TSANG PO KI.

Mr. Tsang is a native of Po On District, Kwangtung Province, where he was born in 1888. His father was a prominent Chinese merchant of long residence in Indo-China, and Mr. Tsang was brought there to receive his early education in his minor age. Later, he returned to China and then came to Hongkong, when he was but fourteen years of age.

He began his career with a low position in his uncle's shop. By his exerting struggles and unwearying intellegence he was promoted gradually, and finally, upon the death of his uncle in 1914, he was promoted as general manager of the shop, which at present stands distinctively amongst its line of business under the name of Ah Yung, Shipping and painters.

Besides this, Mr. Tsang is also partner or stockholder of many other firms.

Mr. Tsang is usually highly populated for his kindness and generosity. As long as charity concerns, Mr. Tsang is quite sure to help with his best part.

He is a member of the Committee of the Chinese Chamber of Commerce, Hongkong. In 1932, he was appointed Chairman of the Tung Wah Hospital and in 1933, he was appointed a visiting Justice to the Po Leung Kuk. At present, Mr. Tsang is also vice-president of the Hongkong Confucian Society.

Married in 1914, Mr. Tsang has seven children. They are receiving their education at local schools.

鄧肇堅先生

肇堅先生○百粵南海九江人○年僅三十晉六○乃已故啟商鄧公志昂之哲嗣○鄧天福銀號之司理也○性秉爽任俠○遇有求助者○必不使人失

人俱樂部新會所華人義務司庫○建築香港仔兒童工藝院籌款值理○孔聖會義務司庫○東華東院籌款董員○研究本港婦女制度委員會委員○一九二四年○任東華醫院總理○一九二七年○任保良局總理○一九二八年○任東華醫院主席○及東院奠基主任○一九二九年○港府以其

MR. TANG SHIU-KIN

皇賞以銀楯紀念勳章○是歲十月三十日○史英謀帝代表英國聖約翰救傷隊總部○頒以 The Venerable Order of St John of Jerusalem Rank of "Officer"○年來港中教育慈善機關○及公益團體○商業鉅肆○莫不以得先生允任委職為榮○計現任者○如九龍城公立義學校長○

精明強幹○特委為太平紳士○一九三二年○聖保羅女書院校董○○委克港大學院○同年○報遠保良局總理○又崇禮督夫人○在本港籌萬國婦女會○及崇禮督夫人總部○先生卽捐任籌捐開辦費，與建築費各一萬圓○一九三三年

赤社堅士提反學堂校董○新界屏山達德學校校董○聖保羅女書院校董○梅芳女中校董○香港大學鄧志昂中文學院名譽副會長○東華醫院永遠顧問○新界無別博愛醫院駐港執行委員○雅利氏醫院董事○廣州方便醫院駐港執行委員○華商總會幹事值理○保護兒童會幹事值理○警循救濟會幹事值理○兒童游樂場幹事值理○管理華人廟宇值理○孔聖堂義務司庫○大埔環兄弟會義務司庫○童子軍會董，兼財政委員○儲備警察華隊財政委員○聖約翰十字救傷隊財政委員會主席，及香港總部信託管理地段委員○健康慈善社董事○南華體育會會董○精武體育會會董○九龍汽車公司主席○華僑商辦中華實業公司主席○宜安煤礦公司總理○均安煤礦公司司庫○百家利公司董事○新界輪船公司董事等職○

三月十三日○見督夫人代表女童軍英廷總部○錫以獎章○起其籌款建設 Sandilands Hut 之功○一九三四年元旦○英廷賜以 M.B.E. 榮銜○同時港府委為國防局紳○又本港創建貝夫人健康院○先生肯捐萬金○以為之倡○為向外勸募數逾三萬二仟圓○一九三五年五月六日○英前

坐○銀金錢時間之損失○在所不計○而對於公益事業○尤悉力以赴○故中西人士○同致敬仰○而榮聞日增焉○益率其歷年貢獻於社會之勞績○以為未稔先生者告○亦冀有志青年○聞風興起○社會多一熱心人物○卽為同羣增進無量福利也○先生叢任鈞索聯安公會主席○籌建某

原院○先生肯捐萬金○以為之倡○為向外勸募檢先生想方少壯○建立事功○當仁不讓○已如上述○想將來造福於僑胞者○史無涯涘也○

Mr. TANG SHIU-KIN, M.B.E., J.P.

OFFICER, VENERABLE ORDER OF ST. JOHN OF JERUSALEM.

Mr. Tang Shiu-kin, native of Kau Kong, Nam Hoi District, Kwangtung, aged 36, son of the late wealthy merchant, Mr. Tang Chi Ngong, is the manager of the Tang Tin Fuk Bank. He is of liberal disposition and generous. He never disappoints anyone who comes to him for help, and even when he has to sacrifice his time and money he does not mind. He always exerts his full energy on undertakings beneficial to the general public thereby gaining the admiration of both Chinese and Europeans. He is enjoying higher and higher reputation in the course of his life. His good work for the community is stated below for the information of those who do not know him. It is hoped that ambitious young men will follow his good example, for every additional enthusiastic worker for the community will help much to promote the welfare of the people.

Mr. Tang was the Chairman of the Luen On Chinese Native Bankers' Association; Hon. Chinese Treasurer of the Committee for the building of the Cheero Club; Member of the Committee for raising funds for the Aberdeen Industrial School; Hon. Treasurer of Confucian Society; Special Officer for raising funds for the Tung Wah Eastern Hospital; Member of the Committee on Muitsai, appointed by the Hong Kong Government; Director of the Tung Wah Hospital (1924;) Director of the Po Leung Kuk (1927) and Chairman of Directors of the Tung Wah Hospital (1928) when he was also Chairman of the Committee for the ceremony of laying the foundation stone of the Tung Wah Eastern Hospital, by the then Governor, Sir Cecil Clementi K.C.M.G. In 1929, he was appointed Justice of Peace, and in 1932, Member of the Court of the University of Hong Kong and Chairman of Directors of the Po Leung Kuk. He was responsible for the contribution of $10,000 for the establishment of the International Women's Club, founded by Lady Southern and a similar amount for the erection of the Sandilands Hut, the Headquarters of the Girl Guides in the Colony. On March 13th, 1933, Lady Peel on behalf of the Girl Guides Headquarters in Great Britain presented him with a Badge of Thanks for the good work he did in raising funds for building the Hut. In 1934, His Majesty the King conferred upon him the decoration of Member of the Most Excellent Order of the British Empire for his distinguished services. In the same year, he was appointed a Member of the District Watch Committee by the Hong Kong Government For building the Violet Peel Health Centre, he took the lead by contributing $10,000. and was instrumental in raising the sum of $32,000. He was a recipient of His late Majesty's Silver Jubilee Medal in 1935. On October 30th the same year, His Excellency the Officer Administering the Government, the Hon. Mr. N. L. Smith, on behalf of the St. John Ambulance Brigade Headquarters in Great Britain, decorated him with the Venerable Order of St. John of Jerusalem, Rank of "Officer".

Educational, charitable and other institutions and commercial organizations consider it an honour to have Mr. Tang among their important officials. At the moment, Mr. Tang is the Managing Director of the Kowloon City Public Free School; Member of the Council of St. Stephen's College, Stanley; Director of Tat Tak School, Ping Shan, New Territories; Member of Council of the St. Paul's Girls' College; Director of Mui Fong Girls' Middle School; Hon. Vice President of Tang Chi Ngong Chinese School of the University of Hong Kong; Member of the Advisory Board of the Tung Wah Hospital; Member of the Advisory Board of the Pok Oi Hospital, Un Long, New Territories; Member of the Executive Committee of Alice Memorial and Affiliated Hospitals; Resident member in Hong Kong of the Executive Committee of the Fong Pin Hospital of Canton; Executive Member of the Committee of the Chinese General Chamber of Commerce; Executive Member of the Committee of the Society for the Protection of Children; Executive Member of the Committee of the Street Sleepers' Shelter Society; Member of the Children's Playgrounds Association Executive Committee; Member of the Chinese Temples Committee; Hon. Treasurer of the Confucian Hall; Hon. Treasurer of the Taipo Rural Home and Orphanage; Member of the Finance Committee of the Boy Scouts' Association; Member of the Finance Committee of the Hong Kong Police Reserve, Chinese Section; Chairman of the Finance Committee and one of the Trustees of the Headquarters of the St. John Ambulance Brigade Hongkong; Committee Member of the Chung Sing Benevolent Society; Committee Member of the South China Athletic Association; Committee Member of the Chin Wu Athletic Association; Managing Director of the Kowloon Motor Bus Co., (1933) Ltd; Chairman of the Directors of the China Merchants Industrial Administration Ltd; Director of the I On Insurance Co., Ltd; Treasurer of the Kwan On Insurance Co., Ltd; Director of the Bakilly Co., Ltd; and Director of the Hong Kong and New Territories Ferry Co., Ltd.

Mr. Tang is young and energetic and is a man of achievements. As stated above, he is never behind others in doing good for the general public. It can be foretold that in his great future he will yet do much to promote the welfare of the Chinese residing in the Colony.

香港・澳門雙城成長經典

陳蘭芳先生

陳蘭芳先生○粵之東莞人○現年五十三歲○初在莞城創立陳泰記號○製造煙竹煙花○行銷國內外○此為先生營權之始○民國五年○蒙香港當局特准○在旺角開設廣萬隆公司○獨家設廠製造○舉辦花旗，新金山，羗吟，南菲洲，及南洋

業前途○蒸蒸日上○內地知省，佛，粵諸城○均有支店設立○仰食者數萬人○合港澳粵內審計之○無出其右者○然先生曾不以此自足○年前，復以振興竹業致志○發起電船○行走澳門，石歧，冰仔，廣灣各處○行旅搆便○先生於商務紛紛之下○對於社會公益○如無不為之為無不力○觀其歷任本港東華三院總理○保良局紳○九龍樂善堂董事○華商總會值理○孔聖會副主席○鐘聲慈善社社長○聖約翰救傷隊名譽隊長○東莞工商總會副主席○及司庫○黨邑東義堂主席○及澳門商會值理等職○可謂賢者多矣○

生先芳蘭陳

翠島一帶，煙花爆竹○副以綢塔日廣○米過芳銷供○後在九龍城碼頭角北帝街七十號○自行建築工廠一間○容積較大○常僱男女織工逾千人○民國十五年○為展拓營業○增設廣興泰，精祥公司，三廠於澳門○繼再設諫隆泰記一廠於佛山○均係捐力銶抱興建○共可容幼男女工四千名○至是而規模大備○近出品暢銷○且普及哥林堡等埠○營為媲仔大王○

又在旺角以個人名義○創辦義學一間○與收問邑失學兒童○免費好業○其熱心平民教育○概可想見○先生和平忠厚○樂善好施○過親友危難○深獲社會人士之同情○故能信孚退過○凡所經營○無不一帆風順○成為港中有數殷商○或且稱之為爆竹大王○良非倖致也○

Mr. CHAN LAN FONG.

Mr. Chan Lan Fong, King of Firecrackers, is a native of Tungkoon district Kwongtung province, and was born in 1884. Immediately after he had finished his school days, he started his business career and initiated the Chan Tai Kee Firecrackers manufacturing Company in his native town. As the products of his factory are excellent in quality and cheap in price, they are welcome and purchased by most people in many places.

In 1916 it was granted by the Hongkong government to establish the Kwong Man Lung Firecrackers Manufacturing Co., Ltd., in Mongkoktsui Hongkong. It is the only concern in the Colony to manufacture all kinds of Firecrackers, Flashlight Crackers, Fireworks and etc. Since then his business has become so prosperous, that his products are exported throughout South China, Indo-china, Dutch E. Indies, Malaya, Siam, South Africa, Philippines, United States America, and Australia.

A few years later, Mr. Chan established and constructed a large manufacturing building in 70 Pak Tai Street in Ma Tau Kok District Kowloon city and employed more than one thousand of male and female workers there. With a view of extending his business Mr. Chan established in 1926 the Messrs. Kwong Hing Tai, Messrs. Kwong Hing Lung and Messrs. Jing Cheung in Macao; and Messrs. Hing Lung Tai Kee in Fatshan. All buildings of the above-mentioned companies were constructed with his own money, thus keeping busy the wheels of industry and making happy about five thousands of workers. He has also established many branches in many places in Kwongtung province. It is said that more than fifty thousand people depend upon him to earn their livings.

Mr. Chan is very prominent in the community. He has held many important positions in different social and benevolent Associations. He is always generous in giving his money to do charitable deeds and has established a free school under his name in Mongkoktsui Hongkong.

劉景清先生

生先清景劉

劉景清先生○籍隸粵海東官○公元一八八七年十月五日○誕於本港○年十五○攻讀於西營盤皇家書院（今易英皇書院）一九零五年畢業○即轉學皇仁書院○迨致將官學生○一九零七年○以優等卒業○旋服務港府清淨局○任太平山疫症驗員○胡歷充中央醫署水師○汕頭地警署○新界之屏山○上水○警署等機關通事○

司自任總翅理外○兼任渣甸燕梳公司諫當洋面燕梳○香港大險燕梳○兩公司港局代理○粵行翹理○榮譽日彰○（先生婟倫胞況溺於紅丸○不惜歷十數月之光陰○而成拒毒會○）熱心辦學也○（先生任席粵東義塾數年○對於堂塾之義學十間○學生五百餘○應付將宜○教有徐裕）責花籌款也○（先生除迨年協助東黨會貴花籌款外○並指示其女于奧挑○為黨花東義塾

廉不力與財俾○贊助公益○慈善○教育○諸事業○先生責性博愛○如勸捐養老院○

院○孔聖會○東華醫院○貴花籌款共四次○均獲全場冠軍○）奔募獻

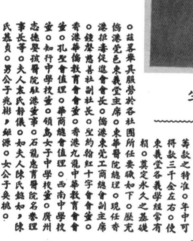

其為如為東黨商會會辦○其至足為人稱頌者○至今猶膾炙於人口○府當局取得每年貴花籌款之特准○年中可將款三千金左右○使東義堂各義學經常有賴○莫定永久之基礎○

益暑舉其服勞於各社團所任要職如下○壓充僑港邑東義塾主席○東華醫院總理○現任奇港扺奉款會會長○僑港東黨工商總會副主席○鏡塘慈善社社長○聖約翰紅十字會副會長○孔聖會值理○華商會值理○香港九龍港商教育會會董○華商教育會會董○西南中學校董○廣州志德慈善醫院院董○石龍惠育醫院名譽理事長等○夫人袁氏靜儀○如夫人陳氏鍫如○陳氏慈貞○男公子兆彬○繼源○女公子奧桃如○陳

職者與五年○均能勝任愉快○僉為上游所器重○原東陸軍測量學堂○暨粵東女子師範等校○聞其賢○基其材○禮聘之回粵掌英文教席○先生遂辭職港○至身教育界○以結學貢獻於州人○時閲兩載○復展香港○初受職於米常商行人○如長安公司○海晏公司○萬祥源行○公源行各號○公安公司○時值一九二二年○海員大罷工○曾為諸行同業挺立不鮮事功○甚社會所稱許○熙啟龍未将雲雨○仍池中物耳○今則大展鴻爪也○除劉海洋船務公

Mr. LAU KING TSING

Mr Lau King Tsing was born in Hongkong on 5th October, 1887, his parents being native of Tungkoon District. He was educated at the Sai Ying Pun Government School (now the King's College) and lately at the Queen's College, Hongkong. After he had graduated from the Queen's College in 1907, he was immediately employed in the civil service for a period of five years. He resigned his position from the Hongkong Government, as he was offered a post on the teaching staff both in the Kwangtung Military Surveying School and in the Yuet Tung Girls' College in Canton. Two years after he came back to Hongkong to start a commercial career. He was Secretary for foreign business in the Cheung On Rice Guild, the Kung On Rice Guild, the Hoi Ngan Rice Guild, the Man Cheung Yuen Hong and Kung Yuen Hong. During the famous strike in 1922 he rendered efficient service and great assistance to the above mentioned concerns.

Mr. Lau is at present manager of the Hoi Yeung Shipping Co. and Foreign Secretary to the Po Tai Co. (Rice Guild). He is a Representative of the Hongkong Fire Insurance Co., Ltd. and the Canton Insurance Office, Ltd. both here and in Canton for native business.

Mr. Lau is well known privately and publicly for his social and charitable activities. He was for two years Chairman of the Tung Yee Tong Educational Institution which supports ten free schools with a roll of over five hundred students and was also Director of the Tung Wah and Affiliated Hospitals (1936). He is at present President of newly formed Anti Heroin Society, Vice-President of the Chung Sing Benevolent Society, Vice-Chairman of the General Chamber of Commerce and Industry of the Tung Kun District, Patrons of the Hongkong Chinese Teachers' Association and of the Hongkong and Kowloon Chinese Educational Association, Vice-Patron of St. John Ambulance Association, Committee of the Chinese General Chamber of Commerce and of the Confucian Society, Hongkong.

Married to Miss Yuen Ching Yee, Mr. Lau has two sons and a daughter all of them are receiving their education at the Sai Nam College Hongkong.

歐偉國先生

歐偉國先生，粵之中山籍。生於澳洲雪梨埠。封翁偉彬。久商於澳。名利兼收。歸國後。歷任上海先施公司總理。乃我國之大實業家，兼大慈善家也。先生幼承庭訓。品質純良。精長

大慈善家也。先生幼承庭訓。品質純良。精長上海商業儲蓄銀行香港分行。乃先生畢券

英京。四歲突署。新知閱歷。兩有進益。一九二五年，返港。克上海先施公司前席秘書。學博如先生。當然勝任愉快。第割雞而用牛刀。遂成大器。良駒未遂伯樂。有屬高材。迨一九二九年，為我國金融鉅子總理上海商業儲蓄銀行之陳光甫實識。聘充該行襄理。以資屏助。是為先生獻身銀行界之始。迨一九三四年，根

香爐島之時。一九三六年，奇港廣東銀行復業。該行董事長宋子文，以非得資望高佳。整經驗宏富者。充當司理。遂禮聘先生任之。羽毛豐滿。旦干青雲。將見敷布鴻猷。為我儕胞組濟集團放一異彩也。

○先生素性。謙和有禮。謙恕尚義。酷肖其先人。對於社會公益之勸助。當仁不讓。現被選為香港中華基督教青年會會長。中華慈善會會長。中華聖公會港粵教區財政部司庫。上海聖約翰大學同學會香港分會司庫。一九二一年，有室。娶羅雪玉簽女士。曾進學於廣州真光女校。後卒業於滬江聖瑪利女校。才德俱備。現有兒女數人。均施

○先修業於奇港聖保羅書院。繼攻讀於聖士提反學校。中英學識。一日千里。將冠。隨父展中江。考進當時最著名之學府聖約翰大學。數年苦勤。三育兼優。畢業時期。衒膺學士。一九一八年，回港。卽能昂展其長。克先施公司秘書。任職凡三載。一九二一年，調陞先施公司倫敦分行司理。每於業餘。不作無謂應酬。報事考察英商業，及財政。計留良好教育。

Mr. DAVID, W. K. AU, B.A.

Mr. David W. K. Au, son of the late Mr. Au Ben, a prominent merchant in China and one of the founders of the Sincere Co., Ltd., is a native of Chungshan, Kwangtung province and was born in Sydney, Australia, in 1898.

He was brought back in his minor years to Hongkong where he took his first studies in St. Paul's College. He did not stay there long and Completed his high school education at St. Stephen's College. Later, he proceeded to Shanghai and continued his studies in St. John's University, where he procured his B.A. degree in 1918.

Starting his business career as secretary to The Sincere Co., Ltd., Hongkong in 1918, Mr. Au was promoted manager of the Sincere Co., Ltd., London, in 1921. He stayed there until 1925 when he was transferred to Shanghai and became chief secretary to the branch there for four years. In 1929, he was employed by the Shanghai Commercial and Savings Bank, Ltd., as assistant manager. Since 1934 he was manager of its branch office in Hongkong. He has been appointed manager of the Bank of Canton Ltd., Hongkong, since it was re-organized in 1936.

Mr. Au is very active in social affairs. He is president of the Chinese Y.M.C.A., and consurrently, president of Chinese Benevolent Association. He is treasurer of Diocesan Board of Finance of the Chinese Episcopal Church, and St. John's University Alumni Association, Hongkong.

Married in 1921 to Frances Louie who is a graduate from St. Mary's Hall, Shanghai, and they have three children.

生先國偉歐

香港華人名人史略（一九三七）

郭贊先生

郭贊先生

郭贊先生〇籍原東粵〇生長香江〇現年三十有四〇為已故殷商郭公少流之第二文郎〇具慧質〇穎奇才〇翩翩風度〇埙篪不孤〇馮世佳公子也〇嘗早畢業於拔萃書院〇繼進香港大學攻商科〇為惡求自立〇不甘以分利份予自居〇一九二四年〇毅然報請〇供職於法國東方滙理銀行〇任事五載〇閱歷湛深〇至一九二九年〇遞進任華組理〇今日港中華僑要膺於銀行界者〇實警有使〇然以年少宰大權如先生者〇未易多覯〇則足如其人之才智非等閒矣〇先生克承父志〇對於公益慈善事業〇均有效力〇一九二五年〇克特務警察〇一九二七年〇政編為後備警察華隊〇服務多年〇吿退後〇切任故隊財政委員及東院總理〇精武體育會副會長〇一九二八年〇任東華醫院及東院總理〇其他如洋行辦房聯合會〇一九三三年〇任保良局總理〇華人游泳會兩屆主席〇拔萃書院舊生會值理〇三水工商會董事〇港大女生宿舍籌備會幹事〇兒童醫院籌款值理〇聖約翰救傷隊會董〇及財政委員〇保護兒童會委值理〇兼司庫〇港大同學會會員〇街童會員〇華商總會值理等職〇先生於為東方滙理銀行推進金融業務外〇於溝通奇港越兩地商務〇多所贊助〇故一九三六年〇越南政府獎以藍佩寶星〇先生遊行興趣亦甚有其導人〇一九二六年〇曾旅行新大陸各埠〇並參觀費城舉行之其國一百五十週年立國紀念展覽會〇至東瀛三島〇荷屬東印度〇美屬菲律濱等處〇均曾留遊其間〇於新知稷益〇吏形豐富矣〇淑配為陳君原伯之女公子〇結婚於一九二九年〇

Mr. KWOK CHAN.

Mr. Kwok Chan, a native of Samshui, Kwangtung Province, was born in Hongkong in 1904 and is the second son of the late Mr. Kwok Siu Lau. He is employed as Chief Compradore of the Banque de l'Indochine, Hongkong.

He was educated at the Diocesan Boys' School, and had commercial training at the Hongkong University.

He joined the Banque de l'Indochine in 1924, and was Chief Compradore in 1929.

Mr. Kwok devoted much time to charitable work and public activities. In 1925 during the General Strike, he served with the Special Constabulary, and in 1927 onwards, when the Police Reserve (Chinese Company) was formed, he continued to be an active member for many years. He resigned from the Force, but was asked to act as Hon. Treasurer and Secretary of the Finance Committee of the Company.

In 1928, he was Football Secretary of the Chinese Athletic Association. In 1930, he was elected director of the Tung Wah and Eastern Hospitals and Vice-president of the Chin Woo Athletic Association. In 1933, he became a member of the Committee of the Po Leung Kuk.

Among other activities, he served on many occasions as Hon. Treasurer and member of the Committee of the Compradores' Association; twice Chairman of the Chinese Bathing Club; committee member of the Diocesan Boys' School Old Boys' Association; director of the Samshui Chamber of Commerce, Hongkong; joint Hon. Secretary of the Hongkong University Women's Hostel Building Committee; member of the Organizing Committee of the Aberdeen Industrial School; Vice-president and Finance committee of the St. John's Ambulance Brigade and Association; Hon. Treasurer and member of the Executive Committee of the Society for the Protection of Children; member of the Hongkong University Alumni Association; member of the Committee of the Street Boys' Association; member of the committee of the Chinese General Chamber of Commerce, Hongkong; and many others.

For his untiring effort in promoting business relationship between the Colony and Indochina, the Emperor of Annam conferred on him the Order of "Chevalier du Dragon d'Annam."

He also loves travelling, and in 1926, visited Canada and United States, and visited the "Sesqui-Centenal Exposition" in Philadelphia. He also travelled in all parts of Java, Japan and the Philippines.

張兆棠先生

張兆棠先生

張兆棠先生○粤之新會人○畢業於廣東陸軍速成學校，及北平陸海軍軍需學校○民國十五年，任黃埔軍事政治學校經理科教官，兼隊長○值北伐軍興○詎國民革命軍總司令部經理處財政科長○簡單北伐○而湘，而贛，而浙，而蘇○遍歷數省○飛勤挽來，為之時○服務於黨國社會之日方長○誠不可多得之材也。

○任經理分處長○及四集團軍成立○卸任該軍總部經理處處長○軍餉之經其手收支者○凡數千萬○曾依法報銷○代清楚○不苟分毫○因之極為李公德鄰，白公健生，所器重○遠廣西銀行成立○以白君志鵬，分任香港廣西銀行經理○現任該行副經理○性忠誠○旅港行經理○數年○信譽甚○今○年復被○貲良有故○故氏現年四十五○正有為之時○詎該民以前所歷○固一廉幹誠信之理財家也○有聲於軍需界，銀行界○姜兼充西南航空公司廣西董事○任團軍總部經理處副處長○旋派駐漢口

生先棠兆張

Mr. CHEUNG SHUI TONG.

Mr. Cheong Shui Tong is one of the most outstanding personages amongst the Chinese banking magnates of Hongkong. He is a native of Sun-wui District, Kwangtung Province and was born in 1892.

He was educated in the Military School of Kwangtung and the Munition School of Army and Navy in Peking.

It 1926 Mr. Cheong was appointed a teaching staff in the Whampo Military and Political School Kwangtung, and concurrently he was captain of the main troop.

Later he became an important figure in the Financial Department of the National Army, following the troop went northwards. Two years later Mr. Cheung was appointed Assistant in the Managing Department of the National Army in Nanking, the new Capital. Before long, he was promoted manager of the sub-department in Hankow.

It was not until the 4th National Army was founded that Mr. Cheung was appointed Chief of the Managing Department of the troop. Thousands of dollars of munition were devised and raised by him at that time; so when he resigned from the post, he was highly recommended by his superiors for his ability and consciousness.

The Bank of Kwangsi established in Hongkong in 1930 and Mr. Cheung was appointed Sub-manager of the organization. In the nearest past, he was promoted manager of the same institute.

In short, Mr. Cheung is not only an adept of Financial administration but also a smart man in politics and in military affairs.

香港華人名人史略（一九三七）

簡熾南先生

簡熾南先生生

熾南先生○南海良沙海鄉周公規初之第五公子也○幼就傅廣州○喜與同學精研典籍○努力上進○常銘勤有功三字於座右○師器重之○及長從父來港習商○勤樸誠實○敏事慎言○其尊人

名譽校長○近年農村敝庶○更擴其眉○婦唯于室○先生愍焉愛之○亟謀有效之救濟○除盡力賞助外○復導以墅強之方○使其循序漸進○故鄉農播以復興其素稱喜衆○斯二者皆先生造福桑梓之功也○民廿四年○先生組織榮泰科有限公司於香港○專營中外各種木料○故懷鉛木規模廣大○同人素仰其為人忠實○智識宏遠○舉為董事衆總○司理○先生亦不貿泉坌○失慎失勤○致力將事○其對於同業也○尤能推誠相與○故民二一年杉木行商會舉為司理○主公正和平○故常務蔚日上馬○且待人接物○皆

亦以免家令子目之○誠者原不為其為年少老成也○先生仍時自勗勉○身心練智○不營年而對於木業已有相當經驗○辭為故行後起之秀○欲一介商人○惟國家觀念彌重○常言辦我國於富後○必以提倡教育為始○遂於民二二年義款理○今歲集本行商會選為正主席○其擁戴之城○于斯可見○先生以年甫而立之人○具此題著才能○其將來發展○正未可限量也○先生昆仲凡十有二○兄友弟恭○怡然相愛○德配劉氏○現有男公子六○女公子二○祥呈麟趾○慶衍益斯○有此美滿家庭○可謂積厚而流光

使萃萃學于○弦歌不輟○鄉人慕德之○乃舉為整理南海第六區小學○聘賢肯教○慮除惡習○矣○

Mr. KAN CHE NAM.

One of the most prominent Chinese lumber-merchants in Hongkong is Mr. Kan Che Nam. He is the son of the late Mr. Kan Yew Cho, and a native of Nam-hoi District, Kwangtung Province, where he was born in 1907.

He obtained his early education from a school in Canton, where he stayed for many years until he was employed as an apprentice in his father's Timber Co., in Canton.

His father died in 1934 and the lumber-yards which he possessed were re-organized. Consequently, Mr. Kan was appointed General Manager of the Wing Tai Cheong Co., Ltd. With his business acumen and experience, Mr. Kan advances the business and to-day, the company is reputed as one ... he most outstanding firms in the Colony.

Mr. Kan is usually very ... ing with social affairs. Furthermore, he is very much interested in educational a....s. In 1933, he was appointed Honorary Principal of a primary school in the sixth District of his native town.

Married in 1925, Mr. Kan has eight children. Except those who are still young, the others are attending local schools.

生 先 川 雨 謝

Mr. TSE YU CHUEN.

謝雨川先生○廣東番禺縣第一區市橋鄉人○現年三十八歲○忠想新穎○雖略堅從○聲譽優良○史嘗江兩堉中之表表人

克盡司賬之職○及一九二五年○始歷本涤美最時洋行之聘○充入口部華人大寫○及總司賬之職○盡忠守職○歷十年如一日○遂於一九三五年○升任華人總理之職○對於社會事業○尚稱熱心○而生平提倡體育○不遺餘力○曾任南華體育會參事○膝任華人體育協進會執行委員，兼副主席○及華人游泳會值理○華人游泳會值理○兼義務總幹事○加入誼會為水港會員○又充華商總會會員○通濟

物也○幼已異凡童○宣讀書○並諸勉功十一歲○倾進香港聖約瑟書院○外攻英文○追歐戰發生○始近廣州對住○翌年○再來港○蛑進聖保羅書院○時兩屆一○故其體檢甚壯也○於一九一九年○已與紫女士結婚○現已生三子○長廣樂○次廣煜○三廣圻○

九一五年也○越兩載○畢業於聖保羅○英文學深○甚為精深○乃進商埠○以謀自立○曾在商業洋行○及港兩華洋行○均年幼○侍親來港○現在廣州培正師業○

公會會員○旅港番禺會所水遊會員○服任反對鴉燁會委員○平生所好○乃游泳一道○無分四季○無間寒暑○堅心練習○

One of the most prominent personages in the commercial sphere of Hongkong is Mr. Tse Yu Chuen. He is a native of Pun-U District, Kwangtung Province and was born in 1899. Having attained a good knowledge in Chinese literature, he entered the St. Joseph's College at the early age of eleven. He remained there until 1914, when Hongkong was heavily effected by the World War, then Mr. Tse returned to Canton. He came back to the Colony in the following year and continued his studies in the St. Paul's College. Two years later, he graduated from the institute and entered the business field.

He started as accountant in the Hongkong Trading Co., and later he was sent to the branch office in Shanghai holding the same post. As that position was not the intrinstic destination of Mr. Tse, so he returned to the Colony in 1925 and employed under the Melchers & Co., one of the most outstanding business houses in the city. At the beginning, he was but chief clerk and chief Book keeper of the Import Department. He worked on honestly and eagerly, discharging duties to every satisfaction. For ten years, he stuck fast in the position and in 1935 he was promoted as Compradore of the firm.

His experience, courtesy and industrious management endear him to all his business associates and friends.

Mr. Tse is publicly known for his social activities. He has been a member of the committee of the South China Athletic Association and Hon. Secretary of the Chinese Bathing Club, and executive Committee of the Chinese Athletic Federation. He is member of the Chinese Chamber of Commerce, Hongkong; Chinese Merchants' Association; and Pun-U Association.

Married in 1919, Mr. Tse has three sons.

香港華人名人史略（一九三七）

79

左達明醫博士

左達明醫師。廣東南海人。現年三十一歲。乃旦英醫學博士。香港著名醫師也。少年時已俶儁有大志。粵語人曰。不

街。然先生猶以為未足。再遊英國畢化甫盧大學研究數年。又得博士學位。D.M.R.E.。近國後。曾充廣州光華醫科專門學校校長。兼任外科及X光綫診斷法教授。連充光華醫院院長。活人無

數。卷之者。輙以華陀比擬也。先生文章亦妙。在英時常有關於醫術著作。投刊於英國醫生理學雜誌。停諳一

為良相。亦為良醫。初進粵東最著名之嶺南大學。苦攻數載。畢業後。再負笈英國。遊愛丁堡大學。專攻醫科。畢業時已得醫科學士學位。後因服務勤謹

時。近年先生在港組織左氏醫院。昆仲分任。名譽極佳。現任中華醫學會肺勞碼組委員。夫人劉氏。乃廣州培道女中高材生。現已有一于名雜鴻。年僅四歲

，及醫術深湛，晉校讀大學醫科博士榮。而天真活潑。甚可愛也。

士博醫明達左

Dr. TSO TA MING, M.B. Ch. B., M.D. (Edin), D.M.R.E.

One of the most famous physicians and surgeons in Hongkong is Dr. Tso Ta Ming. He is a native of Nan-hai District, Kwangtung Province and was born in 1906. He pursued his early education in the Ling Nam University, Canton, and after he graduated he continued his studies in the University of Edinburgh, Scotland, where he passed his Medical Course with the M.B., CH.B. degrees with Honours, and the M.D. degree.

Dr. Tso procured his D.M.R.E. degree from the University of Liverpool, England.

Dr. Tso has been putting on his own practice since he returned to the Colony and not long ago, he has established the Tso's Clinic where he is co-operating with his brother.

Dr. Tso was president of Kwang Wah Medical College, Canton; professor of Surgery and Radiology of Kwang Wah Medical School, Canton; and superintendent of Kwang Wah Hospital, Canton. He is a member of the Committee in Tuberculosis, Chinese Medical Association. In 1930, Dr. Tso was contributing editor of the British Journal of Physiology in England.

Married in 1932 to Lau Mong Ha who is a graduate of Pui To Girls' School, Canton. They have a boy whose name is Tso Wai Hung and is four years of age.

黃訪書先生

生先書訪黃

黃先生訪書○就漢生○蔣繆南海○生而坎壈○遯清光緒壬寅(一九〇二年)畢業於勤頁公模○易廣雅書院為兩廣大學堂○(代史政兩廣高等學堂)拔諸生一百六十人○寫業其中○而先生年最少○凡百科學之名○鹹次乙巳(一九〇五年)選校高才黃訪之二○遂畢鄉立○已浮請書于之名○黃訪學于西林岑公春菼○背學○又遊學預傾科館○其間○先生復與焉○越年，是館政起為兩廣方

Mr. Hanson F. S. Hwang.

Mr. Hwang is a native of Nan-hai District, Kwangtung Province. He obtained his early education from the Kwong Ngah High School in Canton. Two years later, he transferred to a preparatory school which afterwards reorganized under the name of the College of Foreign Languages. He remained there until 1912 when he was graduated.

Realising the advantage of Education, Mr. Hwang devoted himself to the educational circle. He was a tutor in the Sze Mun High School; Nan-hai High School; Kong Yick Girls' Normal School; Sun Yat Sen University and many others.

From 1915 to 1926, Mr. Hwang was employed by the Commercial Press Co., Ltd., Shanghai, as editor of the English Editorial Department. Concurrently, he was instructor and assistant manager of the Commercial Press Correspondent School. He was also a co-editor of the English Student and the English Weekly, both of which were Anglo-Chinese Magazines issued by the Commercial Press.

In 1927, Mr. Hwang was transferred to the branch office in Canton, and in 1936, again appointed as manager of the branch office in Hong Kong.

Mr. Hwang held important posts in different exhibitions, such as the Panama International Exhibition; the Chinese Products Exhibition; the Sze Hu Exhibition; and the Exhibition of Canton.

Literarily, he has written four books in English language. Namely, "The Use of Prepositions", "English Commercial Conversation" "Similarities Discriminated" and "How to Paraphrase".

Married in 1919, Mr. Hwang has six children. They are educated in Canton.

馬國英先生

馬國英先生○別號挖三○粵之台山縣白沙雷洞便平隆鄉人○父諱經典○欵拿大殷商○惜清政之不綱○富有革命思想○張繼理嘗赴埠籌紉○賴其幫助至多○今逖其居○豬見封翁與孫公

○民十三○學成歸里○以先覺自任○即辭雷洞學校○充水遠校董○榮鄉墊樹人之基○隨於是年冬○來港營商○展其抱負○開設廣捷隆金山莊○自任總司理○果然貨殖多能○人莢陶公傳略○交遊日廣○共仰差于高風○緣少年得志○對人態度誅謙○且琭達世情○辦事條理井井

樂趣嚴成○用是備愛師尊嘉許○益為羣樣敬重

○屏身市壓○能輕輕○財重義○接近社會○喜排難解紛○其他關於國家大計○本港公益○靡不諒○至熱心興學○則有前台山縣劉縣長獎勵之文○及充名譽校董於本港南中中學之舉○各同鄉

社團儀其人○莫不倚重○現任廣州台山會館屋業管理委員會委員○僑港四邑商工總局董事○僑港台山商會董事○香港四邑輪船有限公司董事○先生年綫三十晉六○而有此建樹○洵足偉矣○先生配黃瑞芳女士○賢而知書○女錦珠○讀於港眷中女中○于氏幹○亦賦壯鵬燕○前途可

合揆之遺照也○先生禀性沉毅○年少老成○立身向學○克俊克勤○且能紹述父志○平昔黨務○不因讀書時期○精忘定國運動○當辭業台山縣立師範之日○每贊勵黨務於課餘○救國不尚空譚○力行期諸實踐○有足多焉○馬氏日台學會○前此未有也○先生開其先河○且主其事○

當洞閲書報社○歷來所無也○先生實居始創○

嘉○

生先英國馬

Mr. MA KWOK YING.

Mr. Ma Kwok Ying, native of Toishan District; Kwangtung Province, was born in 1901.

He obtained a thorough education from the Provincial Normal School of Toishan, and when he graduated from the institute in 1924, he returned to his native village and initiated the Lui Tung School. Hitherto he has been Permanent Director of the school.

Late in winter of the same year, Mr. Ma came to Hongkong and established the Kwong Jip Lung, an imports and exports agent.

His late father, Mr. Ma King Tin, who was a prominent merchant in Canada, was a zealous patriot and helped a great part in the building of the Chinese Republic. Mr. Ma Kwok Ying himself is a faithful nationalist and he followed the foot-prints of his father. He has rendered his service to the Chinese Government.

He is a man of broad sympathy and every good cause finds him a willing supporter. He is the founder of the Ma's Alumni Association in Toishan; originator of the Lui Tung Library in his native village; member of a committee taking charge of the Property of the Toishan Guild, Canton; Hon. Director of the Nam Chong College, Hongkong; Director of the Toishan Chamber of Commerce, Hongkong; and director of the Sze-Yap Steamship Co., Ltd., Hongkong.

黃卓卿先生

讀孟氏書○至天之將降大任於是人也○必先苦其心志○勞其筋骨○餓其體膚○空乏其身○行拂亂其所為，一節○而如英雄發迹○有自寒微○大器晚成○古今一樣○用述黃棠先生之事蹟

歲月○及歷多大人事○迨無遇問者○遂託先生經理○韓時售貺一空○其任事干脆○誠足驚人○近世有稱之為南中國木業巨擘者○殆指此也○而彼不以利就名成○猶極力研求○以練獨到○前後創設別工夫○黃棠記憶器鋸木廠於港澳粵各地○計連八九家○中英政府，與各大商行，興築宏偉工程○如採用木料○非先生之商店○舉其犖犖大者○在祖國言○若北平之頤和園○鑿各省之鐵路○在香江言○若工務司署○九廣鐵路○各大船塢○九龍貨橋○招商局碼頭○上海滙豐銀行香港分行等○可知先生魄力之雄大也○

以授亞聖之名言○先生字卓卿○粵之順德縣山人也○年尚花甲○慶衍螽斯○生性聰明○紉鈍不露○少年英俊○壯志凌商○初，隻身來港○退九龍貨倉○任管理之務○守法奉公○不取小位○克俊克勤○深得上峯與社會人士器重○有才有識○復遊西人木商某氏處有○陰會風雲○尖沙咀附近○以嘉惠失學之貧氏子弟○最近又將時則駕○荒某商積存巨量木材○賞感不辭○被委充保良局總理○其聲譽可見矣○

於公益贊助○恆其熱誠○教育提倡○尤為盡力○歷任廣華醫院總理主席○建造行商會主席○杉木行商會主席○集木行商會主席○尖沙咀街坊學校校長○德明中學校董等○間不日史由其個人捐辦黃卓卿義學一所於尖沙咀附近○而先生之功業未艾也○

生性有毅驗○所選皆美木○良材矣○鴻毛邊順○駿素宏開○先生之志願能償○彼

生先卿卓黃

Mr. C. H. WONG.

Mr. C. H. Wong is one of the prominent merchants of Hongkong who has achieved success through combats against hardship and difficulty. He is a native of Shun Tak District, Kwangtung Province, and was born in 1877.

He was not born with the proverbial silver spoon in his mouth and therefore could hardly procure a thorough education. When he was but a boy, he was employed in the Kowloon Godown and Wharf. He stayed there for many years and later he began his activities in the lumber line.

A certain European who was manager of a lumber firm had a stock of timber, which he could not find a patron to purchase the lot. Consequently, he confided the matter to Mr. Wong, who showed his business acumen with the fact that the stock was entirely sold out within the shortest span of time.

Since then, his name began to spread in the commercial sphere. Mr. Wong has established, under the name of Wong Tong Kee, altogether nine Saw-mills in Hongkong, Canton and Macao.

Many of the magnificient structures in Hongkong and in China were contracted or supplied by Mr. Wong. Such as the I-Ho Yuan Garden in Peking, which was to be frequented only by the Royal Family of the Ch'ing Dynasty before the Chinese Revolution; the Rail-roads of various Provinces in China; the building of the Public Works Department, Hongkong; the Rail-road of Kowloon Canton Railway; the various famous Docks; the piers of Kowloon Wharf; the Wharf of China Merchant Navigation Co; the gorgeous edifice of the Hongkong & Shanghai Banking Corporation; and many others.

Mr. Wong is Chairman of the Kwong Wah Hospital, Chairman of Fir Merchants' Association; Chairman of Lumber Merchants' Association; Chairman of Chinese Contractors' Association; Chairman of Wong's Club; Principal of the Tsim-sha-tsui School, Director of Teck Meng College, and member of Po Leung Kuk Committee. Mr. Wong has proposed that in the nearest future a free school will be established with his own expenses.

蔣法賢醫師

DR. F. I. TSEUNG

法賢醫師○港故商蔣錦波哲嗣○籍隸廣東新會○生長於香港○行年三十有四○誕應天京○平齊神童之目○曾肄業於育才書社○繼畢業於皇仁中學○旋致港大○以才華早紀○得廣東省府學

中學○旋致港大○以才華早紀○得廣東省府學額○皇校醫醫○性既聰明○志尤篤學○計其在皇仁及港大於業期間○成績優異○獲獎甚多○如庇理羅士，佐領，何福等學額○其最著者也○民十四○卒業於港大○廣內外科醫學士街○隨宪國家醫院內科醫師○為安得區教校助手○任故職十八閱月○卒業於港大○位領，何福等學額○其最著者也○

病診斷及治療之重要」一文○當供職國家醫院時○兼應付門診卻○日常臨証○候逾百人○告退後○即在港開業○仍以糖尿病及理化學等科○展其特長○民廿三○環遊世界各國○觀摩醫學○益求深造○曾在愛爾蘭虛頓遠醫院○倫敦醫院○維律皇后產科醫院○及奧京維也納醫院等處實習○回港後○即與胡惠德醫師合作○趙公之暇○致力於社會慈善公益事業○並具熱心○為普及公衆衛生及預防方法○使人人有醫學常識起見○常在青年會，及播音台演講○富任教中華醫學會及聯青社時○貢貢

遠在聯青社舉辦助日常衛生教育研究班○訓練人才○俾資指導傷病日常衛生工作之責○復與同志叛辦新界醫務會○歷任義務司庫兼司庫○遠故會與受的拯救傷限合辦○成為堅約輪新界附醫會○又宪司理○且加入救傷限為永遠會員○又義務醫官○一二八滬戰時○曾參與組織香港滬戰救護團○並任故團義務秘書○最近在華人慈善會指導之下○對於武高深之研究○曾著有「生理化學檢驗對於糖尿

醫師合作○趙公之暇○致力於社會慈善公益事業○並具熱心○為普及公衆衛生及預防方法○使人人有醫學常識起見○常在青年會，及播音台演講○富任教中華醫學會與男女青年會聯合○組學會及聯青社○貢貢全港健康運動歡次○

遠任三屆義務司庫○港大俱樂部幹事○香港中華醫學會副會長一次○義務司理兼司庫三次○英國醫學會香港分會四屆理事○為華人唯一代表○中華醫學會香港支會秘書兼會計○民十九○港府委宪醫務管理局局員○兩屆共六年○又是年至民廿三○任東華醫院環墅學校義務教校○香港佛學會贈醫施藥所劊料兼資助人○香港聯青社叛辦人○一任幹事值理○三任副社長○四邑工商總局值董事○現任新會商會董事○華商總會值理○商業通濟公會三屆副會長○華慈善社名譽董事○大埔晨化孤兒院副司理○鍵勝港中華醫學會理事○奇江聯青社社長○及聖保羅女校校醫○女青年義務醫師等職○均躍歷著傑代表選舉開宪監察員○西南中學，賢勞○醫師公餘○不事酬應○或博覽中西文學○或作戶外旅行而已○

Dr. F. I. TSEUNG, M.B., B.S. (Hong Kong)

Dr. Tseung Fat Im (prefers English rendering F. I. Tseung), was born in Hongkong in 1903. He received his early education at Ellis Kadoorie School and later at Queen's College. In 1920 he passed his Matriculation Examination and entered the University of Hongkong with the Canton Government Scholarship studying medicine. Both at Queen's College and at the University he had received numerous prizes and scholarships notably the Belilios, Jordan and Ho Fook Scholarships. He graduated from the University in 1925 with the degree of M.B., B.S. He was then offered the post of Clinical Assistant to the Medical Unit working under the late Prof. Anderson at the Government Civil Hospital for a period of eighteen months making a special study of Biochemistry and Diabetes Mellitus and had written an article entitled "Diabetes Mellitus—The Significance of Bio-chemical Tests in its Diagnosis and Treatment." At the same time he was in charge of a large morning out-patient department at the Government Civil Hospital. Since vacating that post he had devoted himself to private practice specialising in Biochemistry and Diabetes. In 1934 he had a world tour visiting medical clinics in Europe and America and also had postgraduate study in Rotunda Hospital, Dublin, London Hospital, Queen Charlotte's Maternity Hospital and Infant's Hospital, London and also in Vienna. Since his return to Hong Kong he entered into partnership with Dr. Arthur W. Woo.

Besides his attention to medical practice Dr. Tseung is well known in all societies and philanthropic organizations in which he invariably serves either as executive officer or committee member.

Realising the importance of mass education in Public Health and Preventive Medicine in China, both at the Hongkong Chinese Medical Association and at the Y's Men's Club he was actively responsible for the organization of Health Campaigns in conjunction with the Chinese Y.M.C.A. and Y.W.C.A. and under the auspices of the Y's Men's Club he was responsible for the organization of a Health Education Class, for the training of a group of intelligent young men to give periodical health talks to the masses. So enthusiastic was he in this work that his lectures were frequently heard either at the Y.M.C.A. or at the Hong Kong Broadcasting Station.

In 1930 when the New Territories Medical Benevolent Society was formed he was one of the founders and Hon. Secretary and Treasurer until the amalgamation with the St. John Ambulance Association to form the St. John Ambulance New Territories Medical Benevolent Branch and is still now Joint Secretary to the latter. He is also a life member and Divisional Surgeon of the St. John Ambulance Association and Brigade.

In 1932 during the Sino-Japanese trouble at Shanghai he was one of the organizers of the Hong Kong Medical Relief Committee and served as its Hon. Secretary.

In 1926 he was graduate representative and for three terms he was Hon. Treasurer of the Hong Kong University Medical Society. He was for three successive terms Hon. Secretary and Treasurer and once Vice-president of the Hong Kong Chinese Medical Association and is at present serving as a member in its Council. He had served at the University Club and Hong Kong University Graduates' Association as a member of the Committee. For four successive terms he has been serving as a member of the Council of the British Medical Association, Hong Kong and China Branch representing the Chinese. He was Hon. Secretary and Treasurer of the National Medical Association of China, Hong Kong Branch. He is a life fellow of the Chinese Medical Association, a member of the American Medical Association of Vienna and also a member of the Fellowship of Medicine, London, England.

In 1930 he was appointed by the Hong Kong Government as a Member of the Medical Board, which post he has held for two successive terms of three years each.

From 1930—1934 he was Hon. lecturer to the nurses at Tung Wah Hospital and for three years he was himself financially responsible for the running of a free medical clinic under the auspices of the Chinese Buddhist's Association.

He was a charter member of the Y's Men's Club of Hong Kong and has been continuously serving for five years on its Board of Directors, having been once its Director, three years its Vice-present and now its President.

In an honorary capacity he serves as Physician to the Si-Nan College, St. Paul's Girls' College and Chinese Y.W.C.A.

Outside his medical sphere he serves as a member of committee in various local organizations such as the Sze Yap Commercial and Industrial Association, Sun Wui Commercial Society and lately was appointed to the General Committee of the Chinese Chamber of Commerce. He has been for three terms Vice-president of the Chinese Merchants' Association, a post which he is still holding. He is an Hon. Director of the Chung Sing Benevolent Society and also assistant secretary to the Tai Po Rural Orphanage.

Recently at the Hong Kong Oversea Chinese Election of members for the coming National Congress at Nanking he was appointed one of the supervisors for the voting papers.

Incidentally it may be mentioned that he is a member of the Euro-American Returned Students' Union, a member of the China Institute of Pacific Relations, and also a member of the Rotary Club of Hong Kong.

He has many other public activities notably Volunteer to the Hong Kong Street Sleepers' Shelter Society etc. Besides his busy practice, Dr. Tseung has devoted most of his spare time in social and charitable works.

He is still single and his hobby is hiking and reading, as well as collecting of old Chinese literature.

香港華人名人史略（一九三七）

陳鐵一先生

MR. CHAN TIT YAT

梅芳中學校長陳鐵一先生。廣東番禺縣人。年境三十八歲。一身係儒，報，軍，政，學，五途。各有建樹。晉享盛名。誠多藝多才之士也。先生早受良好教育。童年畢業於本港聖保羅書院。如在商界。亦有驚人發展。曾料水怡昌瓜哇糖廠。經營兩載。兼任新聞界編輯一年。後歷充奇閒有限公司華人總經理。及華南某某公司華南總經理。泰山人壽保險公司司理。宏利公司華南總經理等職。交遊日廣。信用愈往。社會人士恆以少老成稱之。先生篤於學。持籌握算之餘。糟不輟讀。日必抽暇兩小時。以從事於揣摩政治經濟等書。對於孫總理遺教。尤有心得。民十二。入國民黨籍。民十五。泰本港羣工風潮。乃返廣州。開始政治活動。復以大著遊亞子報章。贊揚乃不絕於人口。良以先生對於國家貢獻。及政治批評。不作唯唯否否之論。不為浮浮泛泛之詞。請者乃心儀其人。為歐大鈞先生。仰其幹練精明之男。時長廣州公安局者。均有兼前眼辣之想。毅沈者。認為不易得之才。特聘之任該局機要秘書。以資贊助。追黨警備司令。亦請參與司令部機宓工作。及錢氏令部機宓工作。領兵北伐時。復薬遠指揮部機要秘書。決勝千里。君與有力焉。決委秘書。遷籌帷幄。亞民十七。其途複陳耀承先生。長國民革命第一軍。希念長才。電召北上。委為軍部軍需長。任。第一軍砲壘留守主任。宓港警備司令部參謀。武漢警備司令部參謀等要職。均能勝任愉快。先生且身軍旅。歷有多年。追入政途。亦如廣東廣州市公安局秘書。兼特務委員。英德籌餉處處長。清化傷區籌餉瞥偵局局長。南韶連等籌餉處處長。上海市公安局特務局摩繁缺。先生對於社會工作具有成績。焉附華僑所屬焉。乃選祿可倖致邪。先生與吳敏屏女士（梅芳女中學校長）結婚於民廿二。即公元一九二三年。鸞合珠聯。尤稱佳偶天成。現育子女三人。長女美虹。現年十四。次于萬端六歲。幺女見虹則辟業於梅芳女子中學初中部。兩子則俱肄業於梅芳幼稚園。

三四屆執行委員會主席。全港學界庭祝教師聯歡聯三屆主席團主席。先生嗜游泳。（按惠抽筋裁至喪身乃止）重發育（曾習中國泰術八歲。日本武士道剣術兩年）精射擊。（曾獲別擊槍章）擅辭令。而於人初學。指教學。病理學尤有特別專長。曾在京港粵各地監獄考察犯罪心理學。及在各大醫院考察病理學。宏證美人。大多數公民擁戴投票選舉。故非德高望重。及歷任社會工作具有成績。焉附華僑所屬焉。况先生為一教育家。筆金賭選。非所屬焉。國民代表大會選舉香港特別區代表。先生得獲國民之博可知。民廿五年。我國政府舉行第一次名計不少。一經品評。均無或爽。則其基名領教者不少。各社會工作具有成績。焉非德高。學之博可知。創料梅芳中學男校於香港。立己立人之利也。久導衆員等。可知干新其邪。固無牲而不利也。先生長。南韶連等籌餉處處長。上海市公安局特務局快。先生且身軍旅。歷有多年。追入政途。亦

壁。史抽徐暇。服務社會。尤苦賢勞。屢任南華體育會幹事。曾軍部主任。學務部主任。香馬商會各區義學校長。一二八全港各界眼港難會主席團主席。兼總幹事。契約翰務傷隊海士隊主任。第二契約敎敎傷隊海士隊主任。奇港華僑敎育會創辦人。兼第一屆監察委員。全港學界庭祝教師聯歡聯三屆主席團主席。先生嗜游泳。（按惠抽筋裁至喪身乃止）重發育（曾習中國泰術八歲。日本武士道剣術兩年）精射擊。（曾獲別擊槍章）

Mr. CHAN TIT YAT.

Mr. Chan, born 1901, is a native of the Pun-U District, Kwangtung. He is one of the most famous and popular Chinese gentlemen now in the colony.

After receiving a high education, he began his business career. He first managed the Wing Yee Cheong Co., dealing in Java sugar. Then, for a year, he was editor of a news-agent. After this, he became, in different times, the Chinese manager of the Hong Kok Advertising Co., Ltd., General Manager of the South China Investment Co., and Manager of the Hongkong branch of the Tai Shan Life Insurance Co., (Shanghai).

However, Mr. Chan was still not contented with his success. He was regularly devoting an hour or two every day to improve himself by reading books on politics and economics and the teachings of the late Dr. Sun Yat Sen.

In 1923, he became a member of the Kuomintang, and during the General Strike in 1926, he went to Canton where he began his political activities. Though unknown to the people there at first, he soon attracted much attention by his wonderful articles appearing in different newspapers giving his views concerning the Strike and the chaotic political conditions of the country.

Meanwhile, Mr. Chien Ta Chun, the then Commissioner of the Bureau of Public Safety at Canton, came to know of the rare talents and ability of Mr. Chan and at once made him his private secretary. Then Mr. Chan gradually became known to many political and military magnates of the country especially when his brother-in-law, Mr. Chan Chi Cheng became the General of the First Revolutionary Army. He was therefore afterwards transferred from one important position to another which he filled with credit and satisfaction.

In recent years, Mr. Chan came back to Hongkong and devoted most of his energy to the work of education. He is now the Headmaster of the Mui Fong College, which under his able management, is rapidly becoming one of the most famous schools in the colony.

Mr. Chan is a man of broad sympathies, and every good cause finds him a ready and willing supportor. He has been the Committee member and Scout Master of the South China Athletic Association, Committee member of the Pun-U Chamber of Commerce in Hongkong, and the founder, and Chairman for the first year of the Supervising Committee and Chairman for the second, third and fourth years of the Executive Committee of the Chinese Teachers' Association. Besides these, he is also a member of many other social organizations.

Mr. Chan is skilful in swimming, Chinese Boxing, Jujitsu and riding, besides being an expert in palmistry and Phrenology.

Very recently, Mr. Chan was nominated by the Chinese Community of Hongkong for the election of delegates for the First Congress of China to be held in the near future.

Mr. Chan married to Miss Ng Man Chee, headmistress of Mui Fong Girls' College, in 1923, and he is now the proud father of three children.

吳敏墀女士

MISS NG MAX CHEE

敏墀女士。母之高要羅人。為遜清御史吳杜丹秋舫之第三女公子。陳君鎮一之夫人。亦即梅芳女子中學校長也。現年剛不惑。幼已秀慧過人。且篤於學。凤聆庭訓。具有師承。早有不

杜。不亞鬚眉。會乃兄陪墓烈士。承 孫總理電召。由德學成歸國。創造魚雷奇巧。參加革命工作。殉難於廣州。女士痛乃兄之慘遊。

復惠團體之淪亡。遂創辦梅芳學校於香港。呂為吳烈士紀念。莫術續乃兄之墜緒。亦呂仲生平之素願。女士人志苦而行孝。務於任事。敏呂耐勞。迨其創辦梅芳女中至今二十載。不

漢，余仕榮，鍾佐廷，林承芬，蕭吉珊，陳樹人，周啟剛，陳春圃，陳公博，曹仲鳴，傅秉常，郭占南，賞賞梯，林菜和，李孝濂，胡耀賢，黃新彥，何世金等。皆分任校董。且現已得為香港傷校向教育部傷務委員會及廣東教育廳立案之第一間學校。復將中英庚款委童事會及中華文化基金會撥附高中部物理儀器金。價值數千元。實開香港傷校受設會共勵之先河。承近進行籌建新式校舍矣。女士於百忙中。史抽開料理社會慈善事業。曹任南華女子部正主任○齊任校董。員生組基綜會值理等職。一二八之後。女青年會少女團主席○籌建香港孔聖堂委員。女青年會少女團主席。現任香港傷教育會教行委員。南華女子部學務主任。香港反對蓄辉會值理等職。近製傷兵衣服二十餘套。運送救奔。十九路軍傷兵受欵不少。一九三四年本港煤災。捐欵。及現製傷兵衣服二十餘套。運送救奔。鼓濟員生出助救護為慈善團體先。且撥校舍一部以收容難民。組救傷應以財醫欵○即分遣救護救傷及身罕員生。女士開受。即分遣救護救傷及身修領夫人特呂大銀杯一庭。劇公開志私四字紀念之。女士復擱升育○尤喜寫梅。高奇華先生曾函索乙愼。則女士之意學深造可知。其創辦學校也呂梅名。呂紀其苦有若耐寒梅也。女士為增見謙改贊展校務起見。最近又橫渡太平洋赴英國致察。行見其將題序所仲。為我國教育界增幸楊馬。

呂人事參差。限境惡芳○及中熙一度工湖之影罄。四次遷校之折屋而小慚其志。或遮親當不足之時。復課抱出其私蓄以奔之。不足則出就校外教席以扼註之。卒能如願呂償。創辦之初○學生不遇七人而己。復呂戚績優越。遂年增加至五百餘人。學級由初小而至高中。且兼辦幼稚園焉。時至今日已料高中華案第六屆矣。其設備之週詳。管教之嚴密。蔚為寄島女校冠。我黨國要人壁本港名流。嘉女士之能廣育人才。無不樂為鼓助。如李明揚，孫科，朱家驊，梁寒操，陳策承，胡文虎，葉恭綽，邵幼庭，周埈年，鄧摩堅，洪興錦，陳行恪，賴璉熙，容光嫩，溫前，李耀

衛遊士之日。再求深造。負笈甲江。果呂戚績最優畢業於塔秀甲西女校。今人徒羡女士之博學多才。豈知為群倫表率。史詢何於而伴天獨厚。寧如女士今日有如此造就。實基於奮志苦學之時。欲惻乎吾國之楨的。端於母教之不健金。竊謂人生不幸而為女子。以等的之軀而能救千戈而守士。亦富偏教育呂救亡。志氣之不

Miss NG MAN CHEE.

Miss Ng Man Chee or Mrs. Chan Tit Yat is the third daughter of the later Dr. Ng Kwai Tan, a high official of the Ch'ing Dynasty. She was born thirty nine years ago in the Ko Iu District of Kwangtung.

After receiving her early education in her native village, she went to study in Shanghai where after some time she graduated from one of the most famous schools.

Miss Ng's ability is a great source of envy to many of her friends but it has been due to the many years of hard work and concentration while she was at school.

She realised very clearly the fact that in order to become helpful wives, good mothers and useful citizens of the society, a lady must possess a good education to help her along. With this point in view, Miss Ng, after equipping herself with the necessary knowledge, cherished the idea, even at her early age, of establishing a school where she could help others by giving them an adequate education. Just at this moment the death of her brother, the late Mr. Ng Pui Ki, who sacrificed his life while serving his country, still more strengthened her resolution to carry out her dormant idea. Thus in 1917, she established the Mui Fong Girls' College with a two-fold purpose in memory of her late brother and to offer the Chinese girls a new home of education.

The college was but a small one at the beginning, but Miss Ng spared no effort to make it a success. After many hardships and struggles, she has succeeded in keeping it running for nineteen long years and making it one of the best Chinese Schools in Hongkong to-day. Under the able management of Miss Ng, the college has won the confidence and respect of many prominent persons in Hongkong, in China and elsewhere. With the ready help of these prominent persons the Board of School Directors have proposed to erect a new school building, and the girls students will find a most up-to-date school in the Mui Fong Girls' College before long.

Outside the school, Miss Ng is very keen in social activities. She has been taking part in many different social organizations and is at present member of the Supervising Committee of the Chinese Teachers' Association, Superviser of studies of the Ladies Division of the South China Athletic Association and Committee Member of the Hongkong Anti-muitsai Society.

She has a kind heart and takes a keen interest in the welfare of her fellow being. To the sufferers of the destructive storm at Swatow and of the horrible Sino-Japanese Conflict at Shanghai, she gave her assistance heartfully. When the disastrous as Tank explosion happened in Hongkong in 1934, Miss Ng immediately sent out her school Nursing Division who were the first to arrive at the scene to take care of the wounded people. She also took a number of the poor sufferers back to the school and supplied them with food and clothes. She fully deserved the beautiful silver cup which Lady Southern presented her as a reward for her kind and ready assistance. She has sailed for America to investigate the system of education while this biography is written.

林銘勳先生

生先勳銘林

林銘勳先生，原籍粵之新會蘆溪牛環○生长於香島○現年三十五歲○乃我國體育界之優秀份子○而本港九龍汽車公司之主委人物也○禀賦明性質○統尚武精神○長讀於皇仁書院○數年

苦修○三育並進○於一九二零年畢業○卽棄學從商○初就職香港環球保險公司○富打字員○繼轉大來輪船公司○充任書記○閱歷日深○學益富○後美實業公司定其才識○聘掌文案事務○凡三年之久○復應其友鄧君次乾之約○合組共和汽車公司○造代理企理其他公司之汽車，及其附屬用品○同時九龍汽車公司○亦以秘

先生富國家觀念○無時而不切齒於外敵侵略○以祖國空防廢弛○飛行人材缺乏○不惜自購一機○痛下苦工練習○提倡見諸實事○敎國不尚空譚○洵不愧為今之志士矣○先生於一九二五年，與畢業廣州榮濟醫院之吳雅英女士結婚○現育子女各二○長男肄業廣州嶺南大學香港分校○餘亦在求學中○

書一席相違○先生雖年少而材多○契方兼顧○游刃有餘也○共和公司，因營業不前○未幾閉歇○乃專心致志服務於九龍公司焉○時半島地方建設○佳其雛形○交通事業○未臻發達○故九龍公司之創始也○屬於試辦○規模甚微○迨一九三三年，公司改組○且享得港府批准專利之權○先生乃膺任總秘書○主持一切○以迄於今○故素推運動之對於球類，游泳，御車，操舟，技術○素加研究○靡一不精○復肯啟身社會○歷充各捷徑務○藍球隊隊長○奇港青年會藍球隊隊長○奇港足球總會之東方體育會代表○南華體育會監球隊隊長○五陵會主席○華商總會值理等席○

Mr. LAM MING FAN.

One of the most prominent merchants in Hongkong is Mr. Lam Ming Fan of the Kowloon Motor Bus Co., Ltd. He is a native of Sun - Wui District, Kwangtung Province, and was born in 1902.

He obtained a thorough education from the Queen's College, where he was graduated in the year 1920.

Mr. Lam began his business career with the post of a typist in the Liverpool & London & Globe Insurance Co., Ltd. A few months later, he worked as a steno - typist in the Admiral Line. He attached to the post for about two years and then turned out to work as Correspondent in the Hongkong Excavation Pile - Driving & Construction Co., Ltd., (formerly Chino-American Industrial Developing Co.)

Three years later, he resigned the post and co-operated with Mr. C. K. Tang and established the Republic Motor Co. of China dealing in Motor Car accessory parts and representing products of the Chrysler Motor Co. The firm did not prove a success to Mr. Lam and a few years later it was closed.

In 1920, the communication of the Kowloon Peninsula was not so well developed. Though the Kowloon Motor Bus Co., had long been established, it possessed only a narrow scope. Mr. Lam was secretary of the company then. After his own business proved a failure, he devoted his main interest in the latter. Until 1933, when the company re-organized and procured the monopoly from the Hongkong Government, Mr. Lam began to put into action his scheme of improving and expanding the business. To-day, the prosperity of the firm reaches the climax.

Mr. Lam takes a great interest in sports. He has been Captain of those famous basket-ball teams such as South China Athletic Association and the Chinese Young Men Christain Association. He likes swimming, and such like games. His interest in aviation is very much, so three years ago, he bought a training-plane and learned the craft of it.

He is the Chairman of the sports Club, committee member of Hongkong Chinese General Chamber of Commerce, & Member of Numerous Clubs & Associations.

Married in 1925, Mr. Lam has two boys and two girls. They are receiving their education in local schools.

何天生醫師

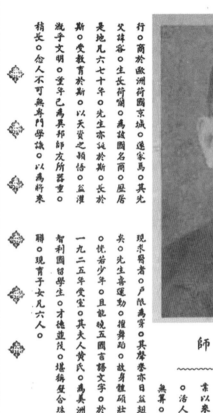

本港著名醫師何天生先生○來粵惠陽人○現年四十二歲○其先祖有大志○作遠

建業基礎○遂在荷國習醫○迨於一九一八年，負笈英國○進蘇格蘭愛丁堡大學○專攻醫科○以期深造○三載精研○迨畢業其業○且授L.R.C.P.及C.P.即S.榮銜○於一九二二年○忽勸至堂而入室○卒業其業○且授

故國之恩湖○胃搏言歸○省識家園之面目○旋

日旋○來港以所學貢獻於僑胞○惟然以濟世為己任○聞素以來○活人無算○

行○商於歐洲荷國京城○遂家焉○其先父諱容○生長荷蘭○為故國名商○屈居是地凡六七十年○先生亦誕於斯○長於斯○受教育於斯○以天資之穎悟○益進漱乎文明○堂年己為異邦師友所器重○

現來醫者○戶限為穿○其摩卷亦日益超英○先生喜運動○擅舞蹈○故身體碩壯○忱若少年○且能晚五國言語文字○於

一九二五年受室○其夫人黃氏○為美洲智利國留學生○才德並茂○堪稱璧合珠聯○現育子女凡六人○

精長○令人不可無專門學識○以為將來

師醫生天何

Dr. HO TIN SANG, L.R.C.P. & S.

Dr. Ho Tin Sang, one of the outstanding physicians in Kowloon and Hongkong, is a native of Wai-yang District, Kwangtung Province, but was born in Dutch Guiana, Surinam, in 1894.

His ancestors had long been living in that country and his father was one of the prominent Chinese merchants there. Dr. Ho studied medicine in Holland and when he had passed the Medical Course he proceeded to Scotland and continued his studies in the University of Edinburgh where he attained the L.R.C.P. & S. degree in 1922. He can speak five kinds of language of different countries.

At the end in 1922, he returned to Hongkong and put up his own practice. His experience and skill have given remedy to many fatal diseases and thus won a good reputation in the Colony.

Dr. Ho married in 1925 to Wong Chi Kin, who was graduated in Chile, South America. They have six children and except those who are still young the others are educated in local schools.

蕭遠嚴先生

蕭遠嚴先生○号之潮陽縣東溪鄉人○現年四十有八○具蛾木奇才○如致高尚義○愛國之商人也○幼時讀書故里○勤學異常兄○十六歲就賣

○與日俱積○富於識見一二八之役○集合同鄉者也○先生輕儚商外人治下○而愛國愛群之熱誠○籌款拯賬○大著賢勞○民二五○戲機尋辭

當謀反正○克恋潮梅先鋒隊部軍需處處長○大功告成○以天職已盡○退海陽○隱於商○迄至現在○身營米業○行昌號其于割業司理

以克實國防○任籌辨員○於米業商會○擔任勤捐○不遺餘力○其於本港社團○亦多貢獻○如創組香港米業商會○充等二兩屆执委主席○現克

香港華商總會值理○旅港潮州八邑商會董事○均蟬聯兩任○旅港潮州同鄉會执行委員○米業同鄉會執行委員○旅港潮州

商會执委○兼詞解部正主任等職○先生於念四歲詞交室○夫人鄭氏○同邑金浦鄉人○現育男公于四○女公于一○長男柏坤○幼讀於鄉○長

向於港○次男柏熙○畢業本島綱布中學○三男柏遜○四男柏修○均蟬索本島香江中學○女玉

奇江○少年忠厚○人以老成日之○當時適清末葉○吏治不修○中原鼎佈○胡率圖謀革命○先生報國情殷○毅然加入○追事機成熟○遠返汕

頭○號召民軍○揭午起義○卒能光復潮汕○任藏保安限部爲刊稱長○時籌廣任追防冠耳○越雲○方退故鄉小學○一家之內○樂也融融○

三歲兩素敗改憲○粤省龍氏勳進梅區○先生復

Mr. SIEW YUEN NGAN.

Mr. Siew Yuen Ngan is a native of Chao-yang District, Kwangtung Province, and was born in 1889.

He obtained his education in his native town, and when he was but a lad of sixteen he came to Hongkong to practise business.

At the end of the Ch'ing Dynasty the policy of the then Government reached its worst and most of the patriots schemed to revolt. Mr. Siew joined into Revolution and went to Swatow to play his activities. Finally, the revolution was successful and the Republic of China was firmly established. Then Mr. Siew became a staff in the Bureau of Protection in Swatow. Three years later, when President Yuan Shih-kai plotted the restoration of a monarchical government, Mr. Siew, who is a faithful nationalist, became Chief of the Munition Department of the Van-guard on the revolutionalists' side.

After this matter was absolutely settled, Mr. Siew resigned every position and returned to Hongkong.

He established a firm under the name of Hung Cheong and deals in rice business.

Mr. Siew is very active in social affairs. He is one of the founders of the Hongkong Rice Merchants' Association and was for two terms chairman of its Executive Board. At present, he is committee of the Chinese General Chamber of Commerce, Hongkong; Director of Swatow Chamber of Commerce, Hongkong; Executive Committee of the Chao-Chow Association, Hongkong; Executive Committee of the Hongkong Rice Merchants' Association, and many other social organizations.

Married when he was twenty-four, Mr. Siew has four sons and a daughter. Except the eldest son, the others are still attending schools.

辛玉銘先生，籍原橫瑯之縣。剛屆中年之年。賦性慈善。熱心教育。傷肥感欲物坐。里黨交稱善人。幼靖於鄉。長商於港。審整我國人之無商棠道德。往往失信。以戾其譽。卒致功敗垂成。莫能

飫其有信。然則後之立身闖關。欲暢其素者。堪資借鏡。先生本其懷抱。致力各種公益事業。當仁不讓。歷任香港崇正工商總會董事。及附設養學校之長。曾所值理，與董事。中山僑商會克任東華三院首總理。鐘聲慈善社社長。現任中山縣六區水豐學校校長。香港聯福行有限公司司庫。華商總會值理等

辛玉銘先生

職。尚德甲戌年間。東華醫院組織善互助社。彼貢獻尤多。故社第一屆馬彩執行委員會。

挽救。故對於信用二字。有若晝之坤西銘睛座右焉。甫出閒世。即受少年老成之目。佳譽日進。乃見知於外商屈臣氏洗水公司。墾亞紅亞出品洋行。現港中上下兩環。以水福二字作店徽。互相辉映者。即先生多年報故之商號。為上列兩家代理。及總怨理之銷埸也。營謀益晉。人方羡欲之多材。棄務興隆。我猶

為崇德報功。本縣繡平原之義。特肘像而裏之贊。曰。為善之榮。煳在好絁。辛公謙怍。中外咸知。熱心公益。見義勇為。互助善舉。竭力難持。籌巨欵大德無私。仰瞻雅範。繁我遐恩。觀此可如其為人矣。德配黃銀女士。內助病賢。現已有男公子三。女公子五人。

Mr. HUNG YOK MING.

Mr. Hung is a native of Chungshan District, Kwangtung Province and was born in Hongkong. After he had obtained an adequate knowledge from a local school, he started his business and established a firm, under the name of Wing Fook, representing products of A. S. Watson's Co., Ltd., and Asiatic Petroleum Co.

His confidence and business acumen soon enabled him to approach the throne of success, and to-day he becomes one of the most prominent merchants in the Colony.

Mr. Hung, though usually very busy with his own commercial tasks, plays an important part in social affairs, he has been president and director of Tsung Tsin Industrial and Commercial Association; committee of Chungshan Chamber of Commerce, Hongkong; and principal of its subordinate school; president of Tung Wah, Kwong Wah and Tung Wah East Hospitals; and Chairman of Chung Shing Benevolent Association. At present he is Treasurer of Luen Fook Hong, Ltd., and committee of Chinese General Chamber of Commerce, Hongkong.

Married to Wong Ngan, Mr. Hung has three sons and five daughters. His eldest son pursues studies in the Far Eastern Aviation School and the other children are studying in local schools.

盧榮傑先生

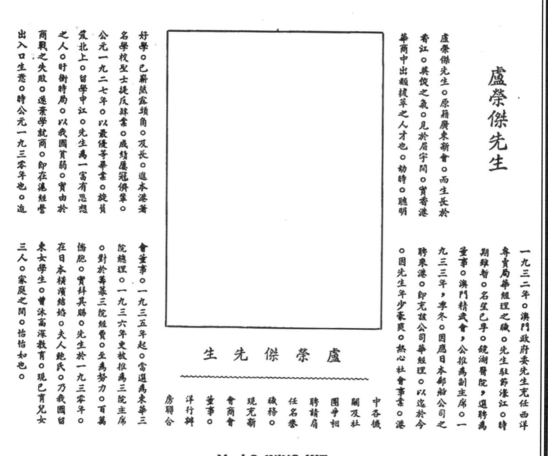

生先傑榮盧

盧榮傑先生○原籍廣東新會○而生長於香江○英俊之氣○見於眉宇間○寶香港華商中出類拔萃之人才也○幼時○聰明好學○已嶄然露頭角○及長○進本港著名學校聖士提反肄業○成績屢冠儕輩○公元一九二七年○以最優等畢業○提資笈北上○留學中江○先生為一富有思想之人○時衡時局○以我國貿弱○商戰之失敗○退棄學就商○即在港組營出入口生意○時公元一九三零年也○追

一九三二年○澳門政府委先生充任西洋專責局華經理之職○先生駐節湛江○時期較暫○名望已孚○銳湖醫院○選聘為董事○澳門精武會○公報為副主席○一九三三年，李冬○因應日本郵船公司之聘來港○即充茲公司華經理○以迄於今○因先生年少氣爽○熱心社會事業○港中各懷
關及社
園學祖
碳務○
現充新
聘請肩
任名譽
董事○
會商會
洋行辦
房聯合

會董事○一九三五年起○當選為東華三院總理○一九三六年史敎授為三院主席○對於籌募三院經費○至為努力○百萬傷肥○賞科其賜○先生於一九三零年○在日本橫濱結婚○夫人鮑氏○乃我國留東女學生○曹沐高深教育○現已育兒女三人○家庭之間○怡怡如也○

Mr. LO WING KIT.

Mr. Lo Wing Kit is a native of Sunwoi District, Kwangtung province, and was born in Hongkong in 1907. He came from a well-to-do family and had sufficient means to obtain a thorough education. He attained his primary studies in Hongkong and later he studied in Shanghai for a short period. Finally, he returned to the Colony and continued his studies in the St. Stephen's College. He remained there until 1932 when he graduated from the institution and in 1930 he started his commercial career in Shanghai as importer and Exporter. His conscientiousness and honesty enabled him to set a foundation in the business sphere, and two years later, he returned to Macao and was authorized by the Portuguese Government as the monopolist of opium in that city.

He returned to Hongkong in the following year and became compradore of the world-famed Nippon Yusen Kaisha Steamship Company. His experience and natural ability are valuable assets to the firm, and his integrity and innate courtesy endear him to all his business associates.

Mr. Lo is very active in social affairs. When he was in Macao, he was director of the Kang Wu Hospital and Vice-Chairman of the Chin Wu Athletic Association. Since 1936, he was appointed president of the Tung Wah, Kwang Wah, and Tung Wah East Hospitals. He is director of the Sunwoi Chamber of Commerce, Hongkong, and also of the Compradores' Association Hongkong.

Mr. Lo married in Yokohama in 1930 and has two daughters and a son.

楊蔭浩先生

生先浩蔭楊

楊蔭浩先生○原籍粵東番禺○生長於香蕊島○年僅三十晷八○擅貨殖才○服膺總司理○壯歲而有老成之稱○辦事富有朝氣○社會人士○交相稱許○以為楊氏積德○迺此路寖之兄也○故就經營○素凡數推○現方力謀擴張○蒸蒸日上○是先生不特守成○且能創業○昔人謂生子當如孫仲謀○何所見之不廣耶○先生個性謙恤○恆視己善○對於社會事業○又復尚力○多所賢勤○現克華商總會等機關會員○以年未瓜乎不惑之人○己將如許進就○其將來貢獻於吾人者○寗有限量○我國商界○誠幸而出此哥材○異域青年○何修而獲斯模範○俊無建樹○鄞多亦英以為○乃不俟卒業○辨而就商○現任香江著名科館之宏記也○先生德配殷眾氏○以賢淑稱○于貢○無訛枝習○服裝致高○少英俊○曾肄業於港中聖保羅書院有年○中英文學問○甚為豐富○先生以學貴能效用○

Mr. YEUNG YAM HOO.

One of the prominent merchants in Hongkong is Mr. Yeung Yam Hoo. He is a native of Kwangtung Province and was born in 1900.

He obtained his early education at St. Paul's College, Hongkong, where he remained many years until he attained a thorough knowledge in English language.

After he left his school, Mr. Yeung devoted himself in the business field. Though stared with a low position, he could easily approach the destination of succcess by means of unceasing effort and carefulness of work. At present, he is general manager of Wang Kee Co., Ltd., one of the outstanding business houses in the Colony.

Mr. Yeung is a member of the Chinese General Chamber of Commerce. Hongkong.

Married to Lo Yun Ling, Mr. Yeung has many children.

葉大楨醫師

師醫楨大葉

葉大楨醫師，祖籍鶴山。乃廣東鶴山。生於奇島。爲是地良醫。濟世有心。活人無算。誠醫界後起之秀也。湖先生誕於公元一九零二年。現年三十有六。童

黔攻讀於本港聖保羅書院。嗣廣州嶺南大學。一九二二年，既冠受業。負笈英京。學道專門。肄業醫科於倫敦大學。冀成一醫之長。將來造福人類。下惟歇哉。有志竟成。迨一九二八年，而獲將倫致皇家內科醫學院執照士。及英國皇家外科醫學院院員。翌年，更膺倫敦大

學內外科醫學士銜。乃歸港開業。斯時也。先生齡未屆乎而立。人恆以年少輕之。迨盎揆況病。逐聲鵲起。而先生臨症不苟。益爲儕儔所器重。乃先生份不自囿。一九三三年遊英時。再進聖巴多羅馬醫院研究。今則業已大起。名勒公卿。

去歲，軍委長夫人宋氏止於天南。舒尊莊港。建門求醫。則其遺詔如

何。必有超出乎尋常萬者矣。彼於業餘。亦龍致力於社會。一九三零年，至一九三一年。充香港青年會董事。一九三五年，晉任故會副會長。又爲聖約翰救傷隊永遠會員。及外科醫生。尊配陳氏慈勞。現育公子二。女佑成。五歲。讀於聖士提反學堂。于承孂。三齡。

Dr. YIP TAI CHING, M.B., B.S.

Dr. Yip Tai Ching, one of the most prominent physicians and surgeons of Hongkong, is a native of Hock-shan, Kwangtung Province, and was born in Hongkong in January 13, 1902.

He received his early education from the St. Paul's College. Many years later, he proceeded to Canton and continued his studies in the Ling Nam University.

Having graduated from the University, Dr. Yip proceeded to London, England, in 1922 and took up the Medical Course in the London University.

In 1928, he was admitted as member of the Royal College of Surgeons of England, and concurrently, licentiate of the Royal College of Physicians of London.

Dr. Yip graduated from the London University in 1929, and obtained the degrees of M.B., and B.S. Returning to the Colony in that year he started his own practice.

From 1923-1929, Dr. Yip studied in the St. Bartholomew's Hospital of the London University.

Dr. Yip is one who interests in public welfares. He was director of Chinese Y.M.C.A., Hongkong, in 1930; and in 1935, he became Vice-president of the same organization. He is also a life member and divisional surgeon of St. John's Ambulance Association, Hongkong.

Married to Chan Wai Fong in 1922, Dr. Yip has two children. The elder one is a girl and is receiving her early education in the St. Stephen Girls' College.

楊少泉牙醫師

楊少泉先生○字祖復○鑽城之下恭鄉北山鄉人○誕於澪江○長於香海○已屆弱冠○始履家鄉○現年五十有九○香港久享盛譽之牙科醫師也○先生喜讀書○尤勤於學○幼隨母居港○攻讀中文書館○及其他團學尊修科○攻讀七八年○業乃大進○乃轉習醫行文○方期英各髮○讀會貫通○不幸學綫兩截○黨以丁母

師醫牙泉少楊

之黃色人種○而能為牙醫先進之白色人種服務○則先生之名符其實可知○而先生尤不自滿○故業餘抒問○乃向牙科函授學堂○求增知識○將批一九一四年○港府頒行牙科註冊則例○得及格○翌年而赴上海美國牙科學堂之畢業文憑○先生重於外○而會於滬上○准府精一技○可自暴自棄耶○且以身被一技○而服身手關上進○隨能力關上進○人可自暴自棄耶○且以身被一技○而服身手○而且不特立身建業○足為後學楷模○而服務社會○兄之於拯教育○有如下述○現任中華內道會香港區醫部值理○沿理家庭○兄女均抱教育○計其獻身於各團體者○有如下述○現任中華內道會香港區醫部值理

憂報讀而工○誠非得已○至十九歲○受業於當時名牙醫徐善亭之門○越兩年○適唐公紹儀南下○倡其師之館○為山海關鐵路學堂招生○乃以學優獲選○派料入校半年○因團匪之亂○份近港之○一再挫折○有志數成○亦已傷已○先生如不能與造物爭衡也○復從徐師治數載○卒偕其秘○至念八歲○乃自設醫館問世○時公元一九零六年也○開業後○以技術優良○人咸信任○遠一九一二年○本港陸軍醫院軍官杒君○重其材○特立合約○聘其外為陸軍士兵料理歯部○以牙醫後學

北山鄉鄉政持會當會長○現任保衛眾常備值理○堅公會議組員○中山僑商會所值理○反對婢制會幹事值理○基督教會興省港副會長○中華國內佈道會香港進部副會長○香港基督教勝會堂事○註港北山楊氏公益社值理等職○先生配牧黃氏○細室羅氏○現代還下女兒○十有一○現由廣州嶺絲教院畢業生陳前俄太太○主持中綺○○先生注重體育○嘗游泳之世人嘗泳於太極拳料之所到○不問寒著○為冬字春字泳之服姑人○故於胖耳順之而精神發絲不遜青年也○

坐法寔社也○計其獻身於各團體者○有如下述○現任中華內道會香港區醫部值理○坐理大光報館伮緯人兼任值理○香港基督教聯會副會長○坐基督教港海西道會值理○坐士夏青年會會長及中華基督教育年會副會長及幹青年會幹事兼記○平氏義學委員○及親青委科○基督教港海西道會值理

趙鶴琴先生

趙鶴琴先生○老儒醫也○現歷春秋○六十有七○粤之新會聯三江鄉人○少從名師呂拔湖遊○久立程門○深知道義○既長○欲精一技以為世○遠歐美醫學東漸○乃修業廣州博濟醫院○後該院因掌教島約翰君逝世告停頓○竟殞一青之功○未屆畢業而退學○轉習國醫於長壽寺僧慧

辦學業訖○已達五次○前後造就人才○千有餘泉○其教校方法○以國醫為性○西醫為用○如古籍所載之醫療理論○有高深莫測者○悉以新學說証明之○故群廣校生徒○無不學成歸去也○先生居粤墨靈之日○曾兼任將弁學堂軍醫○南海中學校醫○教育善堂醫席○遇有暇時○則從事著述○歷年所撰成之諸義○有全體解剖○兄科胎生學○掛症探要○痙症○傷寒論○生理學○方兄科，婦科，脈學，方藥，診斷，眼科，凡十二種○其有功於國醫界良非淺鮮也○先生辦業醫糊口不配儒生本色○自少至老○不甚虛榮○對於扳權附勢者流○尤深惡痛絕○然先生亦非徼物忖才○拒人千里○有能打破階級觀念○而與先生結交者○先生亦樂與過從○蓋欲待人尚無貴族平民之分也○至其醫德○亦有足稱○退貧人踐門求治○拖

生先琴鶴趙

○為期淵博○史向黃赤馬○開潼泗洲○諸名醫領教○既集大成○迨出其所學以壽世○先生以吾國醫者○多自秘其術○不輕易傳諸人○迨為最大之缺點○恐力矯此弊○乃於遜清光緒三十年○創科廣東中醫研究所○時主粤政為岑春公春堂，及王公人文等○多其號嘉惠後學○准予敕立○計開辦後○學生畢業○凡念一屆○洎迄海鶴○繼續努力○亦迪本港教育司備案○迄今

樂贈藥○曾不稍吝○故甚許港粤人士好感○聲譽大著馬○德配於氏○如夫人三○曰何呢蘭○日方煥蘭○日徐美琚○均由先生校以洛人之術○紹粤省衛生局考取前列○曾國素於廣州市迨十年○現育子女十六人○男七女九○次公子名廔○現充國民革命軍第二十八師郎軍長○第六公子名柴氏○現爲壹半石○並習西醫於光華醫院○其餘子女多在各枝讀書○

Mr. CHEW HOCK KUM.

Mr. Chew Hock Kum is one of the most well-known medical doctors with Chinese method in the Colony. He is a native of Sunwui District, Kwongtung province, born in 1870.

He was educated in his native village and when he was grown up he entered the Poh Tsai Hospital Canton after a competitive examination. Unfortunately, the principal of the institute died before he was graduated and he was compelled to leave the hospital without passing his final test. Then he learned the medical course in Chinese method and after many years constant studies, he started his own practition in Canton.

In 1904 he initiated the Chinese Medical School in Canton and in 1925 he removed the school to Hongkong where he is now managing the institution with unweary efforts.

Mr. Chew is not only famous for his skilful treatments but also for his literary works. He has written twelve kinds of books regarding to Chinese medical treatments. Furthermore, he was in the capacity of Resident medical doctor of many schools and government organizations in Canton.

Mr. Chew has seven sons and nine daughters. All of them are well educated and two of his sons are following in his footprints to take up the medical course.

吳志澄先生

生先澄志吳

吳志澄先生○名城波○以字行○廣東中山縣山場鄉人○現年四十七歲○乃奇港商場中上等人才也○幼在鄉塾攻讀漢文○塾師驚其才器○十二歲丁父艱○十六歲隨兄來港○受業於港中已

真○仍聆先生充任司理○在職凡三年之久○乃出而再創光隆公司○尊業備○奇港商業停頓○先生迫將故洋行出讓他人承辦○但故洋行斯膠束○以先生經驗豐富○辦事認

克殖公司分行司理職○但先生不欲遠離奇港○且不願水寄人籬下○遂出而自行創設華貿洋行○組營三載○生寮原有蒸蒸日上之勢○不幸奇港大罷工風潮○發生於西曆一九二五年○當時

一則為畀努力於商業通濟公會之發展○今日故仁書院○年修英文○二十三歲○以最優等畢業道者○先生之力也○一則為勗力於誰侄輩之教育○因先生家庭甚大○以一人之力○維誰全家長大成材○亦先生之力也○其太夫人現年八十

故名儒李賜碩老師○漢學益進○十七歲欽入皇○中西學問斐然可觀○閱年就其樂公司之聘○克仕職員○後改就法團郵船公司及太古船澳職○均歷三年之久○乃應先拖公司之聘○由書記○升至為監察助理○服務凡七年○故公司

影樓具○兼代表歐美各大工廠廠造造品物○生寮發達○且生平坐開住○全港縷契足代表○屆主席○中山商會董事○兼第五通濟公會重要職員○兼第五值理○先生友人言○先生一生尚有二事○自引以為快慰者○

四歲○性極慈祥○先生奉侍唯謹○孝德可嘉○

以其才幹不凡○工作勤敏○擬調往星嘉坡埠○

Mr. NG CHI CHING.

Mr. Ng is a native of Chung Shan District, Kwongtung Province, where he was born in 1890. A few years' early education pursuing Chinese knowledge in his own village enabled him to obtain a fair result in the subject. When he was sixteen, he was brought to Hongkong by his brother in order to continue his studies as well as to further his knowledge. In the following year, he entered the Queen's College and there he stayed until he was twenty-three when he graduated.

In the same year, he started his business career as a staff in the Clark & Co. Then he turned to work in the Messageries Maritimes, and afterwards in the Taikoo Dock. Three years later he worked in the Sincere & Co., Ltd., a famous universal provider, as a clerk. With his ability and intelligence, he was promoted gradually to the position of assistant superintendent of the firm with a long service of seven years. Finally the terminate selection of him as manager of the Singapore branch office forced him to resign on account of his unwilling departure from Hongkong and concurrently his ambition to establish his own business.

He founded the China Mercantile Co., and with his experience he furthered the business in the utmost extent. The famous Strike of Hongkong in 1925 effected him heavily and he was forced to sell the business. The new partners found him very useful in the future promotion of the business, so he was offered with the position as manager of the firm. In 1928, he established the Kwong Tat & Co. dealing with photographic instruments and at the same time, as representative of different European and American Textile manufacturers. His experience and his abilities enable him to make the firm one of the most prominent commercial plants in Hongkong.

Mr. Ng is also very active in social affairs. He has been a member of the committee of the Chinese Chamber of Commerce; Chairman of the Tung Chai Association; delegate of Chinese Piece goods Association; director of the Chung Shan Association and a few others.

蔡惠鴻先生

蔡先生惠鴻○南越銀城人○現年三十二歲本港體育界之領袖也○性聰敏○而喜

場○在各行中○有過人之建樹○居重要之地位○如前任中華娛樂有限公司董事（几五年）也○如現充奇港油蔴地小物公司○及九龍汽車公司董事也○其措極進取○纉有朝氣○宏於造就○不謀老成○

吾知來日方長○先生必有為人之展耳○先生富堂尊觀念○常獻身公共團體○民二一○曾任東華醫院總理○現充奇港中華體育恊進會委員

長○奇港中華體育會委員長○華商總會值理等職○彼為新生活實行家○無不良嗜好○喜偏體育○雅擅足球○求學時期○任嶺大足球隊代表○港粤人士○曾領

讀書○少年絕受高深教育○修業於廣州嶺南大學○雖出身豐家庭○人盏其刻苦自勵○力求上進○未敢以紈袴子弟例之○欲求克紹先人德業○且不徒克紹先人德業○且星其紀投者○廏不如其為此中健將也○

記發揮其天才○出西地轉於遠柴第二市

生 先 鴻 惠 蔡

Mr. CHOY WAI HUNG,

Mr. Choy Wai Hung is a native of Chungshan District, Kwangtung Province, born in 1905.

He was descended from an excellent family and therefore was able to obtain a thorough education at the Lingnam University, Canton. After many years' hard efforts and struggles, he graduated from that institution. Then he came to Hongkong and settled himself in the commercial sphere.

He was Director of the China Entertainment Co. Ltd., and is at present director of the Hongkong Yaumati Ferry Co., Ltd., and of the Kowloon Motor Bus Co., Ltd.

Mr. Choy is very active in social affairs. He was president of Tung Wah Hospital in 1932 and is at present Chairman of the Board of Committees of the Chinese Athletic Federation, Hongkong; Chairman of the Board of Committees of the Chinese Athletic Association, Hongkong; and committee of the Chinese General Chamber of Commerce, Hongkong.

Soccer is the favorable hobby of Mr. Choy. During his school days he represented the Ling-nam University to play in Hongkong.

香港‧澳門雙城成長經典

李焯權會計師

李焯權先生。粵中山良都人。生長香港。現年二拾有九。港中之唯一華人會計師也。父國趨。少商澳洲。現任奇港永安有限公司董事。母蕭氏。乘出望族。深得孟母遺風。教子有方。故先生早年即就飽受家庭教育。民拾捌。辭業

即本所學。設會計事務所於香港永安銀行三樓。並開辦商業會計學院。以養成商業會計人材。蓋鑒於我國舊式簿記之複雜。恆以改良中式簿記為己任。所撰『改良中式簿記大綱』一書。行將脫稿付梓。書中妥義。詳述粵省原有簿記之制度。與乎從華民良之方針。中英義。亦無不分條刊入。將來公諸於世。當大有裨益於商場。溯自香港開埠以來。華人會計師之獲蒙政府特許。有權查特許中西賬目者。以先生為第一人。民國二十五年春。先生為謀聯絡同業之情。利便同業之切磋起見。倡組華人會計師公會。被推任該會首屆主席。任永安銀行查數員。及兼英國商業公會。澳洲會計師公會。兩機關之駐華南總代表。審集閩港同業。開慈善歌舞遊藝大會二次。一萬募款以助兒童保護會。一萬募款絞也。至於體育一門。先生尤提倡不遺餘力。故對於港中小足球賽。曾數次損款獎物。其熱心

於香港皇仁中學堂。旋負笈澳洲。入聖約翰大學。同時實習於澳洲最有聲譽之拍打公泉會計師行。迨加入為澳洲會計公會會員。及英國商業公會會員。對於會計一科。富有經驗學識。用說考列澳洲昆士蘭省會計大試第二名。為我僑胞生色不少。先生以我留學澳洲僑胞之泛無聯絡也。又從而組織留學生會。以團結之。至今仍為旅地人士所稱頌。民念三。返自澳洲。○可見。夫人鄭寶容女士。乃乞故澳洲華僑。前齊山銀行總經理鄭公洵全之女公子。賢淑柔和。○匹配先生。恰成佳耦焉。

小李焯權會計師

香港華人名人史略（一九三七）

THOMAS LE C. KUEN, A.A.A., A.I.I.S., F.C.I.

Mr. Thomas Le is the first and the only Chinese "Incorporated Accountant and Auditor (Aust.)" practice in Hongkong. He is the son of Mr. and Mrs. Lee Gock Chew, a well-known merchant and one of Directors of the Wing On Co., Ltd., of Hongkong.

Mr. Le was born in 1908 in Hongkong. He received his early education at the Queen's College and thereafter went to Australia where he studied for his Accountancy professional qualification. For some years, he was articled to Messrs. Porter and Porter, a well-known firm of Accountants in Australia. After passing his final examination, Mr. Le admitted as membership of the Association of Accountants of Australia (Incorporated) the Institute of Incorporated Secretaries and of the Institute of Commerce (England).

Upon returning to Hongkong, he established his own practice at Wing On Bank Building under the name of Thomas Le C. Kuen & Co., and as a matter of fact he is the only Chinese Incorporated Accountant who is authorised by the Governor in Council to practise as Part 1 Auditor for both Chinese and English firms.

Mr. Le is a keen advocator on reorganization of Chinese book-keeping and accounts. He has written a book in Chinese on "Improvement of Chinese Accounting System" which is in the course of printing.

Besides his professional activities, Mr. Le is the president of Association of Chinese Accountants and Auditors of Hongkong. South China representative for the Association of Accountants of Australia, the Institute of Incorporated Secretaries, and the Institute of Commerce (England). For some time, he was also principal and Lecturer of the Accountancy-Secretarial Institute, founded by him in 1933.

陳福善先生

福善先生。原籍粵東番禺縣。公歷一九零四年生於中美洲。巴拿馬股商陳公肇基第四公子也。其兄福田為美術家。其弟福紀。福浩。福念均為藝術家。就讀香江。敏而好學。每試必列前矛。先生童齡近國。慣英文美術書法。富有藝術天才。年十二。已能為人作英國各種古體字帖。卒業後。為山頓爵士賞識。以其律師模之高級席位相埒。先

頌爵士夫人見而激賞其。特介之加入香港美術會。同人崇拜其藝術超群。旋舉為該會董事。(該會董事其中華人從未染指。至先生始開新紀錄。為英國增光不少)。後又迭獲該會兩屆冠軍獎金。

民國廿四年。實習期不過十數月。以有好奇心。復肯加研究。卒有偉大之收穫。先生之居。西山背水。如在畫圖中。亞柳村波光山景之大。可游目騁懷。出戶則鳥語花香。足以賞心樂事。以天然風景。就地寫生。取之不禁。用之不竭。故其所作之畫。均有得到。山頓爵士夫人尤重金聘去陳列其佳作多幀。以示鼓勵。復又出經貿易。以垂金聘。

民廿四。打洒店舉行其個人畫展。開本港畫界之先河。由山頓爵士夫人主持開幕。並蒙港督史樂詩作序文於畫冊中。肴郁德傑爵士夫人為序開幕。基禮。奇室肅穆其盛儀。於參觀者甚眾外。史寵庆。序文于其畫展開幕。因彼此雅愛藝術。常約觀畫展及諸畫法。切磋砭益。由是求畫者踵相接。而先生大忙矣。先生以學無止境。欲百尺竿頭。更進一步乃於各處成立研究社。如辦香港藝術研究社。與陳宏。黃病碞。等個人畫展。又因多取畫材。曾一度漫遊祖國各地。繪畫主辦六人畫展。時多已借出於先生提倡藝術。尤不遺餘力。就南京北平等處名勝數十幀。當其第二次個展應香港美談結會。及亞院証道學院之邀請而演講也。如發表其所著「一九三六年美術畫法」一文於中西各報也。無不以扶植大雅

生感恩知遇。亦關以中特之學致通顯。誰料今日之成名。在彼耶非此耶。尚未嘗有畫家指來。每心習畫。亦未嘗有畫家指導。僅藉英國美術學校兩年之函授。綜云苦綀。今則一無所人。其成功可知。矣非聰明絕頂不能。欲嘗云「美術之發展。須具有獨立社。方可創其宏作。斯言也。則偏其天才」。以品復學也。以所閒屋所作。請而演講也。畫展討也。故深得各界賞識。而榮閱休悵焉。刀作油畫為最出色。查先生以刀作油畫一幀。尤以用筆。鋼筆。各種美術。無不別樹一幟。先生自謂。刀斫閒居時。雕塑。造像。油彩。水彩。粉彩。鉛是務。

陳福善先生

Mr. LUIS JOSE CHAN.

Mr. Luis Jose Chan is a native of Poon-U District, Kwangtung Province, and was born in 1904.

Though he was born in Panama City, he was brought back to Hong Kong when he was very young. He is at present to be considered as Hongkong's own artist.

He was not at first interested in drawing, but at school he was attracted by Old English Characters. He began collecting different styles of English Lettering, characteristically inventing fancy forms for himself. As a matter of fact, he did not attend any arts school but entered for a course at the Press Art Correspondence School of England.

For some months he drew and sketched in black and white. Then, needing colour, he changed the course to water-colour.

By good fortune Lady Shenton became interested in his work and introduced him to the Art Club. In 1934 Mr. Chan held the first one-man show given by any member of the Art Club.

Early in 1934 he began experimenting with the palette knife. He brought back from a month's holiday in the North about forty pictures and the most of these were executed in Peiping.

In October 1936, he held his second one-man show, which was opened by Lady Caldecott, with great success. His Excellency the Governor wrote a Forward in the catalogue of the exhibition and bought many of his pictures.

Mr. Chan is one of the four founders of the Hongkong Working Artist's Guild, a society of artists organized a little over a year ago.

劉樹聲先生

生先聲樹劉

劉君樹聲○字君任○粵之東官人○學海名流藝林碩彥也○少秉風雅○善畫工書○叔叔有出塵之致○精長○為折衷中西畫理○初索於美洲支加哥大學藝術教育系○墜華盛頓美術大學○數載觀序○學成來港○以發揚藝術○提倡教育為己任○創立萬國美術身科學院○藝花藝術學院○香港華僑美術美術身科學院○藝花藝術學院○香港華僑美術

漢謀，區芳浦，劉石心，張遠峯等各長官○紛紛題詞誌賞○各國畫家蒞場參觀之眾亦眾向所來有○奇港國際美術會主席西畫家容花臣夫人○對之尤表欽崇○除向其商付西畫帆船○國畫墨蝴○陳諳會中○曰待國際名畫家測繪○私人又似其國畫王蜀東一幀與歷○以誌景仰○當特中西報章○均起其事一幀與歷○作者○或刊油畫到前線去○均起其事○而介紹其佳作○易為眼緣美展○造到集○更有為之出倒展尊號者如大光報水彩帆船○不忘倒殺○倒展望日○先生大殺扶物○如大光報是也○先生大殺扶物○

志賢女子中學○均任主持○治事之餘○恆雅集文人○切磋砥礪○奢儕馮師祥，李景康，張谷雛，傅善祥，黎工佽諸名士申書畫合作社○同人推其任社刊編將○奇港華僑教育會○以先生致力文化事業○亦聘之為參議○家藏字冬○奇港華僑美術會開華之日先生皆躬行其倒展○出品有國畫，西畫，書法○著作刊行○現凡三種○(隨中英主管機關簽定，萬國函校兼用之塔就及萬學員)○一日書法述要○一日國畫指南○吾知將來示範於後學青年者○必無量數央○

鉅製油畫到前線去○可知先生藝術感人之切而兩屆月前我首邨二次全國美展○經眾亞入退○尤為港粵擢生之光○若中英文學○苦中英音樂○與夫國扶○以書畫鳴○若○攝影，游泳○均有所長○蓋其倒性好建故○考研究也○先生現方盛年○郵資甚富○著作甚富○奇書○奇研究也○吾知將來示範於

會○志賢女子中學○均任主持○治事之餘○恆雅集文人○切磋砥礪○奢儕馮師祥，李景康，張谷雛，傅善祥，黎工佽諸名士申書畫合作社○同人推其任社刊編將○奇港華僑教育會○以先生致力文化事業○亦聘之為參議○家藏字冬○奇港華僑美術會開華之日先生皆躬行其倒展○出品有國畫，西畫，書法○凡數百倩○我國要人自林主席以降○如于右任，孫科，張群，郵景○朱家驊，黃慕松，居正，王世杰，張賢奎，蔡廷鍇○余

覽○成績甚佳○今年仲春願萬國函校專廣州屆男女學員○及廣州青年會之請○又赴桴市倒展○界人士○凡某先生以書畫孚眾望賢者者○日○臨場實眾者○汽眾千人○此間藝人李全熱等○對先生能以書法描寫蚊蝴○妙筆通案○僅致不置○余如杜省南寧氏國日報亦商刊其富國防性之抉紛○熱心國事○均頌揚不置○粵報多其一再紫畫○李孚公等以○迷頌展

Mr. LAU SHU SHING.

One of the most prominent artists and educators in Hongkong is Mr. Lau Shu Shing. He is a native of Tung-Koon District, Kwangtung Province.

After he had received a thorough education of Chinese literature, he proceeded to America and pursued the course of Arts in the University of Chicago. Thereafter, he continued his studies in the Washington College of Arts, in the capital of the United States of America.

Then he returned to Hongkong and founded the International Correspondence Fine Art Academy and the International Academy of Arts. Besides these, he is also founder and principal of the following institutions, namely, the Ngai Fah Art, Academy the Overseas Chinese Fine Arts Association, Hongkong, and the Chi Yin Girls' Middle School.

Mr. Lau held his one-man art exhibition in the Chinese Art Club in December 1936 when the Club celebrated its opening. This exhibition was a successful one and many of the famous officials in China wrote complimentary notes to him. The exhibition continued in the following day, with the object of raising funds for the relief of the refugee and sufferers in the North China.

In February, 1937, he was requested by the Chinese Y. M. C. A., of Canton to hold a second one-man show at Canton. This is also successful, and was highly recommended by the leading newspapers there.

Mr. Lau is a councilor of the Hongkong Chinese Educational Association. Recently, Mr. Lau has written a few books, all of them are on the theme of arts.

曹思晃牧師

師 牧 晃 恩 曹

香港銀崗聖保羅堂主任牧師恩晃先生〇誕於澳
江〇前澳門議例局員曹善案之第四文郎〇本港
前任華人代表曹善允之肥姪也〇忱況歇〇喜讀
書〇幼攻國學〇家聘專席名儒〇精長〇智葡文
於澳門政府公學〇西一九一〇年〇益學英文於

培義會背骨封先生為牧師於敖廣州主堂〇斯時
除服務會外〇兼任大良〇石岐〇江門〇三區
總巡〇一九二三年〇應澳難多利省美利濱埠
李會督允之〇〇尤充華人教會主任牧師〇躡聯五
栽〇旅澳之日〇曹參加全澳教會大會議〇復
好從各科學專家遊〇新知直進〇於一九二八
回港〇是年二月十一〇由吳寿增會督主禮〇與
真光中學教員何女士玉瑛結婚於誠校禮堂〇三

月八日〇奉杜結義會背骨
〇委為本港聖保羅堂主
任牧師〇先生乃倡議展
拓堂址〇進於其側附建
牧師莊一間〇費共四萬
金〇尤推華人禮拜堂之
巨擘〇先生向來不作無
益身心之消遣〇最愛讀
〇故世界著名演講家艾
迪博士〇鍾士德博士等
來港佈道〇恆賴先生
作舌人〇現業廣州協和神科大學演講學講師
〇而對於社會職務〇尤樂於接受與負責〇如國聯
會香港分會董事〇聖保羅男書院董事〇聖保羅
女書院董事〇香港真光分校董事〇香港基督教
聯會英文秘書〇反對蓄婢會值理〇南華聖書會
值理〇中華國內佈道會總會贊助會員〇港粤教
區常備委員會委員等〇現年四十有一〇于三人

奇港聖保羅書院〇修業期間〇感基督教理之薰
陶〇心馬嚮往〇於一九一三年四月十三日在聖
保羅堂受洗禮〇五月十四日受堅信禮〇學成後
從事教育〇先在母校工作年餘〇嗣求深造於廣
州協和神科大學〇至一九一九年畢業〇旋就
白烈士會史長之〇〇為秘書〇助理英國聖公會南
第差會幹事宜〇是年屆月〇〇偷會督乃冊立先生為
會史於齊港聖約翰大禮拜堂〇一九二二年〇杜
〇長安邪〇次安道〇幼安民〇

Rev. P. S. F. TS'O,
THE VICAR OF ST. PAUL'S CHURCH.

The Rev. P. S. F. Ts'o who is the fourth son of the late Commendador S. I. Ts'o of the Portuguese Government, a member of the Legislative Council of Macao, and who is also a nephew of the Hon. Dr. S. W. Ts'o, was born in 1895 in Macao, to which his ancestors migrated from Chung Shan District, Kwangtung.

Coming to Hongkong in 1910, he studied in St. Paul's College, till he graduated. After his graduation, he joined the teaching staff of his mother school for two years.

Then he left Hongkong for the study of theology at the Union Theological College Canton. After he graduated from the Union Theological College in 1919, he became a secretary to Archdeacon E. J. Barnett, who was then the Secretary of the Church Missionary Society, South China.

In 1923, a call came from Australia. He responded to the call and accepted the invitation from the Mission of the Epiphany, Melbourne. He went there as Chaplain to the Chinese Mission and worked under the late Archbishop H. C. Lees. When he was there, he was able to attend the Australia Church Congress in 1925.

He stayed in Australia till the year 1927 and landed in Hongkong in January, 1928. On the 11th of February, in the same year, he was married at the True Light Hall by Bishop Mok Shau Tsang, to Miss Amy Hoh, a teacher in the True Light Middle School. He was inducted as vicar of St. Paul's Church by Bishop Duppuy a month after his marriage.

Mr. Ts'o is known as an able interpreter. During the visits of Dr. Sherwood Eddy and Dr. Stanley Jones to the colony, he was asked to be their interpreter. His Hobby is reading. He takes great interest in the Art of Preaching and Psycho-analysis.

Mr. Ts'o is a tutor of the Union Theological College' Canton on the art of Preaching, a councillor of the League of Nations' Society Hongkong, a member of the Council of St. Paul's College, of St. Paul's Girls' College and of the True Light School, Hongkong, an English Secretary of the United Council of the Hongkong Chinese Christian Churches, a member of the Standing Committee of the Kwang Yuet Diocese of Chung Hua Sheng Kung Hui, a director of the Anti-Muitsai Society and of the Bible Society of South China, and a member of the Assistant Committee of the Chinese Home Missionary Society.

士女瑛玉何

曹忠晃夫人，何玉瑛女士。原籍粵之達平人。於耶穌降生一千八百九十八年。生於廣州市。為雲山珠海靈氣所鍾，咯鍾毓地。已丰姿秀媚。英氣逼人。惟命遭不辰。父早見背。遺孀六人。賴母鞠育。女士居長。爹友性成。念母氏之劬勞。顧他年之生計。故每日除助家務及

投攝弟妹之外。遭饑孜孜求學。日無暇務。埋頭苦幹。作學費之代償。殆孟子所謂苦其心志。勞其筋骨者歟。稍長致進南中國最著名之眞光女校。身受師範。呂將來得天下女才而教育之為己任。在校時。每於假餘。均於研究鄉聖道。西歐一九一六年畢所業。以女士品學優異。聘充該校教職。二年之後。冀求深造。一九二〇年果呂最優等畢業。且留校富

教席兩年。呂所得來修作投大學準備。一九二二年致讀嶺南大學。身攻文科。業得教育科身證書。卽於是年應眞光中學之聘。一九二五年又任。女士篤信耶教。服勞於基督『非徒役人乃役於人』之說。常其在中學及大學肄業時。喜與同學組城村服務團。聯班結隊。往附近村落。舉行衛生演講。及兒童識字運動。故當時白鶴洞及康樂一帶村鄉之婦人孺子。莫不親炙女士其人。而樂與之親近。一九二六年曹代表該村教仵道

該分校校長。女士生平與兒童為友。對兒童愛心理學。兒童故事。兒童圖書方法等。小學教育。尤為熟諳。一九三五年之廣州眞光中學分校長於小學教育資。呂女士富於師資。常方法等。送歡然應聘。港中各界威虔誠教席將才人。

表南基督教育會議。赴申出席全國基督教育大會。一九二八年曹代表香港女青年會到上海出席全國代表大會。一九三〇年之久。一九三〇年聘女士為廣州眞光中學分校長。一九三四年起被推為香港女青年會長。均歷任數屆。呂迄於今。一九三六年史祝被推為香港反對蓄婢羅堂女服務園副會長。及港聖保羅堂女服務園主席。總此呂觀。女士菩於求學。樂於育才。勇於服務社會。實港中婦女界之偉大人物也。

Mrs. P. S. F. TS'O, B.A.
President of the Young Women's Christian Association, Hongkong.

Mrs. P. S. F. Ts'o, whose maiden name is Amy Hoh is a native of Lingping, Kwangtung, born at Canton, in 1898. When she was 13 years of age, her father died, leaving six children behind with but little means. Being the eldest child in the family, she needed to find money not only for her own education but also for her brother and sisters. She managed however to study at True Light School, Canton, which is the oldest educational institute for girls in South China, having been established 60 years ago. After graduation from the school with unusual honour of being the first in every class, she took up the normal course and finished the course in 1916. Saving some money from her salary as a teacher at her school for two years, she again joined True Light Middle School, Pak Hok Tung, and was again engaged as a teacher of the school for two years after her graduation there in 1920. She entered Lingnam University, Canton, in 1922 and graduated with the Bachelor degree of Arts and with the educational Diploma in 1925. At the request of True Light Middle School, she joined the teaching staff and remained in the post until she married Rev. P. S. F. Ts'o, vicar of St. Paul's Church, Hongkong, in 1923.

She is an earnest Christian, and her life motto is, "Not to be ministered unto but to minister". That is why in her school days, she organized a Service League for the villages. She went very regularly with a number of girls into the villages near Pak Hok Tung and Lingnam, teaching and preaching. She taught the villagers, particularly the women and children, about hygiene, about book and, above all, about God. Consequently, she was a well known figure among the village people.

In 1926, she was sent to Shanghai for the National Christian Education Conference as a delegate, representing Kwangtung Province.

Since her marriage, she has lived in Hongkong. She was engaged as a teacher in St. Paul's Girls' College for three years.

In 1930 she was invited to attend the National Young Women's Christian Association Conference at Shanghai.

When the Council of True Light Middle School Canton decided to open a branch school in the Colony in 1935, she was repeatedly asked to be the Principal of the new school. It is said that as she is known as a born teacher and is richly equipped with knowledge of Child Psychology, Story-telling, methods of teaching, School Administration, and with ten years' experience of teaching, it is a great pity that she does not take up education as her life work. Finally, she accepted the post.

As to her social activities, she is the President of the Young Women's Christian Association, Hongkong, Vice-president of Anti-Mutsai Society, and the Secretary of the Diocesan Women's Auxiliary, these three posts she has held ever since 1934. She is also the President of the Women's Auxiliary, St. Paul's Church.

柯應李先生

柯應李先生○名宏楊○粤之潮陽縣洋內鄉人也○現屆中壽之年○為本島汕頭花邊公司創辦人○歷兼總司理○性況敏○志不凡○少曾肄業於香港青年會○敏而好學○成績為同儕冠○精敏

計氏生焉○先生為發展其業務○送分設支號於汕頭北平等處○於推銷其故鄉萬餘婦女所成之抽紗製品外○復搜羅湘粤以及北平各地之刺繡絨工○蔚為大觀○用備具邦來遊者所採擇○故一歲之中○周遊國內○長征償償○不以為苦也○先生雖忙於商務○對於社會○亦肯服務○

香港青年會○敏而好學○成績為同儕冠○精敏

民十一，曾受孫大元帥委充潮梅善後委員會委員○同年八月，汕頭抽紗同業公會○因交涉免稅事○請其代表○赴平稅務處請開○卒得成功○同業受益不淺○氏十七，參加菲律濱加年海賓會○菲律濱華商總會先派其代表出席○兼陳教信主任○彼為基督教信

徒○向來注重培養體育與教育人才○氏七，於原籍創設進德學校○且年助經費百金○迄今不替○又為本港華人游泳會贊助員○旅港潮州中華基督教分會○贊起人○其對本港各教會○及海面傳遊會○捐助亦不貲○是誠有心世道之士○未可以其一介

念人貴自立○萬般讀從商○本港為遠東第二市場○商界奇才○威集於此○先生果何所恃○而能馳聘數十年○以躋今日之地位耶○是亦有故○蓋彼有遠大眼光○復想深長遠底○營謀方法○以提倡工藝為主○將吾華巧妙之美術鈹繡○

代各地女同胞取償最優厚工值○實大有裨於國光○從而兩人兩沾祝之也○

柯應李先生

Mr. KWA ENG LEE.

Mr. Kwa Eng Lee is a native of Chaoyang District, Kwangtung Province, born in 1886.

He obtained his education at the Y. M. C. A., Day School, Hongkong, and after he was graduated, he began to practise business in the Colony. He established the Swatow Lace Company in Hongkong with the main destination to promote the Chinese drawn work and embroideries, which are highly recommended in the Western Countries. His able management enables him to further his business to such an extend that to-day there are branches of his company in Swatow and Pieping.

Besides his commercial activities, Mr. Kwa has been devoting a lot of his time and interest in dealing public weal. He has been appointed by His Late Excellency Dr. Sun Yat Sen as a committee in the management of the affairs of the Chaochow and Mei-hsien Districts. In 1928, he was appointed representative for the Chinese Chamber of Commerce Manila P. I. in the Carnival Exhibition of the Philippine Islands. He is one of the founders of the Chinese Bathing Club and a patron of the Chinese Swimming Club, Hongkong. In 1920, he established the Chin Tack School in his native village and contributes to it a yearly fund.

He is a faithful Christian and is one of the original members of the Chaochow Chinese Christian Association, Hongkong Branch.

Married in 1905, Mr. Kwa has two sons and four daughters. All of them have received a thorough education.

黃燕清先生

MR. WONG YAN CHING.

燕清先生○名熊超○字俊英○列著言情○行三○粵高要金利鄉人○現年四十有六○為本港開埠富人黃瑞生公之文孫○錦塔公之哲嗣○生而秀麗○甫神童稱○讀於官立英漢文學堂○（今易英皇中學）博知篤行○在校大考十次○名未嘗稍降○且將全校綜分最高之特別獎○

學臺仁○繼辦廣東高等師範○學成囘港○就金臺洋行華經理職○時粵清季○革命思潮澎湃○先生囘熱血之士○年十六○已加入同盟會香港支部○後竟捧擔保證金萬五圓○已星駿○從事革命○聯絡各方○迢攻哥哥署之役失敗○李公煜堂亨○為喚朏園姚○徐越三○主其事○時此間有茶保及黨候閣報從文○題為「中國應否革命」懸合

讀詩○於是中國○世界公益○新少年等報○率起聞之○先生謀伐尤力○某報送業於國人○及民國成立○從事革命者○多作官去○尤以報界為泉○惟先生獨留○未幾新少年報停版○遂改充民國新報編輯○旋骨總編輯○後亦因某事停版○乃先復創香海女校○後請開辦民報○及南後報○此後蔣君瘐粵○蔣君壽石某組討賊軍○功成某港○任奇港農事○期年○復創新江報○香港有說報○自與現象派○及同志辦中華女學○威聯先生任其事

適其岳父溪深森○病遊江門○先生赴弔○有感於是地教育之落漠○遂創江門女子中小學校○同時值溪水為災○乃人鑒於粵港實物眼災會之具有成績○學校各界有水為災○乙人鑒於粵港貢眼災會之具有成績○學校各界有俊英三字○送辭侍於革者根據執行○而黃江門人士之口○題詢後張君祝樵○同組四

邑商報○先生任總編輯○時歐戰初起○某公司假招華工為名○運赴戰地工作是實○其組理某御命來此○以巨資向各方疏通○先生首拐於報章○學東蔣萊代某公司私許先生二千金○先生竭卻○反感勁之○某經理知敗而退○四邑人不致枉死異域者○斗先生賜也○後張氏祝樵○任五邑廿料處眼線○骨料玉菜○勒撫工作○王不

○適其岳父溪深森○病遊江門○先生赴弔○有感於是地教育之落漠○遠創江門女子中小學校○同時值溪水為災○乃人鑒於粵港貢眼災會之具有成績○學校量身報學兩界○泡二十年○除上遠外○討先生董事會○在祖閣偽委員○整教育部立案○成立他教席之者○尚有育江之術深○朝報○與廣州之公評○新園華○現象○珠江，廣東，東方○起然○中和○南方○奇江，工商○南俊○民報等等另○尤相小說家言○旅行社會歡迎之○計有紫綠勤○駕當擊，大小俊合侍○新西遊記紀詞單行本○在編慕中○俊笑史，大風，閣脂虎，老娘奴上下集○大俊笑史○大

博於張○先生告退○旋該報為王所買○張憝留○旋訂聘先生仍留該報○熊先生不復留○惟失志於教育○猶自滋黃寶之戚正者○復致波○陳鞭南等○以先生為報界之戚正者○復致請開辦民報○及南後報○比龍街後粵○蔣君壽石某組討賊軍○功成某港○任奇港農事○期年○復創新江報○香港有說報○自與現象派○及同志辦中華女學○威聯先生任其事○黃車二君合料中華中學○四年後○等報偏輯○又與黃車二君合料中華中學○四年後○等報偏輯○又與現象派○及光中女小學○學務發達○一日千里○去年秋○史符黨四兄熱心華偽贊助○成立小學，及光中女小學○學務發達○一日千里○

於人○先生著為清鄉事忠告王骨料一篇○王不聽○故極為港僑所尊敬也○先生現育子女凡九人○

於人○先生著為清鄉事忠告王骨料一篇○王不聽○故極為港僑所尊敬也○先生現育子女凡九人○學界運動會委員○華商總會與孔聖會舉辦之壽辰○眼綜○及義學費花○等款○皆勢力以赴○兼宣傳部主任○出任中華教育會常委也○先生近倘各社區志盧深惑○待人接物○莫不出於至誠○錢酱慈善社宣傳部主任○全港故牂鄉事忠告王骨料一篇○王不

Mr. WONG YAN CHING.

Mr. Wong Yan Ching was born in Ko Iu District of Kwangtung province in 1892. He was first educated in the King's College Hongkong and then in the Queen's College. Later he was transferred to study in the Kwangtung Provincial Higher Normal College, Canton. After graduation he was for some time the compradore of a foreign firm Hongkong.

As he was a faithful follower of the late Dr. Sun Yat Sen, he made great efford in forming the Republic of China. He was either chief editor or associated editor at different times of the various Newspapers in Canton or in the Colony.

Besides being a well known journalist Mr. Wong is also an enthusiastic educator. He has been a teaching staff of many famous schools in this Island. About a decade ago he founded a girls' school in Kaingmoon and later he founded the Kwong Wah Middle school, the Kwang Wah elemantary school and the Kwang Wah Girls' school. He is now the principal of these schools.

He is noted for his activities in social and charitable affairs. He is member of the Committee of the Kowloon Chinese Educational Association and of the Chung Sing Benevolent Association. He has written many Novels which are so interest and are welcome by most of the young people, so he is also called as a Novelist.

The readers of his humourous novels may easily think that Mr. Wong must be a very funny man; but, on the contrary, he is a man of dignified appearance. He talks very little yet works very much. His sincerity and honesty endear him to all the people with whom he associates.

During the beginning of the establishment of the Republic of China most of the journalists of the Kuomintang, the national party, were appointed as officials in the Government; but Mr. Wong declined all the posts offerred to him. He does not mind very much about wealth and fame, but he likes literary works and teaching best.

生先成振郭

郭振成先生

郭振成先生，百粵之中山縣人也。年剛而立。為香港振成商科專門學院之創辦人。兼監督。

壯歲鷹。志不凡。幼肆業於德濱。每試輒冠其儔。

先生抱不屈不撓之精神。弗以曲高寡和而小餒其志。卒也期年而生徒大增。一九三一年，港中各大西報均為

九二八，漫遊華南北。從事攷察教育及實業。放其遠大銳利之眼光。深感商言人材之重要。於一九二九年春，在港舉辦振成打字專門學院於澳卑利街。斯時規模甚小。就學者僅六人。

文甾逸其打字技術之新奇與敏捷。衆時增設商科。積極擴充。無

如院舍辟拓。仍感不敷。再於一九三五年夏，而遷中環鐵崗現址。開辦迄今凡九載。培養商材泡千人。先生之素願能償。而先生之雄心未已也。教授態期速成。儀器亦顏完備。先生因見。乃遂實感街。象。欲為普及起。

之新奇與敏捷。後。復以學員畢業後。各商行機關。紛爭聘用。成績顯著。從遊日。

書。極得郎次之愛戴。其商學造詣。對於簿記等科。顏具心得。閒日，輒于，打字法。尤有神出鬼沒之妙。故能致授英倫商學會優等文憑。迨先港上各中西商行委辦。年任及冠已也。

即任某大洋行司理。行內職員逾二百。奉命於社會工作。素感興趣。精明能幹。且和藹可親。審當各社團委辦。對維護。吳藪拉稅。足見其多藝多才矣。公元一

Mr. KWOK CHUN SHING.
A.A., A.R.I.P.H., F.COM.SC.A., F.C.I.

Mr. Kwok is a native of Chungshan District, Kwangtung Province, who is the Founder & Director of the Chun-Shing Institute of Commerce, Hongkong. Having obtained a fair knowledge at his town, he proceeded to Shanghai and continued his studies in the Ling Nam College, where he stayed until was graduated.

He began his commercial career in a famous business concern in Shanghai. Late in 1928, he had a tour throughout North and South China to investigate education and industry. Realising the depression of trade would soon be spread to the Orient, Mr. Kwok, since that time, had a firm decision to establish an institute of commercial subjects, where pupils may be trained with a technical profession before they start to face the depression.

In 1929, he established the Chun-Shing Institute of Commerce in Hongkong. At the beginning, he was little sympathized by the public and he had but six students. This weak start would have disappointed most people. But Mr. Kwok had the optimistic foresight that he could not fail if he tried hard. So he did, notwithstanding bad circumstances and the handful number of students. In the following year, the number of students increased rapidly and at present the institute is considered to be one of the up-to-date Commercial Institutes in the Colony, and its testimonials are well recognised amongst local banking and business concerns.

Mr. Kwok Chun Shing is also deeply interested in the social affairs and is now holding various positions in different Associations of the Colony.

生先海輯譚

譚輯海先生

夫功名富貴○固宜炫赫一時○而忠孝廉節○尤應流芳百世○譚輯海先生○事親孝○與士信○臨財廉○取予義○此其犖

生亦善書○世以小歐稱○且楷行篆隸○學寫大字○蝇頭小楷○無所不能○有索書者○咸忻然許之○絕未經潤面○曾不靳惜○蓋先生素性恬淡○薄榮利○凡見惡求者○龍利物濟人○有任俠風○凡有急者○必百計應之○故人皆顧讒荊○先生少西

犖之所以被徵西列於是書也○先生乃順德龍山人○其尊甫藻川孝廉○為朱九江先生弟子○素有理學名○先生學其淵源○牲尤孝友○生平非先王之言不敢言○非先王之行不敢行○方弱冠已以「道學」見稱於卿黨○又其尊甫素工八法○而先八人。

不殉力以赴○至今桑梓樂道之○先生又曾寧嶺南學校教席○桃李遍於門下○近歲偕寫香江○所交者皆名流雅士○其貽蘭蕙之校契歟○淑配盧氏○有銀行之溫恭有禮○勤儉持家○井井不紊○生子女

避八桂
陽朔平
樂○山
水波連
採索疾
十年○
光緒末
束歸○
肩荷地
方公益
慈善事
業○歷

Mr. TAM SHIU HOI.

Mr. Tam is a native of Lung-shan District, Kwangtung Province. He is prominent not for his position but for his high learning in Chinese and great virtue in old Chinese Style.

His father was a learned man and had obtained the scholastic degree of How Lian. Mr. Tam inherits the gift of talents from his father. He showed his conscientiousness in his studies when he was quite young. He had obtained a good knowledge of Chinese literature before he started his business career.

He was a teaching staff in the Ling Nam University, and at present he is a staff of Messrs. Ts'o & Hogson, a famous firm of solicitors in the Colony.

Mr. Tam is a man of broad sympathy. He is ready to give assistance whenever he is asked to. Besides, he has partaken many social and charitably affairs in his native town and in Hongkong.

Mr. Tam has eight chidren and all of them acquire a thorough education.

關心馬醫師

關心馬先生

關景良醫師。字心馬。粵之番禺西塱村人也。年近古稀。本港西醫之老前輩也。乃祖尤著公。自闢港使來此間營銀業。至父元昌公。為港粵牙科醫師之先進。先生初讀於拔萃書室。至一八八七年。乃攻醫學於雅麗氏醫院。附設之香港華人西醫學堂。時掌教席者。為西人白德力孟及。唐士嘉德利。賀爾瑪。威原容諸醫生。在故校同學者。為孫總理逸仙。陳公少白。

不聞其參預日。先生性孝。慈命致違。（太夫人蔡氏。諳英文。在雅麗氏醫院曾通事。待人和藹。有大眾慈母之稱。習聞孫總理革命言論。復見前來與孫陳容談者。如尤少紈王孟琴與簡楊鶴齡楊衢雲諸人。均以捕滿為己任。惟事不成而禍及也。約束先生。惟恐不謹。）且救氏於水深火熱之中。與沽人於痛苦呻吟之下。道韓其西而功同也。先生於一九〇三年學成。翌年服務於邯打賞醫院。當軍院發

聘之。四國往江陰沿江砲台總醫官。坪聯四載。至一九一一年間世。先生淡泊名利。泡歷三十有七年矣。先生曾與孫總理為摯交也。先生少紈楊鶴齡四人。在雅麗氏醫院三樓相對。同榻一影。時鶴齡模樣。同攝一影。逃清光緒十三年九月初六日也。即公元一八八七年十月十日也。惟其心致志於本業。民國成立以來。未嘗名於仕版。惟恥最喜。影片在復幅。）先生對於本港社團商業。亦肯致

力。嘗連任華商會所主席。暨奇港油蔴地小輪公司主席等職。現仍任華商會所值理。奇港油蔴地小物公司董事。甚有聲絕。于淑配江氏恩梅。任吉隆坡廣盆銀行董事。供職本港無線電台。克我首都紅十字會醫官。榮譽。星崇坡棠商。榮賢。胃腎于奇港大學。榮展。攻讀于英華書院。榮社。卧棠于培正分校。榮元。女慈馨。遠林慈珍。慈莊。讀於米利厚書院。讀於小學。女慈馨。遠林慈珍。慈莊。讀於米利厚書院。任民生中學教員。

江君英華。劉君泅楷等三十餘人。先生與孫總理同一宿舍。共晨夕者凡五年。極相友善。理舉所業。即出而致力革命。盡畢書楷用具。以贈先生。或曰。先生為恩怨極新之人物。觀其與陳君于袁。陳君賓東。登起剪髮不易服會。早在民國紀元前兩年。（即滿清宣統二年冬月初三。假座華商會所舉行。是日聘定以關西樂隊百廿人奏樂行禮。敦請六老人為公証。到會者五六百人。禮成谷會。並遊行本港各馬路。故會成立紀念影片在復幅。）何以照次革命

Dr. K. L. KWAN SUN-IN.

Dr. K. L. Kwan Sun-in has the distinction of being the Chinese Medical practitioner of longest standing in the Colony. He received his English education at the Diocesan school and was the second graduate of the Hongkong college of Medicine. In 1893 he was appointed house Surgeon to the Nethersole Hospital and in 1907 he entered the service of the Chinese Government at Nanking as an Army Surgeon for three years. Dr. Kwan returned to Hongkong and commenced private practice in 1911. He was chairman of the Chinese Club Hongkong in 1921-1922 and 1935-1936 and Chairman of the Yaumati Ferry Company 1933-1935.

Here the author must mention that Dr. Kwan was a schoolmate and a roommate of the late Dr. Sun Yat Sen, the founder of the Republic of China. Dr. Kwan lived with this late great revolutionist at the same room in the dormatory of the Medical College for a period of five years. In the next page we can find a picture of five persons who are the late Dr. Sun Yat Sen, the late Mr. Yau Lit, the late Mr. Chan Shiu Park, the Late Mr. Young Hock Ling and Dr. Kwan. This photograph was taken on the front of the second floor of the Alice Memorial Hospital Hongkong.

Being a roommate of the late great revolutionist Dr. Kwan had an intense hatred of the cue which was a special token of the Manchurians who reigned over the Chinese empire at that time. He originated "the League of Cue cutting but dress remaining unchanged" in November 1909 in the Chinese Club. The Late Mr. Kwan Yuan Chong, father of Dr. Kwan, was the first man to cut his own cue on that day and more than five hundred men followed. On the next page there is a picture of the important members of the league at that time.

THIS PICTURE WAS TAKEN IN OCTOBER 1888 ON THE FRONT OF THE SECOND FLOOR OF THE ALICE MEMORIAL HOSPITAL HONGKONG.

斯照展片，為心馬先生所珍藏，編者以此中人物，一斤為革命元勳，關係民國史實，鏡有價值，特商借刊之，

前排自右至左為尤公少紈，陳公少白，孫總理中山，楊公鶴齡，復排為闗先生心焉，

DR. KWAN SUN-IN.
THE LATE MESSRS. YOUNG HOCK LING, SUN YAT SEN, CHAN SHIU PARK, AND YAU LIT.

剪髮不易服會成立紀念

導團中興之前表也。

贊成人為王元琛，闗元昌，吳秋湘，胡禮垣，溫清溪，區鳳墀，六老。實我挷復後之光磐。

此會港准當地政府設立。於宣統二年冬月初九日。假座本港大道中六四號二樓華商會所開業。贊起人為闗心焉，陳寶東，陳子農三君。

<table>
<tr><td>某君</td><td>陳寶東</td><td>闗心馬</td><td>黃江波</td><td>陳子裴</td><td>曾李彭</td><td>某君</td><td>郭之翼</td></tr>
<tr><td>胡禮垣</td><td>闗元昌</td><td>王元琛</td><td>吳秋湘</td><td>溫清溪</td><td>區鳳墀</td></tr>
<tr><td>(垣錦律師之郎父)</td><td>(心馬醫生之父)</td><td>(宪忠博士之祖)</td><td>(天保醫生之父)</td><td>(宋先生之父)</td><td>(斯港醫生之父)</td></tr>
</table>

THIS IS A PICTURE OF "THE LEAGUE OF CUE CUTTING BUT DRESS REMAINING UNCHANGED" WHICH WAS ORGANIZED IN NOVEMBER 1909 BY DR. KWAN SUN-IN.

(98)

復排 前排

闡潛德之幽光

盧伯禎題

香港已故華人
名人史畧

何啓爵士

THE LATE SIR HO KAI

○何啓爵士○科原百母樓西○於公元一八五九年○生於香港○乃此間設有學問及最令人愛戴之已故聞人也○幼英俊不凡○曾肄業本港官立中

學○注復到理○數年肆讀○狀死其習○遠程故而與松者○必先貢以大義○從俗代為和解○故得衆數十命○仿兩利清夷也○爵士生平於心社會○務於設持○无政府機制○華僑因世故不以影劇之任相推○或名巻之後見后○雁○爾不以設劇之任相推○或名巻之後見后○座

央書院○精長○爲刑壯志○貧笈英倫○先進巴盧麻學校政設○組入阿城旬大學習醫○貸既隨大學與科學士○及外科研士而學位○富得有英雄貴族刑蠶名雅麗者○定為高才○夫不以其爲貴

八八二年始○政款大律師案○彼持躬公正原潔○常謂爲富不仁○爲仁不富○遇兄弟世庄盛名之雅麗氏○吳院也○爵士自榮退時○以醫閉世○自一交港府○廷一士德延名立夫○公餘復從事著述○計刊行者有『中國之訴論』『賠與祝』『中國基礎與改革』『致廣州稅務司赫博士之中國地稅及陸海軍計劃書書信』『原有君政見之評論』『中國政革之進步論』等文○及與英國巴公爵討論開放門戸之女函○與翰先生討論養護之公開畵件字○爰有心人也○爵士共生兄女十二人○于名水茂○水元○水亨○水利○水良○水魚○水樹○女名金○玉○珠○錫○鈿○玉苑○讀于港大學○保寶官司學○水貞○當我到三連教訓恩養束之原○任外交部次女婚洛開監時○

士天才活溌○不宜以醫自固○勤其政習申轉之學○欲開以身相勗○爵士可其請○即進英國林肯法科院○努力精研○卒後故院高級法律學士資格○而與雅麗熱成伉儷焉○一八八一年○爵士孚其新婚夫人返港○尋肯一女○不幸夭折○○夫人傷之○不久亦棄世○○爵士遂其遺爲採八年制者不同○人以其成功速○多樂就之○教育司檢查○其學級採六年制○校以（二九。等判科聖士提反書院○以保存祖國之禮敎文化爲目標○爲華人唯一獨立敎育機關○不愛當地○爵士選定遠爲一八九二年○與廷爲妃爵士勤前○校以（二九。（二勛章○一九一○年○復錫以爵士榮街○爵士德延名立夫○公餘復從事著述○

色人種○而有所茶等○屢向之表示慇慰○且以賢士天才活溌○不宜以醫自固○勤其政習申轉功善俱○又爵士於任華人代表時○曾與曾苦无閒華人者○亦悉以諭之○其溝通覧方脈膜○厥十年○不特徇肥唯其馬苣是照○即港府遇有事充保良○圍防，太平，三局神士○定例，議政色人種○而有所茶等○屢向之表示慇慰○且以賢，兩局議員，束華醫院顧問董事等○在港垂三

THE LATE SIR HO KAI.—C.M.G., J.P., M.B., C.M., KT.

Among the Chinese there are many who have profited by a thoroughly sound and high-class European education, but there are few who have had a more education, but there are few who have had a more distinguished academical career, or who have used their advantages to better purpose than the late Sir Ho Kai.

Born at Hongkong in 1859, he was the fourth son of the late Rev. Ho Tsun Shin, of the London Missionary Society. He was educated at the Government Central School in Hongkong and subsequently in England at Palmer House School, Margate; at Aberdeen University, at St. Thomas' Medical and Surgical College, and at Lincoln's Inn. He took the degrees of M.B., C.M., Aberdeen. Then he became a member of the Royal College of Surgeons, England, and was Senior Equity Scholar, Lincoln's Inn, in 1881. Upon returning to the Colony he started to practise medicine but found that the Chinese were not yet prepared to avail themselves of Western treatment unless it was offered free. Sir Ho Kai therefore presented the Colony with the Alice Memorial Hospital, named after his late wife, Alice, eldest daughter of the late Mr. John Walkden, of Blackheath. Sir Ho Kai then commenced practice as a barrister-at-law, and he was so engaged since 1882. He served as a member of the Sanitary Board for over ten years and on the Public Works Committee for five years. He was a Senior Non-official member of the Legislative Council, and was for many years a member of the following public institutions:—The Standing Law Committee; the Examination Board; the Medical Board; the Po Leung Kuk Committee; District Watchmen's Committee; the Governing Body of the Free Hospitals; the Tung Wah Hospital Advisory Committee; the Governing Body of Queen's College; the qualified Architect's Advisory Board; the Interpretation Committee and the Advisory Committee of the Hongkong Technical Institute; and Rector's Assessor of the Hongkong College of Medicine of which he was one of the founders. In short it may be said that he had the distinction of serving on the Committee of almost every public board appointed during his last twenty-five years; and that his time was always given ungrudgingly in the public service no matter at what sacrifice to his own interests as a professional man. For upward of twenty-six years he was continuously resident in the Colony; for twenty-six years he was a Justice of the Peace for Hongkong and for three terms (eighteen years) represented the Chinese community on the Legislative Council. Hence it was not a matter for surprise that he was looked to by his fellow countrymen for advice in their dealings with the Government, and was also often consulted by the Government in their transactions with the Chinese community. On the occasion of both visits of the Duke and Duchess of Connaught and of Prince Arthur to the Colony, he received and welcomed their Royal Highnesses on behalf of the Chinese and in recognition of his many public works and services he was created as C. M. G. in 1892. He was conferred with the honour of Sir in 1910. Among his publications are:—"A Critical Essay on China"; "The Sleep and Awakening"; a letter addressed to Lord Charles Beresford on "The Open Door"; "An Open letter to John Bull on the Boxer Rising"; articles on Sir Robert Harts' Memorandum on the Land Tax of China and his army and navy scheme, 1904; the "Foundation of Reformation in China"; criticisms of the views of Kang Yau Wei, 1898; criticisms of the views of Viceroy Chang Chi Tung, especially on his recent work, "Encouragement to Learning", 1899; Persons responsible for Reformation in China; and Two Critical Essays on the Progress of Reformation in China.

Died in 1914 at the age of Fifty nine. At his funeral thousands of persons followed his remains to the cemetery and many social organizations held a memorial service in honour of him, showing how many lives he touched.

韋寶珊爵士

韋玉爵士，字寶珊。粵之中山縣。於公元一
八四九年。生於香港。父韞光。歷任本港有利

THE LATE SIR WEI YUK, BOSHEN.

時打學校。越年。轉進蘇格蘭大衆書院。僑業
四歲。成績優異。師友敬。剞後進求人士投
考該書院者。皆蒙青睞。寶爵士曾給該院一好
印象故也。爵士爲我國留學歐西之第一人。於

相將請充名譽或重要職位。莅署畢其願。著者述
之。一八八一年。爲東華醫院首總理。一八八
三年。爲太平局紳。一八九三年。爲定例
局議員（此局乃由爵士倡辦者）一八六六年。爲定例
局議員。一九〇八年九月。晉授英國 O M G 勳
章。一九一一年。英廷以其勤績殊錄。錫以爵
士榮銜。又爵士卒年已有從九龍築鐵路至廣州
直達北京之獻議。惜清廷官吏不之計。刷廣九
鐵路興築。實與其原定計劃一部份相同。今中
英政府有廣九粵漢兩路接枕之磋商。將屆實現
○此後遠抵北平。當非致事。豈非爵士龍洞燭
先機之明証耶。爵士於一八七二年。娶前本港
定例局議員黃勝之長女爲室。（黃勝字平甫，
本港定例局議員華人議員之第二人。）爵士有第二

追悼。即進有利銀
行供職。屑助乃父
。以學問及才幹兼
優。至爲富華人所
器重。至一八七九年
。其父棄世。故行
倚之史服。一八八
二年。遂使繼父職
。而�M0爲華總理

○計其父連續與故行發生關係者。爵士迨六十
年。可謂勤將矣。而勇於服務。廉不貲
除銀行本職外。凡港中社會公益善舉。靡不贊
助。故政府信任。備肥受戴。各機關團體。爭
律耶。○四安。田培。均藩於法學。爲當時港中著名

銀行華總理。爵士出自富裕家庭。總角受書。
名僑身席。某甫十歲。漢學功深。繼進本港官
立中央書院身習英文。融會新舊文化。學後悉
形豐富。年十八。欲浪衆風。赴英肄業於利些

THE LATE SIR WEI YUK, BOSHEN C.M.G., J. P., Kt.

As a conscientious worker on behalf of the Chinese community of Hongkong, and as a man who did a great deal to produce the good relations existing between the Government and the Chinese, the late Sir Wei Yuk's name deserved to be specially remembered by all section of society in the Colony. On many occasions he was of invaluable assistance to the officials and his counsel was largely instrumental, notably at times of riots and strikes during the past half of a century. In settling matters amicably before they assumed the serious proportions which they threatened to do in several instances. Sir Wei Yuk was a Cantonese (Chungshan District), born in Hongkong in 1849, and came of excellent family. His father, the late Mr. Wei Kwong, was a well-known banker, and formerly compradore to the Chartered Mercantile Bank of India, London, and China, in Hongkong.

After ten years' study of Chinese, under private tutors, Sir Wei Yuk commenced his English education at the Government Central School, under the late Dr. Frederick Stewart, LL.D., and in 1867, at the age of eighteen years, he proceeded to England and attended the Leicester Stoneygate School for twelve months. In 1868 he went to Scotland and studied for four years at the Dollar Institution. He soon became a favourite with both masters and fellow pupils, and the impression regarding his nationality that he made and left behind him became a tradition in the school, ensuring to others from the Far East a most friendly reception at that institution. The late Sir Wei Yuk was one of the first Chinese to go abroad for Western education. On his return to the East in 1872, after a European tour, he entered the service of the Chartered Mercantile Bank of India, London, and China (now the Mercantile Bank of India, Limited) in Hongkong, and on the death of his father, in 1879, he (after a temporary retirement, according to Chinese custom) took up the vacant position of compradore. Sir Wei Yuk and his father served the bank for fifty-three years in Hong Kong—that is to say, since it was first opened.

In 1883, the late Sir Wei Yuk was appointed a Justice of the Peace, and, in 1896, became an unofficial member (representing the Chinese community) of the Hongkong Legislative Council. He worked in the greatest harmony with his colleague, the late Sir Ho Kai, C.M.G., M.B., Kt. and while not noted for long speeches, was regarded as an invaluable adviser in connection with all legislation in any way touching the interests of his fellow countrymen. In many other capacities also he had striven for the public good. He held numerous appointments, and served on may committees, for when his help was required for the furtherance of the public weal it was never withheld. It is impossible to give a complete list of his appointments in a brief biographical sketch such as is here essayed, but a few of his appointments may be mentioned. He was chairman of the Tung Wah Hospital (Hongkong's leading Chinese charitable insitution), 1881-83 and 1888-90; a permanent member of the committee of the Po Leung Kuk for the protection of destitute women and children (of which he was one of the founders) since 1893; a permanent member of the Hongkong District Watchmen's Committee (which was formed on his suggestion); and a member of the Standing Law Committee since 1896.

Moreover, he served on all the commissions appointed by the Government to inquire into matters affecting the Chinese since the commencement of his public career. The Chinese Government was indebted to him in no small degree for the assistance he rendered in bringing to justice Chinese criminals who had fled from Chinese territory to Hongkong and elsewhere. For the services which he rendered during the plague epidemic of 1894, the general public of Hong Kong presented him with a gold medal and a letter of thanks, while the Chinese community also addressed to him a letter of thanks.

Sir Wei Yuk may be regarded as the father of the Sanitary Board. For many years, previous to the formation of the present body, he took greatest interest in sanitary matters, and he was the friend and adviser of Professor Chadwick when that well-known authority visited the Colony to report on the sanitary condition of the city of Victoria.

He suggested the construction of a railway from Kowloon to Canton, and thence to Peking. He spent large sum in furtherance of the scheme which failed however, owing to the obstacles placed in its way by Chinese officials, who at that time strenuously opposed the introduction of anything from the West. During the past decade, however, several lines of railway were constructed, between the places named, and they follow closely Sir Wei Yuk's original plans.

The Honour of Knighthood was conferred upon him by the British Empire in 1910.

香港華人名人史略（一九三七）

劉公鑄伯

THE LATE HON. MR. LAU CHU PAR.

鑄伯劉公○寶安縣人○性聰穎○甫七歲○即就學○以家貧○肄業於西營盤之富義學○苦讀不報○試輒列前茅○堅卻膏火○十二歲長父○賴母勤事女紅○以供俯膌○未幾○兼習旁行文○益自刻苦○獲獎免費生○捷叙進皇仁書院○

○學益大進○試輒獲獎金○學費衣履○皆有以自給○十七歲畢業○獻身社會○初浮沉于士商者十年○而學行言論○已懇懇具於衆○中西人士○咸倚重之○每遇踟組○輒不煩其心力○為屢任地方委職○人數十計○為傷肥連福○當其被選為東華醫院總理也○同時被任為香港清淨局員○會役甚○遇病者○即昇入醫院○療與醫

精研政治法律○故於立法行政○多所獻替○壓任凡九年○傷肥以公一言而殘安居樂業者不復○吏債敫數○局外人固不盡知之也○公卒生長香江○學成後囘未嘗一日忘祖國○遂清戊子○應台灣巡撫劉中丞之聘○任淡水西學堂教席○兼洋務委員○越二年○港充殖教員○乙巳○應北洋大臣楊制府之招○任漁家紹科○徒以當時國

○兩衛生局，巡警局○皆資助理○聽夕勤勞督察○遠病者○即昇入醫院○療與醫

遠○入者多死○欲速內地○又為法令所禁○且惠疫之家○例須燻洗○鄰遂十餘戶○家具擡殘○不可以日○居民民援○至有景庇不顧○伺陳逃去者○全港黃徭○如蛙蟹墓○伺報仕進○傌出亦何補○故終不願去鳴婷○非數時勢○傷出亦何補○故終不願去鳴婷○非數

○其以閒於港史○不與清淨局力爭○當黃洗時勢○傌出亦何補○故終不願去鳴婷○非數以是鳴高也○閒者雖其言○而元肓及雜史○益知其賢○遂權聘為綱同○公辦無官守言實○然為國致力○曾不少懈○如勸學也○（公與嘉道理醫生集資二十餘萬○設育才社於港澳粵○以培育華人子弟○廣州之有公立學校○自公始也○其後港大學等款遠七十餘萬○亦公贊助之力為多○）如徵教也○（公偏設義學三十餘所○以為發倦育孔聖會於香港○附設義學三十餘所○以為發倦倡孔教之地○就學者歲逾千人○海外之有孔聖會○亦自公始）○以興邦為主旨○論者謂其如何先務焉○公既完其國○尤愛其鄉○當廣九銀路改近其故里平湖○公請於粵省局○將原定路軌方挺慎初○於其地故車站○而路亦不紆○又鄉人稱便○鄉人稱使○困於重息○于女多沒為奴婢○公設恩賞局○儲賞出貸○農貧苦○時以于女質殘○困於重息○于女多沒為奴婢○公設恩賞局○儲賞出貸○農貧甚附○）一以興邦為主旨○論者謂其如何

局凡十二年○局例有不始定○漸復舊觀○公在便者○必娘理辦爭○學局員也○所以為華海諜者○益復富屬○遠革原晴不勝舉○此則其故著者也○當其被安居樂業○亦見○一如其在清淨局時○故華傷除受其福者○所阿附○斷然以風骨自於此閒利病附失○復背

○兩衛生局，巡警局○皆資助理○徒以當時國禍○公以義當指卷○以資銀仙○氏二○漢陽浮張兵其不煩力捐卷○以資銀仙○氏二○漢陽浮張兵莫不煩力捐卷○以資銀仙○氏二○漢陽浮張兵○實安兩會○廣華醫院等○其衆若中外凶災○所○樓經局○公立醫局○華商總會○來兗而會○成一模范村馬○其抱於鄉有如此者○其閒在○立工廠○建醫院○附以農林實業○規模粗具○公除陳省史○小試於其鄉○創市場○故學校江○學成後囘未嘗一日忘祖國○遂清戊子○應○寶安兩會○廣華醫院等○其衆若中外凶災○福○公以義當指卷○以資銀仙○氏二○漢陽浮張兵襦付災區○存活極衆○閒者嘉之○歐洲戰起

吾國參焉○公依國民外交之義○惬大有紐鈕關聯軍以飛機一架○乙則贈以紅十字庫托車一輛○而中英邦交○益加親睦○論者咸以為誼大誼云○公歷任治安局員○國防局員○公立醫局副局長○保良局副局長○東華醫院歷年顧問○保良局總理○撲童椅審查值理○衛生局則例審查員○裁倉借樍核值理○微收物料稅務用品值理○保壹工程師局員○法例審察員○英國欽設工藝進研究會會員○北帆鳥工藝製造會水道會員○華人水道境培幹事值理等○貪重事繁○心勞力瘁○其病站平伏於此矣○公性恬淡○徒以榮視故○納衆得問知○乸以到中丞表保加知府街○以道員候○乙卯順直賑捐出力○栴制肘表保○以有功民退加知盬運副街○貫換花剣○鼎荤徒○以有爲圜○奬給四等嘉禾章○袢晋給二等大紋嘉禾章二等寶光嘉禾章○以褒袋國內公債○以裹共○實給樂善好拖，慈公好義，等區額○以裹辦港事○奕善分紛○其延侍帑嘉其○許鈌給二等寶生○公著力摩事○猶念食貨者○圜之大命久不下○各一卷○士戌午春○海員罷工事起○鎮○公公力所事○先徒割社經好凡十有二○世界者○有自治須知○西檀須知○社會主義平首婦公主持於○治事之眼○亦問事蒿遂於刊行於倚海大局計○商民交困○華推公出任調停○公為華外亦多有不及知者○衆情不諛○致訟交集○迫事搜解○而公之心力益庠以至不起矣○公於士戌四月七日仙逝港寓○享壽五十有六○哲嗣四○長子德詩○現在本港寫有盛名○

THE LATE HON. Mr. LAU CHU PAR. J.P., C.M.G.

As the successful career of the Late Hon. Mr. Lau Chu Par may be an encouragement and an insperation to every poor youth, the author has endeavoured to collect the materials and write this biography.

The late Hon. Lau Chu Par was a native of the Bo On district in Kwangtung Province. He was born in Hongkong in 1856 and was gifted with a high talent for learning. As his parents were so poor, they were compelled to send their child to study in a free school in West Point. His father died, when he was only twelve years old. He had a very good mother who realized that a higher education was necessary to her child and tried her best to send him to the Queen's College.

As the late Hon. Mr. Lau was a good and obedient son, he understood that the school fee he paid was obtained by his mother's hand works, he made his hardest efford in studying. Consquently, he was always stood first in his class and was much praised by his teachers and school mates. The bounties and prizes he received every year from the college were sufficient to cover his school fee, and thus he lightened the burden of grief of his mother.

After he had been graduated from Queen's College at the age of seventeen, he began, at once, to give his efficient and trustworthy services to his community. He held many appointments and served on many committees. It is hard to give a complete list of them here. However, a few of important ones must be mentioned. He was chairman of the Tung Wah Hospital; Member of committee of Po Leung Kuk; Member of committee of the Hongkong District Watchmen; member of the Sanitary Board (Now Urban Council) and member of the legislative council of the Hongkong Government. He was also made as an official in the Ching Danasty.

He died in 1922 at the age of fifty six.

李公煜堂

THE LATE MR. LEE YOK TONG

李公煜堂○原籍粵東台山東坑○後遠居同邑西關隻龍舟里○幼研經史帖括之學○抱泉風破浪之志○年十八輟讀○附帆舶俗行○留心考察商務○往○孝及遠西富強之術○在香江小焉肆業○旁及遠西富強之術○在香江小焉肆業○

金利源水利源等藥材行○善於擇人任事○歲獲厚利○值清李甲午之役後○公深慨列強陵暴○華夏板蕩○益知復興之不容緩○遂所資經營工商業○如廣州電力公司○及機器麵粉公司○泰山源出入口貨莊等○事咸草創○艱於開始○成效斑斑未彰○而公志曾不稍餒○公又以保險事業效斑斑未彰○而公志曾不稍餒○公又以保險事業有裨民生○園人不之抹煞○時當母財外輸○漏卮實鉅○乃竹創香港聯益保險公司焉率○而

康年，聯泰，上海聯保，羊城各公司，踵其後○今仍與外商遞迴○抵抗其經濟侵署○他如寧陽鐵路公司○香港廣東銀行○四邑輪船公司○粵航輪船公司○安樂園食品公司○上海新新百貨公司○漢口穗豐紗業打包公司○杭州西冷飯店等○咸組手創○咸任督偏○均被推焉董事或主席○信乎其規模從心○斯輪老手○聲宏實大○闔堂煜然○公畢身處開園○兩目營八表○凡

○康年，聯泰，上海聯保，羊城各公司○踵其後○今仍與外商遞迴○抵抗其經濟侵署○他如寧陽鐵路公司○香港廣東銀行○四邑輪船公司○推○屢集義規復○未知所定○公披露肝膽○開陳利害○各償權人咸為之感動○復業之議遂決○而公竟棄是愛養成疾○至於不起○老成凋謝○國人咸其辰恩○公生平素性惻怛恭謙○言行不二○其待人也○恂恂如也○其處人也○介○俾而好施○樂以濟力○用之於公益教育慈善諸事業○如嶺南，執信，青年會，鋼紀慎○各學校○及廣州公醫院○南京日增○分售廣及中外○抵值百業凋敝○行務中○

風箏報國之志○乙巳○香華政府侮華工入口案○公憤國人咸咸加入同盟會○以制以制以制○其一○北平台山會館之哈爾濱廣東會館○台山男女青年會○奮有力焉○相與策到○香華生輕德○正焉社會人士所共聞共見者也○其於○卒成立十二條款○藥例○相與策到○約會○美商惠之○請和解○厄其何焉喉舌之中國報○兩年漏於危○公俱資承斜○自由，之請○出資承斜○馮國內橫閣園體充任要職○曹焉大元帥府參議○總統府參議○南京兩廣迎賓館○哈爾濱廣東會館○台山男女青年久○廣戍，廣州新軍起義○事敗○黨人焉遇者董事○中央財政委員會委員○廣東實業園所倜○泉以焉家○公又以舊業金利源藥料公於歐戰復興之努力○焉視察列強從事實展工商業焉業人集令中樞○自三月廿九日廣州一役至以而謀復興之勢力○周避廣東各國○曾著『九園遠民元園府成立○海內外軍需之出納○器械之赴日本美圖或香港廣州內地各學校籌業○國民避記』一書○用資園人傳誦○蓋欲茂國覺李之貯藏○皆焉金利源是賴○廣東光復○同志爭公於民國廿五年一月一日○享壽八十有五○終剩几十七八人○男女各半○男勸堂○環請出長財政司○時軍需孔亟○一夕之政府迺念前徽○於民國廿五年八月十四日明給心○老而益煜也○劉公生於民國紀元前六十年項○集款八十萬圓○士抛心勛○歡圖�歌績○在政府追念前徽○於廣東省台山各縣○李煜堂○撰裝斛之○照準於后○輸助革命○勒斛濟餉○焉策畫之時給○輸助濟餉○焉策畫之時給○以昭激勸○

任六月○以積勞引退○嗣後多致力於商務○偶厥平生○殊堪嘉尚○特趄給與獎斛○以昭激勸

香港・澳門雙城成長經典

THE LATE Mr. LEE YOK TONG.

The late Mr. Lee Yok Tong was a native of Toishan District, Kwangtung Province, born in 1851.

He obtained his education at a school in his native village and when he was eighteen years of age, he followed his kinsmen to America, where he started his commercial practice. When he had acquired sufficient experience, he came to Hongkong and established the Kum Lee Yuen and Wing Lee Yuen, dealing in Chinese drugs.

After the Chinese Fleet was absolutely annihiliated by the Japanese in 1894 the late Mr. Lee realized that it was difficult to restore the prosperity of our country besides the promotion of her industry and commerce. For this sake, he went to Canton and organized the Electrical Power Company; the Mechanical Flour Mill, and the Tai Sang Yuen Imports and Exports agent.

Later, he organized the Luen Yik Insurance Co., Ltd., in Hongkong. This is the first Chinese insurance enterprise in the Colony, and years later there are the Hong Lin Life Assurance Co., Ltd., the Luen Tai Insurance Co., Ltd., the Shanghai Fire and Marine Insurance Co., Ltd.; the Luen Po Insurance Co., Ltd.; and the Yeung Shing Insurance Co., Ltd., all of which are established with Chinese capital and are at present severe competitors of European insurance firms in Hongkong.

Besides the above mentioned, Mr. Lee is either a founder or a promoter of the following business firms:- The Ningyang Railway Co., Ltd; the bank of Canton; the Sze Yap Steamship Co., Ltd.; the Yuet Hong Steamship Co., Ltd.; the Sun Sun Universal Providers, Shanghai; The Shui Fung Cotton Packing Co., Hankow; and the Sze Lang Hotel, Hangchow.

Mr. Lee is a zealous nationalist. He joined in the national party long ago and rendered great assistance to the revolution of China.

In 1905, when the government of the United States of America announced the restriction of Chinese imigration into that country, a meeting was held in Hongkong by those prominent merchants who had close connection with the American trade to respond to this matter. Mr. Lee was appointed one of the committees of that assemblance. Consequently, the Americans were afraid of this resistance to justice, so the restriction was far less rigorous.

Before the establishment of the Chinese Republic, Chinese were divided into two parties. The nationalists who achieved the revolution on one side and those who plotted restoration of a monarchical government on the other. It happened that the China Post, which belonged to the nationalists, was endangered by the latter, and the situation was very hazardous. Mr. Lee undertook the enterprise and preserved the dorment force of the former.

At that time, the Ch'ing Dynasty Government had put a rigorous search on the nationalists, but Mr. Lee, who was one of the members, made his own shop, the Kum Lee Yuen Drug Store, a concentrating centre for his comrades so as to avoid the views of the Ching detectives.

When the Republic of China was just established, Mr. Lee was appointed as Treasurer of the Kwangtung Province. Mr. Lee, raised $800,000 in the shortest span of time for the purpose of supplying munition for the army. Six months later, he resigned from the post and came to Hongkong, where once more he set himself in the business sphere.

Mr. Lee was a man of broad sympathy, and every cause of good will finds him a willing supporter. He was in close connection with the following institutions:— The Lingnam University, Canton; the Chih Sin College, Canton; The Chinese Y.M.C.A., Canton; The Hong Kong Kong Kee Son School; the Public Hospital, Canton; the Kwong Shui Hospital, Canton; the Liang Kwang Association, Nanking; the Cantonese Guild, Harbin; The Y.M.C.A. and Y.W.C.A., Toishan; and the Toishan Chamber of Commerce, Peiping.

Mr. Lee was a counsellor of the Commander-in-chief, China; counsellor of the President, China; Director of the Industry Guild, Canton; Committee of the Board of Finance, Nanking; and member of the Chinese National Calamity Convention.

Mr. Lee had a tour around the Western countries and had written a book entitled "A travel over nine nations."

Mr. Lee died on January 1st. 1936, with a ripe old age of eighty-five. He had eighteen children and all of them are well educated. Mr. Lee Chi Chung, his eldest son, is the General Manager of the Shanghai Fire and Marine Insurance Co., Hongkong.

簡公耀初

THE LATE MR. KAN YEW CHO

竊太上不朽○立德，立功，立言○天下達尊○爵一，德一，齒一○尙一○仕宦而至將相○至公卿○意者尚已○而生前則榮○歿則已焉○惟簡公耀初○手澤難毀○國人皆以富致富○等卜式之輸財○國人皆曰賢○交游拓其信○億則屢中而貨殖○愛其所親可謂仁○其此

雄才○微爲戲行○宜必邦三公位○字萬鎭祿○勒請舞鼎○著之折肱○方足以樹之風聲○昭茲來許哉○然則將其生平○撰成得筈○宜惟德之被及社會者深○抑亦義之表指善行者宜也○自古其雄姻起○多由貧賤○衆傑樹立○半出寒微○勝爲之魚鹽○傅說之版築○固無論已○近或起家寒素○生擁厚封○瞻諸族人而迹舊而無遺○文正義田○自官失其取○未發麻摄魅○就必數路其巢穴○先生之志碩樓○守錢虜之○往往殺之○先生之少也○家徒四壁○

臣浸○乙卯水災○海成澤國○吳占魚蟹○詎免鴻嗷○先生瘵懷絮屈○批撥千章○財用匱詘其多塞○爲一鄉謀桑田之草圍○以鸠力障杯里之安危○用能慶安集於秋潦○派怨咨於善冊○此其一也○二日衛鄉閭○往行之害○甚於天災○卽民陷其情○先生之瓴樓○以杜奸完之前○蚨寰

門不容車○旣靲錫彔○爲陸烏卷○年十七○籍燔揀青火之資○爲家墅束備之奉○軋軋紡車之響○濛濛依然○落葉添薪○古桃是仰○機○二截○江革以行檐供母○亦足悲已趟○厚澄影○圖畫依然○遭逢如此○耐卒耳○也才高挾举○街擅莑等○故卒載緒○指揮不凑○惟簡公耀初○手澤難毀○解說史料於餅铋○○于顗毀毁○國人皆曰賢○交游拓其信○億則屢中而貨殖○愛其所親可謂仁○其此

水興街○簽報之始○銳意遠征○長袖之工多○財善舞○又復寸獻拓○器讓宏通○香海一島○圈十二年○壓任香港橘民

以助守望之力○故圍墙○以杜奸宄之前○蚨寰

THE LATE Mr. KAN YEW CHO.

The late Mr. Kan was a native of Nam-hoi District, Kwangtung Proivnce, where he was born in 1867. He was bred up in a poor family which could scarcely afford him a thorough education. His father died when he was yet an infant and it was his mother who went through hard and soft to rear him up. It would be surprised to learn that the late Mr. Kan received no other higher eduation than his homely tuition when he was young, yet he could become a rich merchant later. When he was seventeen years of age he was sent by his relations to go to school. It spite of the short span of two years in school, he obtained a fair knowledge in writing and counting. Before he was known to his community he had been an apprentice in Canton, and through his frugality he could accumulate a little savings.

In 1891, in partnership with a kinsman, Mr. Kan established a lumber firm in Canton under the name of Wing Cheong. Through his able management and foresight, this shop soon prospered to such an extend as enabled him to initiate a firm of his own in Hongkong. This ambitious and industrious man worked on energetically and before his death in 1936, he owned nine lumber shops and five go-downs, and was considered to be one of the most influential lumber magnates in Hongkong.

In his life there were many good deportments and charitable deeds and the following descriptions are the most popular ones. First of all is that he was generous in contributing a large amount of money to build a dike in his native village, which is located on the bank of a river and is often threatened by floods. Secondly, about half of a century ago, his village was threatened by bandits who used to rob and made disorder every now and then. The late Mr. Kan gave his own money to build many ramparts and earthworks to resist the robbers. Therefore, though all the neighbouring villages were deeply afflicted by the outlaws, Mr. Kan's village was always in the safest situation.

Lastly, the late Mr. Kan paid much attention to education. He spent considerable time and money for the purpose. In 1910 he was a director of the Kok Man School, and in 1935, just a year before his death, he founded a school in his native village with his own means.

Commercially, Mr. Kan was a committee of the Chinese Chamber of Commerce, Hongkong; Chairman of the Lumber Merchants' Association; President of the Tung Wah, Kwong Wah and Tung Wah East Hospitals; and committee of the Nam-hoi Chamber of Commerce, Hongkong.

馮公平山

馮平山先生，諱朝安。廣東新會縣人。以商業起家。生平樂善好施。尤熱心捐財興學。近世言慈善者必稱之。少讀書於家。年十六。景儔業商。從其亨父之遺蔭。既壯有室。其地有資人業茶。見先生軀俊偉。計為大器。欲以其女為妻。並持其產鉅萬治奩具。先生婉詞謝之

THE LATE MR. FUNG PING SHAN

者甚泉。後居香港。每年先與群善事業。遂被選為廣東華醫院首總理。及永遠顧問。保良局首總理。團防局紳董。太平紳士。香港大學永遠校董等職。初先生經理東華醫院時。為院廣闢財源。繁其彩票。值歲丑軍興。香港金融缺。醫院有積存之資。先生游於歐美。考察商業。旁及教育之事。見吾國教育。多不如人。貢獻所得。於銀號卽須提取。先生慨卽提款。一提存款。泉集卽須提取。先生慨卽提款。必力開商場競融。勸以穿起鈤鑼。銀業益濫蒼涼。乃以其產業文旅為質。保不提金。銀市卒賴以安。自是益為富

大學經費。大學圖書館建築及開辦費。兒童工藝院建築費。曾出銀資。練紀相助。而景堂圖書館。為紀念其先人者。題榜尤大。景堂其先德字也。計先生用於教育之費。凡百餘萬金。其義舉殊星小款。尚不與焉。先生游於歐美。考察商業。旁及教育之事。見吾國教育。多不如人。貢獻所得。故備辦理。至其言行。尤堪矜式。先生幼時。於先世遺產。少嘗過問。實回。人能於分占財物時。視為父母多生幾子。於有產出資時。則必無爭執。又揣處世為人。第一不可欺人。第二不可為人欺。又以古人格言。乃橫學經驗之語。斟事不眠。當其七十生辰時。親友捐款於慈善事業者。不多課也。當其七十生辰時。親友賀者。以現金。故其遇事堅定。見全蘭生先生所釋格言聯雙乙。喜其簡要。恆記誦其語。以行事己之則。人之一力。往往以一人之力成泉。其本格言曰。律身行己。恃取而常懼之。與人謀和。以視賀者。乃舉年謀議英。就之成泉。人智謂律身行己。恃取而常懼之。先生就亦勇於任事。往往以一人之力成泉。其本蔣新會書院。白沙公園之建築。象山公園之建築。象

成之。廣東政府當軸闢先生名。倭欲聘為顧問。先生諍不習為政。均不受命。先生少時好學賴先生之力約地人士所推重。多每舉辦公益。必請先生與成之。於其邑城附立貧民義塾。科教育事業。於其邑城附立貧民義塾。學校。景堂圖書館。平山小學。及捐建蓮勸場孔聖會中學。香港商總會圖書館。其輪財而不親其事者。於廣東高等師範附屬小學校建築云。旅港新會商會之成立。多賴先生之力約為有勸其兼營之。先生不為勁。光緒士辰年。先生至港數載。愛育善堂。及各善院紳董。及其各院紳童。乙巳先歲大歉。泉拯先生往港縣來。先生誠篤。先與米。不卽索值。做氏料以存活

費。香港大學堂基本金。與圖書樓縣書費。漢文云。生恐家庭紛多故。亦不育。五南後而其子汝材。亦早天。側室李氏小。生於汝桃村。生五子。生汝材氏。德配李氏。生於汝桃。不育。五南後而其子汝材。亦早天。側室鄭氏。生女八人。長子慶流亦泉華。卒業於香港大文科。生子慶瞞。廣州中大附中小學開會。先生亦不育。其子汝材。亦早天。側室鄭氏。廣州中大附中小學開會。先生卒於港寓。以自壽年七十有二。中外人士。民國念五年六月十九日。聞先生之其卒於港寓。以自壽年七十有二。中外人士。民國念五年六月十九日。聞先生之其不悒悒。瞑目。享壽七十有二。中外人士。恩請患以現金。求學中。歧疏異子。常人。諸子幼承庭訓。克承亦蒸蒸。為世所重。稽考之家。成下其必昌大

○清光緒癸未。丁外艱歸。服闋。以選羅商業。未足發展所長。乃北湖大江。過武漢。踰三峽。以入巴蜀。每歸供采辦剝之理。以此優有藏貨。時蜀商多以運殖片致富之道。以此優有藏貨。時蜀商多以運殖片致富。有勁其兼營之。先生不為勁。光緒士辰先生至港數載。任方便醫院。及各善院紳董。歲大歉。泉拯先生往港縣來。先生誠篤。先與米。不卽索值。做氏料以存活

香港・澳門雙城成長經典

124

THE LATE Mr. FUNG PING SHAN, J.P.

The Late Mr. Fung Ping Shan was one of the most prominent Chinese merchants in Hongkong. He was born in 1860 in the District of Sun-Wui, Kwangtung Province. In his early youth Mr. Fung was deprived of the opportunity of completing his education on account of poverty, and consequently, when he was only fifteen, he followed his uncle to Siam where he started his business career.

It was some years after that he returned to China to be married, and after his marriage he returned to Siam to continue his business. While in Siam he came in close contact with a certain rich merchant who took a ready fancy to him, deciding to betroth his daughter to him, with the promise of the rich dowry. This generous offer, however, Mr. Fung declined without hesitation.

In 1882 Mr. Fung's father died, and he returned at once to China to attend the funeral. Shortly afterwards, he went to the Szechuen Province, where he started a business of his own, dealing principally in Chinese drugs.

After making a fortune, he returned to Canton in 1891, and was at once elected Director of the well-known Fong Pin Hospital, and many other charitable institutions. In 1904 there occured a severe famine in Canton, whereupon Mr. Fung, amongst a number of other philanthropists, was asked to deputise for the Hospital and proceed to Hong Kong to purchase rice, which would be distributed among the sufferers. The rice was purchased, but the necessary fund was not fully subscribed in time. Yet the rice merchants trusted Mr. Fung and delivered the rice to Canton without delay, thus saving many lives from the disaster.

A few years later, when he settled down in Hongkong, Mr. Fung served on several occasions as Chairman, Director and Adviser of the Tung Wah Hospital and Po Leung Kuk. He was an unofficial Justice of the Peace, a member of the District Watch Committee, Life Member of the Court of the University of Hongkong, permanent adviser of the Po Leung Kuk, and a life member of the Chinese Chamber of Commerce.

Himself a self-made man, Mr. Fung's great desire was that those who came after him should enjoy the opportunities that he had missed. He initiated Free Schools and Vocational Institutions both in his own town and in Hongkong. He gave generously to the building fund for the Higher Primary School of the Normal College in Canton; and in his native district he established the King Tong Library to the memory of his late father. He was mainly instrumental in the establishment of the Aberdeen Industrial School in Hongkong, towards which he donated $100,000.

To him it would seem monstrous that Chinese boys and girls should grow up in ingorance of their cultural heritage. He was one of the founders and staunch supporter of the now defunct School of Chinese Studies of the University of Hongkong; and the Fung Ping Shan Chinese Library is an abiding testimony to his devotion to Chinese learning.

In commerce, the late Mr. Fung was one of the founders and a permanent Director of the Bank of East Asia, Ltd., and many other public and private Companies. Besides his many commercial activities in Hong Kong, he had numerous connexions in the principal trading ports in North and South China, as well as in Siam, French Indo-China and India.

Owing to his genial disposition, Mr. Fung, both in his private life as well as in business, was much liked by all classes and nationalities with whom he came in contact.

He died on the 2nd August, 1931, at the ripe old age of 72, and is survived by three sons and six daughters.

香港華人名人史略（一九三七）

陳公子丹

THE LATE MR. CHAN TZE TUAN

同人胼胝修粵江人物志。時賢之嘉言懿行。已廣事徵獻。古哲之潛德幽光。將增編賴太史陳熙先生，為誥封光祿大夫子丹陳公撰行狀。茲錄於后。

公諱健埗。字子丹。一字幼缶。至覲先公。乃繁之饒平縣居莫鄉。越十一世。其先自閩遷粵之

宅前澳。即今所居也。曾祖有狀。祖慶璘。父煥榮。嘗以世德清望梅於鄉國。累晉封胙為通奉大夫。而煥榮公史以樂善好施坊純表。煥榮公有三子。長步堦以樂善貢公。次步貢公。公其季也。步堦公既父組商成偉案。而皆雅重文行。尤喜勉成偉案。而皆雅重文行。尤公善體父兄志。蕃熟成偉案。出就有司試。輒升其曾。桷博士弟子員。食廪餼。舉俊行。自居上舍。益勤往來精進。知學問之道。非徒卽充切磋攻錯。成就不能遠大。乃貨筴遊涽方。

績其詩陳列會所。售資優厚。公躬以績詩名其樓。史輯集師友文字。凡簡牘酬答。詩詞唱和。以至敦于課本。治家訓言。罔不備列。彙為三十六種。亦名績詩樓叢書。其志趣可觀矣。睦姻任邮。為公素行。而於尊祖敬宗賻族。尤所措求。身留旅外。心必一辭。展墓祭祠。建蘭必偕。修舉規約。訓示禮法。

歲。廣東水災。島人會集偏為賓物等眼。公躬與其役。弁走呼號。偏救慈善。時有女于絲懰。以勤人哀作為詩歌。開寫哭情。以

言。弁走呼號。弁贈聯。每年萬額節。必衣冠坐閣甲申。則賡合多人。迻致貢獻。值大婚修慶諸大婚。而科舉亦承貢各嘉。賞頗貤戴。則貢獻先緒。寵貴特厚。公正純摯顙御書楊方毒方。公正純摯喉。時父兄所營商業。日益興盛。步堦公主持于選羅。公則偕煥榮公初躍維主持於香港其生母劉太夫人以壬戌年終。其別營閩伍西肄定之。以己與妻之娥附諸左右兩交游。尚風義。礬氣宏遠。公廣四方名流至者。必欣勤款洽。而於駢入墨客。講宦遺民。戊甲官遺民。尤加禮重。或遇有義必梅之問。必梅豈有義之問。必梅力協助。

而未嘗或報。遭國變後。寬身孤島。足缺不履都悶。居恒齶齶。遺有重憂者。每年萬額節下。與澄海陳芳汝南。潮陽蕭郡鄧瓊珊。訂文字交。討論講習。復集合多人。迻統初元。討論講習。始以明經貢于國。而科舉亦統初元。討論講習。始以明經貢于國。而科舉亦已厭止。公乃捐葉帖括之學。而致力於詩古文辭。與海內名彥。馳聯文園。間。名乃大喋。時父兄所營商業。日益興盛。步堦公主持於選羅。公則偕煥榮公初躍維主持於香港其生母劉太夫人以壬戌年終。於禮不得合葬。父母皆晉諸左右兩禮矣。公處身行事。不拘苟禮。得生母劉太夫人以壬戌年終。於禮不得合葬。

彥方。遠氣世。逃居海外。曾閱越俗薰凝。藝學街。皆有趣遠流俗氣慨。世間。曾閱越俗薰凝。其音論平允。岸然有以自異。乃與深談。公乃發為海賓。余既有以自異。乃與深談。行文學見重於時。遠齔以倏。自是斫斷夕逐訂交。自是斫斷夕逐訂交。偶或述三數日不見。則間二紀。而未嘗聞歇。甲戌夜。公偶癭喘逆。至此奉忠孝之誠。有名儔老師不能盡喜。公乃奉忠孝之誠。有名儔老師不能盡喜。至此奉忠孝之誠。有名儔老師不能蓋喜。公亦孝而違于庭。王

令獨的。而相與談笑。則彷知往日。再以讒枝作劇。配李氏。繼配陸氏。則彷知往日。再以讒枝作劇。配李氏。繼配陸氏。蘭增桷。於增桷。配李氏。繼配陸氏。女二。長適王。次適陳人生于五。李邦先公卒。曰定邦。側室孫四子。曰昌邦先公卒。側室楊氏生。選邦。側室曾氏四中學。用中。嵩齊。由勁女二。長適王。次適陳人生于五。李邦先公卒。曰定邦。側室孫四子。曰昌邦先公卒。側室楊氏生。選邦。側室曾氏四中學。用中。嵩齊。由勁欲以獨的。而相與談笑。則彷知往日。斫斷夕訂交。其辭若陳列舉世次行實。請李為之狀。卒于回。是歲庚戌夜。公偶癭喘逆。至此奉忠孝之誠。卒于回。是歲庚戌

所為復死。必光與先死者作狀。斯配信也。記昔年公與約。吾二人交至密。知敦身也。記昔年公與約。吾二人交至密。知歃為後死。必光與先死者作狀。斯配信也。記昔年公與約。吾二人交至密。知諉撮錄其生平本本。撰為此狀。

增城翟熙撰狀

THE LATE Mr. CHAN TZE TUAN.

The late Mr. Chan Tze Tuan, grandfather of Mr. Chan Yeung Chai, shipping manager of the Kin Tye Lung 27 Bonham street west, is considered to be a learned merchant in the past.

The late Mr. Chan Tze Tuan, born with a literary gift, was under tutor of the Chinese old classics at an early age. He was arrayed with a formidable scholastic degree as "gung Seng" in the Ching Dynasty when he was still within his "teens."

Later, he came to Hongkong with his father, and settled in the Colony as a merchant. Though he was in the business field, yet he continued to do his literary works.

He was a man of broad sympathy. His humanity and generosity might be seen from the fact that during the disastrous flood in Kwongtung Province in 1908, he raised a large amount of money by means of selling his literary works and contributed all the money for relief.

In the family, he was an obedient son and a strict father. He taught his children in such a way, that all of them are good, obedient and diligent.

As to his ancestors they were originally natives of Fukien Province. They removed to live in Yau Ping District Kwongtung Province about two hundred years ago. So the late Mr. Chan Tze Tuan may be called a Cantonese or a Fukienese.

He was died in 1934 at a ripe old age of sixty five.

郭公少流

郭公少流

郭公守怡。字少流。廣東三水人。生於遜清咸豐九年。幼習中英文於本港。新舊學均精通。年十七輟讀。遂赴廣州營商。旋赴小呂宋等地經商。公元一八九四年。法國東方滙理銀行開設分行於香島。公即進該行任華經理。且至一九零六年。以衰老告退。旋行固留不獲。乃懇其萬賞接替。仍任保家。一九二九年。由其子郭賢君接任華經理。計與該行前後有四十餘年之歷史。公退隱後。惟致力於公益善舉事業。光緒兩申年。曾任東華醫院總理。戊戌。任保良公局總理。庚申，谷亥。復兩任該局前總理。俟港府史仙遊。享壽七十有八。一九三六年六月。在港寓所。

委為該局永遠總理。其他如港大校董。基督教聯校校董。雅利氏醫院值理。聖約翰救傷會董事。及財委。華人後備警察委。華商總會顧問。旅港三水商會樂就。而於提倡教育。更力與財俱。無不悅捐鉅款。如興保聖士提反女校郭少流大堂。及創立香港大學生理學綬等。此均為港中人士所共見者。尤為共聞者也。至於遊橋鄉土者。足稱。尤為和善廷三水得定留醫院。與決留旅院。購置。

港三水工商會會址。均能悉力以赴。色人甚德之。港府敬公重公。特委為太平紳士。復給以榮譽獎章。法屬越南政府亦錫以龍佩寶星。公平生雅喜遊行。嘗周遊世界。凡名勝之地。靡不有其足跡。始佻善養其浩然之氣。故碑於本港古院總理。戊戌。任保良公局總理。庚申，谷亥。復兩任該局前總理。俟港府史仙遊。享壽七十有八。

THE LATE Mr. KWOK SIU LAU.

The late Mr. Kwok Siu Lau, a native of Samshui, Kwangtung, was born in Hongkong in 1859 and received his early education here.

At the early age of 17, the late Mr. Kwok started his business career. He held positions in Canton and Manila. In 1894, when the Banque de l'Indochine opened its branch here, he was elected the first compradore, and remained with the Bank as such until 1906. He continued to stand surety, but retired from active work. In 1929, his son, Kwok Chan succeeded as compradore. His connection with the bank lasted forty odd years.

After his retirement, he devoted much time for philanthropic work and public activities. He also travelled intensively, and had made visits to all parts of the world.

He was a member of the Committee of the Tung Wah Hospital thirty odd years ago, and the committee of the Po Leung Kuk. He held the position of Chairman of the committee of the Po Leung Kuk on two occasions, and was nominated Justice of the Peace and also permanent director of the Institution.

In the cause of education, the late Mr. Kwok donated large sums for the erection of the Kwok Siu Lau Hall in the St. Stephen's Girls' College, and the founding of the Chair of Biology in the University of Hongkong.

He also devoted much attention to matters in Samshui, and helped largely to the Hospitals there. He also purchased the present site of the Samshui Chamber of Commerce in Hongkong and gave it to the Chamber.

He was a member of the Court of the Hongkong University; a member of the Committee of the Church Missionary Society Associated Schools; member of the Committee of the Alice Memorial and Affiliated Hospitals; Finance Committee of the St. John's Ambulance Brigade and Association; Finance committee of the Hongkong Police Reserve (Chinese Company); Adviser to the Chinese General Chamber of Commerce, Hongkong; Permanent President of the Samshui Chamber of Commerce and Committee member of the Society for the Protection of Children.

He was awarded the Certificate of Honour by the Government of Hong Kong, and the "Officer du Dragon D'Annam" by the Indochina Government. He was a member of the Septuagenarians, and died in June 1936 at the age of 78.

陳公任國。廣東省台山縣水南鄉人。七歲至十七歲。在珂里從師習經史之學。年十八。業備入商。就同邑沖蔥盛普濟堂藥肆之聘。華華不倦。服務三年。旋改應新昌埠歧生堂藥肆之微。未約三載。美國三藩市致中和藥肆聞其館。

○公不好名○自民國啓建○從不以革命先進自稱○一志經商○不求宦顯○來港創辦陸海通有限公司○務拓寶業○以利民生○當組織時○親歷美洲各埠○所到之處○華僑皆表歡迎○大股遂集○繼而陸海通人壽保險有限公司○陸海通旅館○陸海通銀行○陸海通飯店○六國飯店○彌敦酒店等○先後紛立○刷以年事日高○而智制行祥君○辭事輪煥○免耀大志○遂使總理公司事務○若遇委公○份須商承之也○公除任陸海通有限公司董事會主席外○並充上海聯保水火險有限公司董事○生平樂善好施○關心教育○當公七秋開一慶壽時○於廣州公醫學院○台山水圓○則正學校○曹慨捐款巨萬○又公深捍基督教義諦○忠厚

國 任 公 陳

特廷之往○公為紹述父兄向外發展之志○欣然就道○受任後○整理有方○營業大進○任事六年○為謀獨立進展計○乃婉辭告退○在三藩市自設保滋堂藥肆○駕輕就熟○業務日廣○時當滿清末葉○當地戚某偽入境○公以己國衰的○異族主政○莫奈之何○遂傾向革新自後事業

和平○與人無忤○故鄉人美其名曰阿婆○以其兄弟具有姿心○足為後輩楷式也○公年過六旬○娶鄺氏為室○生二子一女○長男符樂○年五十五○曾讀於上海南洋公學○及廣州嶺南學堂○次男元喜○年四十一○畢業於廣柏林大學○屑醫學博士○胡公生於遜清同治元年正月念三日○於民國念五年九月初三日○享壽七十五歲○

同盟會為會員○歷次起義公債捐款○均樂輸將○革命首領孫總理引為同志○來往甚密○加入

THE LATE Mr. CHAN YAM KWOK.

The late Mr. Chan Yam Kwok was a native of Toishan District, Kwangtung Province, born in 1861.

He acquired his education at his native village and when he was eighteen years of age he worked in a Chinese drug store in his neighboring town. Three years later, he transferred to another shop and again he remained for three years.

Then he crossed the oceans and proceeded to America, where he worked in the Chee Chung Wo Chinese Drug Store, San Francisco, California. He stayed in the post for six years and when he had accumulated sufficient means to be independent, he established the Po Chi Tong, which was also dealing in Chinese drugs. His experience and business acumen enabled him to become prosperous in the shortest span of time.

Mr. Chan was a faithful nationalist. He had helped a great deal in building of the Chinese Republic. He was an intimate friend of the late Dr. Sun Yat Sen and had for several times assisted the latter in revolutions. After the Republic of China was firmly established, Mr. Chan did not boast for his merits but ran on his business as usual.

Then he came to Hongkong and devoted himself to the commercial field. He initiated the Luk Hoi Tung & Co., Ltd.; the Luk Hoi Tung Life Assurance Co., Ltd., the Luk Hoi Tung Hotel and Restaurant; the Luk Hoi Tong Dispensary; the Luk Kwok Hotel; and the Nathan Hotel.

Besides the above mentioned, he was also director of the Shanghai Fire and Marine Insurance Co., Ltd. He contributed a large sum of money to the Public Hospital in Canton and the Chik Ching School in his native town.

Married at twenty, Mr. Chan had a couple of son and a daughter. He died in 1936, with a ripe old age of seventy-five and to the mournfulness of most people of the Chinese community.

THE PROMINENT CHINESE IN HONGKONG

BY

Prof. WOO SING LIM

PRICE; $ 3.00
$ 5.00 (Cloth)

THE FIVE CONTINENTS BOOK CO.

63, HENNESSY ROAD, WANCHAI,

HONG KONG

All Rights Reserved

中華民國二十六年六月初版

◉ 中英合璧 香港華人名人史畧一册

每册 硬面定價 伍元
軟面定價 叁元

編著者　中山吳醒濂

發行者　五洲書局
香港軒鯉詩道六十三號

承印者　聚珍印務書樓有限公司
營業部：香港威靈頓街五十號
工版：灣仔洛克道卅二至四十號

◉ 此書有著作權翻印必究 ◉

書名：香港華人名人史略（一九三七）（中英合璧）
　　　The Prominent Chinese in Hong Kong（1937）
系列：心一堂 香港・澳門雙城成長系列
原著：吳醒濂 編著
主編・責任編輯：陳劍聰

出版：心一堂有限公司
通訊地址：香港九龍旺角彌敦道六一〇號荷李活商業中心十八樓〇五一〇六室
深港讀者服務中心：中國深圳市羅湖區立新路六號羅湖商業大廈負一層〇〇八室
電話號碼：(852) 67150840
網址：publish.sunyata.cc
淘宝店地址：https://shop210782774.taobao.com
微店地址：　　https://weidian.com/s/1212826297
臉書：　　　　https://www.facebook.com/sunyatabook
讀者論壇：　　http://bbs.sunyata.cc

香港發行：香港聯合書刊物流有限公司
地址：香港新界大埔汀麗路36號中華商務印刷大廈3樓
電話號碼：(852) 2150-2100
傳真號碼：(852) 2407-3062
電郵：info@suplogistics.com.hk

台灣發行：秀威資訊科技股份有限公司
地址：台灣台北市內湖區瑞光路七十六巷六十五號一樓
電話號碼：+886-2-2796-3638
傳真號碼：+886-2-2796-1377
網絡書店：www.bodbooks.com.tw
心一堂台灣秀威書店讀者服務中心：
地址：台灣台北市中山區松江路二〇九號1樓
電話號碼：+886-2-2518-0207
傳真號碼：+886-2-2518-0778
網址：http://www.govbooks.com.tw

中國大陸發行　零售：深圳心一堂文化傳播有限公司
深圳地址：深圳市羅湖區立新路六號羅湖商業大廈負一層008室
電話號碼：(86)0755-82224934

版次：二零一九年四月初版，平裝

定價：　港幣　　　九十八元正
　　　　新台幣　　四百四十八元正

國際書號 ISBN 978-988-8582-65-5

版權所有 翻印必究

心一堂微店二維碼　　心一堂淘寶店二維碼